WHEN IT RAINS

First published 2024 by
FREMANTLE PRESS

Fremantle Press Inc. trading as Fremantle Press
PO Box 158, North Fremantle, Western Australia 6159
fremantlepress.com.au

Cover images by Brad Wooler, bradwooler.com; Shutterstock,
shutterstock.com/image-illustration/smoky-abstract-background-218842384
Cover design Nada Backovic, nadabackovic.com
Map by Christopher Crook.
Printed and bound by IPG

A catalogue record for this
book is available from the
National Library of Australia

ISBN 9781760993177 (paperback)
ISBN 9781760993184 (ebook)

Fremantle Press is supported by the State Government through the
Department of Local Government, Sport and Cultural Industries.

Fremantle Press respectfully acknowledges the Whadjuk people of the
Noongar nation as the traditional owners and custodians of the land where
we work in Walyalup.

DAVE WARNER
WHEN IT
RAINS

 FREMANTLE PRESS

For Sandy Holliday

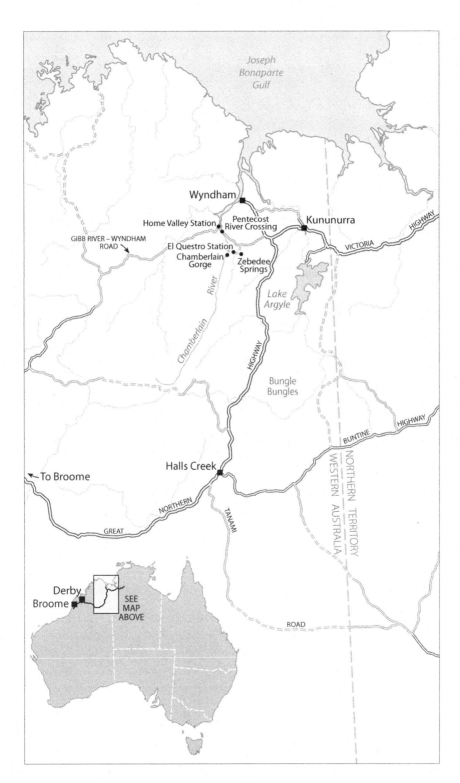

THE KIMBERLEY, WESTERN AUSTRALIA

1

Her first conscious thought is diffuse, shaded by a sarong, like she used to do to the lamp back in the Surry Hills flat when she was expecting a 'gentleman caller' as Bronny her actor-flatmate would joke. She hasn't thought of Bronwyn in years. Wonders what she is doing now. Aspirations of playing Sydney Theatre Company, scored a couple of ads. Lives diverge. Best friends are gone from the radar. Nobody can be bothered with the upkeep. Weeds in a rental's garden ...

She drifts in dark grey mist for a while, then the bulb in her head brightens. Where is she? A vehicle of some kind. With who?

She tries to sit up but can't. Her legs are bound together, and her hands. Panic floods her.

'Let me go!' she screams as the vehicle bumps over rough ground. When there is no answer, she bellows, 'Helllp!', drawing out the sound as long as her breath can hold. Fear is sprouting by the millisecond, wrapping her up, strangling her. She has had too much to drink anyway. Plus, those joints. Tonight, just one more in life's spilled ashtray.

Dancing at the pub: she remembers that. Then – what? It's blank as the sheet of paper noting her lifetime achievements. She screams at least three more times. Then stops. It is pointless.

—

Light from a half moon spills into the back of the vehicle but otherwise it's pitch out there. This is as far from artificial light as you can be. No roads, no petrol stations. No people. She envisages the car's headlights probing a black, endless belly. No chance of confirmation possible from here on the gritty surface she's lying on. Has to be a four-wheel drive, for out here where there are only tracks, even gravel is a rare luxury. She understands now, in some ethereal way, that this night has long been promised her.

She should never have listened to him. Wasn't doom squatting in her heart the moment she heard his message?

Despite her bound feet and her hands tied behind her back she manages to roll on her side. She fights to get her torso off the deck, stretches her neck up at a weird angle.

'Please, I'll do anything you want.'

Her words are soaked in desperation, but she can't bring herself to believe they will change anything. The bullet had been fired long ago. All this time it has been travelling unerringly to the target she'd painted on her own chest.

The driver pays no heed to her, does not tell her to shut up, does not slow down, or even reach around to clip her. For all she knows he has earphones in, listening to music.

Perhaps it is the drugs, but she feels an inability to offer any further physical resistance. Hers is a resignation, near total. For eight years her life has been a shadowland. It seems that will soon come to an end: the creeping anxiety, the paranoia, leaves whispering in accusation, the derisive hiss of combers on even the most deserted of beaches.

Another wave of anguish surges through her.

'Anything!' she screams, going through the motions, but deep inside knowing the torpedo tube door is already welded shut. The lassitude settles over her again. Bronwyn got a part in a mini-series, didn't she? She'd forgotten that. Remembers now a wrap party somewhere near Taylor Square, genuine coke off toilet lids. They'd gone their separate ways when the lease ran out. Nine years. Bronny might be a mother by now.

—

That first trip to the west had been a high point ... no pun intended ... opportunities stretched in front of her like ... like endless lines of coke. Shitty analogy. There is no invention in her now. Hasn't been for years. Her mouth opens to cry out but this time all she manages are sobs.

An image of a long-ago Christmas Eve comes to her: satin pyjamas and coloured lights around her family garage, snacks laid out for visitors; white Christmas, nuts, pretzels. She'd helped her mum. It made her feel grown up. She'd waited in bed long after the guests had gone, and her little brother had stopped chattering and plunged into dreamland. She'd waited full of determination and expectation, alert for the sound of reindeer hooves. And then she'd drifted towards oblivion, just like now.

Finally, she had capitulated, her vigil unsuccessful.

—

The car slows and stops. Her muscles tighten. Terror has formed a mould around her, a full-body death mask.

A back panel opens, air blows in and she smells the bush and … moisture. A river or a creek. She feels a presence looming over her.

'Please,' she starts before something pricks her neck. A thought struggles out: maybe this is for the best …

The veil descends over her …

—

Her next conscious thought is she has wet herself. It is dismissed almost the same instant. She is in water, waist deep. Her hands remain bound, only now they are looped around a rough wooden post at her back. She yells into the cavernous night, her eyes adjusting to the moonlight, picking out wooden stumps encircling her like cricket fielders, perhaps the remnants of a jetty. But her legs, what's with them? She tries to lift her feet. They are heavy as lead. Suddenly she understands what has happened to her, the situation in which she finds herself, the awful symmetry of what has been prepared for her.

This time when she screams, it is with a power that can only be generated by the most intense, primal dread.

They are out there, those prehistoric creatures. Her galloping heart taps out its telegram: 'Not this death, anything but this'. Before she can wail again, she hears that slight suction sound when the massive reptile pulls itself from a muddy bank. She does not hear it enter the water but even as she screams anew, she can feel the resultant ripples running up under her ribs.

Her cry is still thrusting from her throat towards the moon, her tongue still trilling when the monster strikes, severing her body in two.

2

Of all the Friday-night drinking holes Josh Shepherd would have chosen to spend his Friday night in, the Picador ran last. He'd lost count of the number of times he'd been called out here as a young uniform. The pool cues had higher IQs than the blokes wielding them, and a large portion of whatever brains they had wound up spilled on the sticky carpet, or on the bitumen in the carpark because of a dumb argument over house rules on the eight ball.

Now he was a detective sergeant, Shepherd didn't have to bother with that crap, but what do you do when you are nominated best man, and Robbo, the upcoming groom, wants to get a few of his mates together for a drink, and suggests the Picador because Robbo feels quite at home here? Okay, normally you tell your mate, 'Sorry, no can do,' and suggest some other venue. Or you make up an excuse, like your toe has gone gangrenous from where that turtle snapped it. Trouble was, Robbo was also captain of the footy team, and Josh was astute when it came to sucking up.

At the start of the last season Josh had initially been pissed off he'd been moved from the glamorous centre half-forward position to anchor the defence at centre halfback. He'd been mollified, however, when Dutchy, one of the committee, had leaked the news to him privately during a urinal visit at a Sunday recovery session, that he was leading the club best-and-fairest. This he had duly won. So, in the interests partly of team unity, but more importantly of maintaining his status come the next season, and possibly winning back-to-back b&f medals, Josh hadn't said boo when Robbo nominated the Picador as venue for a pre–bucks'-night piss-up.

—

It was around nine-thirty now and Shepherd was ready to head home. Saturdays he liked to rise early and polish off a ten-k run before a long and relaxed breakfast topped off with a swim. Most of the clientele of the Picador had been drinking since Friday early knock-off and things were getting untidy. A lot of FIFOs had absconded from their Pilbara and Kimberley dongas and headed to Broome for shore leave. That always made for a tinderbox. Even though the numbers of women working the mines had increased a lot over the last couple of years, most had the good sense to steer clear of here. He supposed those rare women who did venture here enjoyed having their drinks bought for them. Predictably, however, their scarcity encouraged claim-jumping. That, or arguments over the pool table were the matches that invariably set the tinderbox ablaze.

'Fellas, I'm off,' said Shepherd, rising from his bar stool. He parried the demands of 'one for the road' from his three remaining teammates, visited the gents and, having relieved himself, headed into the sultry October air to his car. A couple of bays from it, two blokes and a young woman, listing like boats in a marina, were in what passed for conversation.

'Come on. We can drop you back after.'

'I dunno. I mean youse nice and all but ...'

The bigger of the two blokes with a mass of curly hair was doing the talking. 'You'll have the night of your life. I'm telling you the gear we got will blow your fucking—'

Shepherd's head had turned at that and the big bloke had spotted him.

'What are you staring at, dipshit?' The big bloke.

See, this was why Shepherd hated the fucking Picador.

'If you're talking about illegal drugs, which is what it sounds like, then you best leave it.'

The big bloke advanced. Shepherd was taller but this bloke had the back and shoulders of a gorilla.

'What's it the fuck to you?'

'Detective Sergeant Shepherd, Broome police. I know your number-plate. Enjoy the rest of your night. Legally.'

Shepherd turned back to his car and was about to zap it when he felt a tremendous blow to the back of his head. His knees buckled, then a fist powered into his kidney, and he sagged. He was hit in the side of the head and his knees dropped onto the bitumen. A boot struck him from the right, then he was hit somewhere near the eye. He was kneeling now, and the blows were still coming. He toppled, tried to shield his head. Kicks pummelled both sides of his body, at least two bastards going him. His ears rang. His head was light, empty, most of his consciousness had fled already but the waves of pain in the rest of his body were undiminished. Where was he? There was no land beneath his feet, no horizon, no beacon. An ocean swirled around him. He fought to stay afloat but wasn't strong enough. The depths claimed him.

—

These Friday nights at the Derby house had become a routine. A much better one, thought Clement, than the norm of the previous eight years: drinks at the Anglers, usually with Bill Seratono, a chicken curry takeaway finished off solo with a half-bottle of wine in his small pad above the chandler on the wharf, evocative Brian Wilson songs turning him to mush. Nostalgia, futility, an invasive sense of failure, dehydration, fitful sleep.

He looked across, admiring the curve of her naked right buttock, her long legs scissoring the sheet, one above, one below, so that only the right one with the tattoo of the archer on her calf was visible. Copied from an artist named Kirchner, she'd told him. The one on her left leg was of two blue horses. Apparently, it too was a copy of a famous painting by another German artist, but he couldn't remember the artist's name.

'Why did you pick those particular paintings?' Clement had asked.

Lena, in nothing but a leopard-skin thong at that moment, had stretched back, looked at him through those smoky green-grey eyes of hers and said, 'The tattooist graduated from the Berlin School of Fine Art and Design. His name was Manfred. He specialised in German expressionism. This kind of art. He is the best tattooist in Berlin, probably Germany, maybe the world, and …'

'Why is he doing tattoos?'

'Why do you think? He makes a shitload of money. But you interrupt me.' Lena could be very blunt, very German. It was a lesson he'd learned early on in their near three-month relationship.

'I apologise.'

'The other reason I pick them is the colour. Blue is the best tattoo colour, right? The horses are blue in the painting, so I figured why alter that? And the archer is blue, mainly. The archer aims for something. Maybe they hit it, maybe they don't, but they are aiming, not searching. I like that.'

Yes, thought Clement, Lena was decisive. She doesn't drift like me, the untethered rowboat. She'd ridden into town on her motorcycle like a movie cowboy. Her long finger tapped the tattoo on her left leg.

'The horses are free. But still, they are together. Because they wish to be.'

The tattoos were quite large, and yes, very high quality compared to what Clement was used to, but he was pleased she had only the two. He asked her if she was going to get more.

'I don't think so. I don't want to be defined by my tattoos. I don't feel that need. Like people who need six sunglasses, or ten hats. That's limiting.'

She revealed she had thought of getting a 'tubist' image on her arse. 'A Franz Leger or Max Ernst. Like *Celebes*, you know?'

He didn't. She found a photo on her phone. It looked like a large vacuum cleaner. He was glad she had decided against it. It was silent outside. She loved it here, the place in Derby that he'd originally bought as a weekender where he might play dad to Phoebe. How quickly the time had gone, how much of life he had squandered.

He continued to study her, dark hair fanning over the pillows. Most nights they were together he found himself contemplating if this was the inevitable midlife crisis playing out as the cliff that was his fiftieth birthday loomed. Lena was, he believed thirty-six. He was worried about asking her for specifics in case it turned out she was younger still. He didn't believe her youth had anything much to do with his hooking up with her. If anything, that had acted as a deterrent.

I shouldn't be worried about people judging me, he thought, but I am. Especially, he'd been concerned what Phoebe might think if he began a relationship with a much younger woman. Phoebe was eighteen now, probably she didn't care but he didn't want to embarrass his daughter.

He had thought everything was under control with Susanna, his previous … what did you call them? 'Lady friend' sounded ridiculous and girlfriend sounded wrong. Whatever the word was, it had appeared he and Sue were going to work out. In a place like Broome the fact was most of the prospective love interests you met were young. It was a transient population: tourists, young people on gap years, young professionals on internships. When he'd finally motivated himself to look at meeting somebody single, he had discovered that there wasn't a big pool of available females close to his own age. Sue – she preferred Susanna – had in fact been older than him by two years, and that hadn't bothered him in the least. It had initially been refreshing to have the same cultural touchstones. Like movies: shared Maltesers, shared experiences of youthful love, holding hands watching the latest blockbuster. When he'd been courting Marilyn, *Runaway Bride* and *Notting Hill* made lasting impressions on him. According to Sue it had been the same with her ex, although they had already been married by then.

Of course, Sue had never heard of Doctor John – that might have been expecting too much – but she loved Michael Jackson and 'Horses' and U2. Clement had let that slide but for the life of him he couldn't match up those three. Did it just mean Sue's music taste was whatever other people seemed to like? He'd behaved himself, tempted as he was to bemoan 'Sunday Bloody Sunday' as the most overrated song of the modern era. Sure, he thought it was an okay song, perhaps even a good song. He'd said nothing, and to be honest that had seemed the wise choice as the relationship had bloomed. Sue had replaced his threadbare towels with fluffy ones and decorated his bed with cushions. He had almost forgotten that part of living with a woman. It was comfortable, it was pleasant not being on your own, the house no longer smelling of sweat and worn runners. But. The strength of being the same age was also the problem. Sue's twenty-four-year-old son carried on like he was sixteen. Jordan lived in Sydney and bled her for money. 'Bludged', Clement's old man would have said. He couldn't keep a job or girlfriend, did drugs, lied. This upset Sue greatly. Foolishly, Clement had stuck his nose in where it wasn't wanted, said the boy needed tough love. Once, when Jordan rang, Clement picked up Sue's phone and told him this to his face. And that was the end of Sue and him. It had crumbled quickly.

When you're our age, ruminated Clement, there is too much history: spouses, kids, habits. At least though he had Sue to thank for making sure he now had decent manchester. She had headed back to Sydney, but the fluffy towels remained.

—

It was surprising how quickly after the demise of the relationship he had fallen back into the old ways. In fact, if his memory was correct, it was on a Friday night after the Anglers, in the midst of a curry and a large glass of one-too-many wines, that he had received an overseas call from Mathias Klendtwort, a former German policeman he'd come to call a friend even though they'd never met in person. Mathias' former colleague had been brutally murdered eight years back, and Clement had called him for background on the victim. The two had hit it off and every six months or so one would call the other, Klendtwort because he was a little bored, Clement because he was lonely. Clement found it so much easier to confide in somebody thousands of kilometres away than to an office colleague, even a good friend like Graeme Earle. They had shot the breeze for a while, then Mathias had come to the point.

'Listen, the reason I am calling is my niece, Lena, is coming to Australia, and when she said she was going to visit Broome, I mentioned you.'

Clement was already running through his brain where he might recommend that she stay. Di Rivi, he could ask her, she might have a few suggestions.

'I'm warning you well in advance,' chuckled Klendtwort.

Now Clement was imagining some young prima donna.

'How old is she?'

'Thirty-four, thirty-six, around there. I'm telling you, Dan, Lena is a real firecracker. She's got tattoos, she's smart as hell and she devours men. So, you've been warned.'

Clement readjusted his ideas. 'She can look after herself then.'

Mathias roared. 'Dan, you're the one who will need protection from her. She's been working a bar in Bangkok, she's ridden a motorcycle around America, she carries a flexible riot baton, she can take care of herself but even so, young people, especially young women, can get overconfident. You know what I'm saying?'

Clement did. Phoebe was just embarking on her parent-free life. No way was he paranoid but there was always a thin layer of silt at the bottom of his mind where concern could be stirred in an instant.

'It is always good to have a friend who can help if things go bad.' Klendtwort coughed and lit a cigarette, Clement could tell.

'If she needs anything, I'm here.'

That had been back in May. Clement had forgotten all about it by late July when she'd turned up at the station, black motorcycle leathers, a helmet in her hand, thick hair cascading over her shoulders. She'd been touring Australia on her own on her bike for five weeks and already had organised a place to stay in Broome, so Clement suggested he show her around the town and take her to dinner when he finished work.

—

Mathias was right. Clement conceded it from that first moment he saw her standing there in her leathers. She would be able to claim dominion over most guys without a shot being fired. She was tall, taut, smoky eyes. Her chin was defined, slightly masculine, her face maybe a fraction long to have been the traditional cover girl. She was sexy as hell, but Clement had no design to be anything but a good host.

She was waiting at the motel and had changed into shorts and singlet. You couldn't miss the tattoos. Clement took her to a Chinese meal and insisting on paying. He drove around town, peppering the drive with stories of notorious criminal interactions. They visited Cable Beach of course. Lena peeled off her top and had a dip despite Clement's warning of the temperature.

'I can live with hard nipples,' she laughed.

Clement tried to avert his eyes when she came running up to him. He offered the towel and she hit it like a runner breasting the tape, carried on into him.

'Don't worry, Mathias knows what I'm like,' she laughed, reading his mind.

On the way to the Roebuck, after she'd dried off a bit, though her hair was still wet, she pointed at the CD player in his car. He would resist Bluetooth as long as he could. You could pick used CDs up for nothing and his player was always loaded and pumping.

'What's this?'

She must be younger than he'd supposed. 'A CD player.'

'I know what it is. Hey, I'm not nineteen. I mean the music.'

'Charlie Haden, Liberation Music Orchestra.'

'It's super cool,' she said.

'You like it?'

'What sort of music do you think I like?' she turned, facing him, that set jaw demanding of him.

'Eminem?' Taking a pot shot. This millennium was a musical blackhole pretty much for him.

'You're right, I like Eminem but also Miles Davis, Beatles, Bowie.'

'Doctor John?'

'Shit yeah!' She sang a line from 'Right Place Wrong Time'.

That was incredible. That was also dangerous.

—

At the Roebuck, she had joined him in a beer. 'People look at me, they see the tattoos, the motorcycle, they think I'm some wild chick. Okay, I like sex, you got me, but I don't do drugs, I don't drink hardly. I'm conservative. Apart from the sex and travel, I could be a nun.'

Once more Clement cast his eye over her slumbering body. She wasn't like any nun he'd ever known. Mind you, how many nuns were there these days? It had taken a little over a week before he'd succumbed to the inevitable. That first week he had caught up with her: a couple of lunches, a couple of dinners. Work was slow, his colleagues curious. Shepherd had naturally fancied his chances, though the difference in ages between Lena and him matched that between Lena and Clement, but in the opposite direction. Shepherd had got her into his gym. Like a criminal burying the bloodied shirt he'd worn and thinking that solved his problems, Clement tried to deny to himself he was jealous. He'd strongly suspected Lena saw through him.

'You're a good-looking guy, you know?' she'd whispered out of nowhere, around about day eight, as they sipped a juice at a wobbly iron table.

'Thank you.' He'd tried to be neutral, like an umpire or a diligent journalist. These days he never really thought of himself as attractive or not. He assumed that any women who would entertain the idea of him as a lover would be basing it on whether he might be loyal, attentive, interesting, and yes, earning enough. Middle-aged women don't want poor blokes, he'd decided. Not even hunky surfers or sensitive songwriters. That was strictly for young women.

'No, I mean it. Sexy. I'd like to fuck you.'

Firecracker. That was the word her uncle had used.

'I don't think that would work.'

'And you're such a good judge of what works for you.' She'd raised her eyebrows, licked her straw. 'How long now have you been living the high life?' Lacing those two words with deadly irony.

He'd already given her the basics of his life. He'd had nothing to hide. It hadn't been like he was trying to clean up a messy bedroom for a prospective lover. So, she knew the important stuff: Marilyn, a daughter, the Anglers Club.

'It's best we don't go there,' he'd eventually managed.

'Yes, best we don't talk. At least not about important stuff. I'll just say this: I like you, you like me. And if we try to judge what's best for us by using the same failed logic as what has proved in the past to be no good for us, well …' She'd shrugged.

'And has sleeping with every guy you had the faintest fancy for worked for you?'

'When I was in my twenties, I made a lot of mistakes. I don't make those now. I learned. So now, I regret nothing.'

Yes, he thought, though she hadn't explained the archer tattoo to him at that stage; she looses her arrow, and strike or miss matters not to her, because she has determined that at least she knows what she's aiming for.

—

The inevitable moment came when her prepaid accommodation ran out and he told her she was welcome to stay at his house in Derby. He explained he only used it on weekends, and recently not very often at all. In fact, he'd not used it since Susanna, around three months back. Lena was grateful, looking forward to having the chance to explore out of Derby. She followed him to Derby on a Honda Africa she'd bought second-hand in Sydney for sixteen thousand dollars. She explained that she found it more economical to buy a vehicle and then sell it.

'I don't know how long I'll stay,' she said, and Clement realised it was the first time they'd canvassed in any way the duration of her trip, although he supposed they probably had talked about it that very first night. But how could you concentrate on anything with Lena there, after she'd just thrust her part-naked body into you?

Had he secretly hoped things would turn out how they did? Only now did he dare to peek under the tarpaulin he had been laying down for weeks, only now did he dare to scrutinise his behaviours, what they said about him. Had it been his plan all along for him and Lena to get together sexually? The nod and wink between his bodily desires and medulla, or whatever part of the brain controlled that stuff?

Or was it, as he preferred to believe, the inevitable outcome of the proximity of two personalities that was bound to manifest itself at some unpredictable point in history?

That point was reached when she stepped from the bathroom

wrapped in nothing more than a towel, said, 'I love these fluffy towels,' and, unhooking it, let it drop to the floor.

That's all she wrote.

—

At some point during that weekend, he realised that the negative team's arguments in his internal debate – that the age gap was too great, that he was being disloyal to Mathias, that he enjoyed her company and might jeopardise the friendship, that his colleagues would judge him poorly, et cetera – were all spurious.

There was only one true reason: he feared he might commit to Lena, only to discover he was no more than a challenge, another notch.

It was so pathetically simple, so unoriginal, so 1960s-teenage-girl, that his skin crawled when he was forced to own it. Though own it he must. For he had slept with women younger than her, he really didn't give a rat's arse what his colleagues thought, and Lena's and his friendship, nice as it was, was still nascent. So that left the impact on Mathias. Clement suspected Mathias knew what outcome might eventuate when he involved Clement.

He stroked her shoulder now, silently confessing: That's my problem, simple as that. The time might arrive when you have no use for me, and when you knock me down with the words 'we're over', I might not be able to get back up off the canvas.

However, he had come to admit that despite this fear, she was absolutely right when she'd told him that whatever compass he had been using these last ten years had been defective, leading him nowhere but in a large circle. Maybe he would tip over the edge of the world, maybe he would strike the mother lode? At least he had ceased drifting ...

His phone buzzed. After eleven on a Friday night, any call could not be good news.

3

When Clement arrived at the hospital, Scott Risely was waiting. Risely, his superintendent since Clement had returned to Broome, had been notified he was to be promoted to regional commander in the New Year. Even if that transition had already taken place, Clement knew Risely would have been there. Pretty much the whole way from Derby, Risely had been calling, feeding Clement updates. But as recently as ten minutes ago the picture was still unclear on Shepherd's situation. They were doing 'further tests and scans', one of those phrases that sent a chill down Clement's spine.

Risely didn't bother with a greeting. 'They don't think there's any skull fracture but there's swelling, so they're working on reducing that. As far as the head injury goes, it might be a bad concussion and no worse.'

A bad concussion could still have grave long-term consequences. Many a footballer had been forced to retire because of ongoing headaches, tinnitus, nausea. And Shepherd played football. Maybe he was already vulnerable before this. However, compared to what Clement had been dreading, the news was good, and the possibility there was no fracture, heartening.

Risely was continuing. 'Definitely fractured ribs both sides. Could be a beating or kicking. You heard anything?'

'I told Jo and Graeme to call me if they had anything important.' From personal experience, Clement knew that a superior constantly demanding updates could be a pain in the arse, taking up valuable time of those on the ground investigating.

—

It had been Jason 'Gimmy' Moore, the night sergeant at the station, whose phone call Clement had taken in Derby. Moore had been notified by the hospital about Shepherd being brought into Emergency semiconscious after apparently suffering a beating. Unaware that the detective was now in Derby, Moore had called Clement first. Despite having consumed two substantial glasses of wine, it had not crossed Clement's mind to delay his departure. He'd roused Lena, informed her one of his men had been bashed and that he needed to leave now.

'I'll be back when I can,' was all he'd said. They'd kissed. He'd left. She had her cycle there, so she had transport if she needed.

The highway had been deserted as an abandoned runway. Earlier, on the way to Derby, the two-hundred-and-twenty-k trip had taken him two hours fifteen. Now he was back in Broome in under two. He'd requested Moore call Jo di Rivi and get her on the case. Figuring his usual partner Graeme Earle might still be up, Clement had called him personally. Earle had only just gone to bed. Striving for calm in spite of the clamour going on in his head, Clement had managed to brief Earle without histrionics.

'I asked Gimmy Moore to get di Rivi working on it.'

'You know where this happened?'

Moore had no idea. Earle remembered Shepherd complaining about how he was having to go to the Picador for a pre–buck's night gathering. Shepherd was always complaining about something; however, on this occasion Clement was sympatico. The Picador would be a good place to start any investigation.

Half an hour later as Clement sped to Broome, Earle had called back. Shepherd had indeed been found in the carpark of the Picador and he and di Rivi had arrived there. All of this Clement had passed all on to Risely.

And now here they were in the flesh.

—

'If there's no skull fracture, he's going to get out of this okay,' said Risely.

Shepherd's mother lived hours south in Geraldton. Clement asked if Risely had notified her.

'Yes, don't worry. I'll look after that. There's no point you hanging around. You should get out to the Picador. I'll let you know any developments.'

Clement would have liked to see Shepherd, satisfied himself about the state of play, even though he'd be able to tell nothing of Shepherd's condition. He'd be unconscious, entrapped in a web of tubes.

Some of us get to offer succour, thought Clement; others, like me are the avengers. It was his job to hunt down the transgressor. He strode back out into the hot night. His car, still getting its breath, ticked like a bomb.

Or perhaps that's me, thought Clement. He was angry, sick of yobs who bashed medics, cops, good people, and did it with impunity. Actions by a handful of redneck cops in America gave a spurious justification to these arseholes. Anybody could find any excuse these days to do whatever they wanted. Well, not on Clement's watch. Whoever did this, he would crush under the full weight of the law. That was a promise he made to himself as much as to Josh Shepherd.

—

Crime-scene tape was always a sobering sight. Knowing it signified where one of your own had fallen didn't help. Shepherd's car was still there in the Picador carpark under the glare of Lisa Keeble's lights. She was in her crime-scene suit squatting down, scrutinising the bitumen. Clement parked on the street. The night's hot, clammy fingers groped the t-shirt he'd been wearing when Moore's call had come through. So far, he hadn't found the time to change but he'd thrown a clean work shirt into the car before leaving Derby. He went to circumnavigate the carpark, but Keeble motioned him in.

'It's okay, we've got everything worthwhile. How's he doing?'

Clement knew he'd be running through this spiel more than a few times in the next little bit, but duly reported what he knew. Keeble nodded, pleased at what seemed benign news.

'I've dusted his car. It doesn't look like it was opened. I found the keys right here where it looks like he fell. Have dusted them of course.'

Clement was already speculating. If it was a robbery or carjacking, surely the car would have been taken, or at least rifled through, unless the assailant or assailants had been interrupted. He pulled himself up. The others might already have established a scenario based on fact.

Keeble said, 'I've sent Janene to the hospital. Our best evidence repository could be Shep himself. She'll give him a going-over once she gets an all clear. You were in Derby?'

Graeme Earle would have already told her. Keeble was inner sanctum. She knew all about his Lena romance. Keeble never judged. He liked that about her. Her own long-term relationship had folded just a week or so back. That had been a surprise, Clement confident it would have gone the distance. Not one for gossip, Clement had nonetheless quietly asked Graeme Earle if he knew what had happened. Earle had shrugged. Clearly Clement hadn't asked quietly enough. Shepherd, who'd materialised from a toilet cubicle, had leaned in and said, 'Boyfriend,' pushing the finger of one hand into the circle made by a hollow fist, in a fairly universal gesture for fucking. Whether Shepherd was on the money was moot. It could have been just him surmising, making out like he knew more than he did, a particular Shepherd trait.

And now here was Lisa Keeble, analysing the minutiae of the attack on Shepherd. So far Clement had refrained from asking Lisa why she and her musician boyfriend had busted up.

'There's not much more for me to do here,' she offered.

'Grab some rest then. If we arrest anybody, you'll be fresh.'

—

Clement continued to the Picador's front door and pushed in. The large bar was deserted now except for Earle and di Rivi sitting on bar stools with notes and phones spread out, and a pasty-faced man about fifty who gave the vibe he wanted to finally lock up and get home. Clement brought his colleagues up to speed.

'This is Harry, the manager.' Earle gestured.

Clement shook hands, turned back. 'What have we got?'

Earle let Jo di Rivi paint it. Shepherd's mates said he'd left the bar a little after 9.30. A patron going to his car had spied Shepherd about ten to fifteen minutes later, sprawled and bleeding in the carpark. The Picador had CCTV but not in the exact area where the assault occurred.

'But we have got coverage for each of the exits,' put in Harry, eager to establish the pub was up to scratch. 'And we have one over the bar, there.' He pointed about halfway down the bar.

Di Rivi did not break stride. 'Judging from our interviews with those staff, and the couple of patrons still here when I arrived, we have three persons of interest. Two males, one female. Thirties. Could be Caucasian, Indigenous, not Asian. They were drinking here from about eight. They left the bar here about ten minutes before Shep.'

'Not locals,' interjected Harry.

Di Rivi slid a sideways glance at him that said, 'Shut the fuck up, mate.'

'The men weren't locals, but one of the bar staff, Andrea, said she was pretty sure she had seen the woman in before. Didn't know her name or where she might live, but she reckoned she has served her before. We have viewed the footage from the CCTV over the door when we left because we could get to it quickly. It's not great for detail but it's better than nothing. Just the back of them as they walk away. You want to see it?'

Clement waved that off. If these guys didn't recognise them, he wouldn't. But the footage would come in handy later if they were able to arrest any suspects. He told Harry they would need all surveillance footage.

'Whatever you need, you got.'

It was better, thought Clement, to sift through the footage calmly. This trio were a good lead as suspects or witnesses, but it was still possible they'd neither saw nor done anything. Right now, it would be better to stuff himself with general information, try to build up a picture of what may have gone down. Plenty of times in his career he'd missed the forest because he was spending too long studying the trees.

As if reading his partner's mind, Graeme Earle entered the fray.

'They paid cash, so no card we can run down. They didn't interact much with the other drinkers but sat over there by themselves for most of the night. One of the blokes was wearing a Darwin t-shirt.'

'One of the patrons thinks they arrived the same time as he did in the carpark. Vague on the time but reckoned around seven thirty.' Di Rivi was checking notes. 'He couldn't swear to it but was pretty sure he saw two men and a woman get out of a Landcruiser. Thought the colour was cream, white or beige.'

It didn't narrow things by much. Half the cars up here were Landcruisers. But again, a little information was a whole lot better than none.

Earle said, 'We've got a BOLO out for two men and a woman in a light-coloured Landcruiser.'

A good start. That would at least get all police in the region alerted. 'We should get any cameras picking up that car on its way here, or after it left.'

'Jo's already onto that,' said Earle. 'She's asked Gimmy to pull everything he can get his hands on.'

'And I've asked all uniforms to keep an eye out for two men and a woman in a Landcruiser, or acting aggressively,' added di Rivi.

That was good thinking too. This could have been a meth-fuelled attack with little rhyme or reason. Shepherd may just have been, like Doctor John sang, in the right place at the wrong time.

The sight of the table numbers on a bench behind the bar gathered like egrets prompted a new idea.

'Did they eat here?' Clement directed this at Harry.

'No.'

Clement was thinking that likely meant they had eaten elsewhere earlier. Tomorrow they should chase up all the restaurants in Broome. There weren't that many. Tonight, they could at least try pizza places, burger joints and anywhere else that might still be open. If they hadn't eaten earlier, maybe the trio would drop in somewhere for a late snack. Clement made his decision.

'Jo, you go back to the station and start checking any road cameras we have, and any servo footage. If they are from out of town, they might have filled up and that could give us a numberplate. And get someone ringing motels, hotels and caravan parks for two men and a woman in a Landcruiser. Graeme, you and I can do a run through town.'

Earl said, 'If these are meth-heads we could lean on our bikie friends.'

Another good thought. The bikies supplied most of the meth, and they know we know, thought Clement. But they must also be aware that any attack on a cop would increase the usual amount of grief tenfold. They might be prepared to point them in the direction of a maverick just to get things back to normal. Earle and Clement could be persuasive when they wanted.

—

Under the halo of a dim cabin light, Keeble was in her car making notes and, by the looks of it, labelling sample bags. The window was open for air, but what air there was was like an old dog refusing to head out for a walk. Clement stopped by.

'Could you grab the hard drives for the exits and the bar? Dump them on Manners' desk.'

Keeble barely looked up. 'No worries. You get anything?'

Clement told her the little they knew. 'We're heading into town, follow up on this group of three.'

She wished them good luck. 'Janene was able to collect Shep's clothes from the hospital. Plenty of blood. Hopefully not all his.'

—

Clement followed Earle back to his place where he dumped his car, then Earle joined him, and they continued. Even with the windows down it was stifling, like being inside a costume. A lost memory was dredged to the surface, a fancy-dress ball with Marilyn in Perth, Clement in a bear suit. How long since I dressed up like that for a party, wondered Clement. Twenty years? It used to be quite the thing, fancy-dress parties. Then when you got older and believed yourself more sophisticated, dinner parties. French onion soup for starters. Lasagne for a main course. Where do those days go? He supposed all social activity got sucked into the maw of parenthood. Instead of dinner parties, you found yourself on canteen or barbecue duty. You lost track of your old circle and became Phoebe's father.

That costume had been incredibly uncomfortable, yet the parties were fun. Would he dare to go to one now? And who would he go as? Would Lena find it pathetic? He was sure Marilyn would. She had enjoyed being Little Red Riding Hood, or Alice. Something that had a pretty outfit as part of it anyway.

Lena, he had no idea. Maybe she would enjoy the challenge, ask him his opinion on who she should go as. He smiled at the thought. He would recommend the Terminator for her: German accent, a motorcycle, and abs hard as concrete.

—

Despite the humidity Clement resisted going to air-con. This was the very start of the season. He needed to toughen up. They had just breached the main drag when Gimmy Moore came on the radio.

'What's up, Sergeant?' Clement spoke into the mike, swapped looks with Earle. Was Shepherd okay? A fist had seized Clement's heart; by the look of Earle, his too.

'Just had a call from the night manager at the Hartog. Young woman bashed, possibly raped.'

The Hartog Motel was less than ten minutes from where they were now.

Friday night, start of the build-up, Shepherd's assault fresh. It never rained but it poured.

'No worries. We can attend.'

'Reason I mention it,' Moore with a dramatic pause, 'the night clerk said the room had been booked by two blokes.'

The same two who bashed Shepherd? Maybe. If it was, the pattern might be escalating. Clement accelerated.

4

The Hartog was one of the cheaper motels, two-storey, concrete, no-frills, metal keys and wobbly doorhandles. The carpark was full, mainly utes. A few nosy guests had gathered outside their units. Some were drinking beers. The air a blood clot. The ambulance had already left but the patrol car was still there, the uniforms who had responded, having been asked to wait by Clement while he was brought up to speed. Clement guessed the night manager was also the day manager, only difference being that after hours the manager was in her adjoining unit instead of the office. She was mid-forties, carrying extra kilos that showed in shorts despite the oversized t-shirt. Thongs on her feet, straggly hair. Clement cut her slack: she'd been fast asleep when she'd been woken by thumping on her door.

'Guests are supposed to call the number but a lot of them know I live here,' she explained. As a gloved Clement and Earle checked the first-floor room, she ran commentary from the balcony outside, where she'd been asked to stand.

About half an hour earlier, a couple returning to their room after a night out had found a naked young woman bloodied, collapsed on the walkway outside room fourteen. While the woman guest had called triple 0 from her phone, her partner came down and had woken the manager. She had rushed up with a medical kit she kept for minor injuries but had realised that was hopelessly inadequate.

'The best I could do was grab a sheet and cover her.'

The men had cleared out. No clothes, no bags. Empty beer bottles and a takeaway chicken box in the bin. Great for DNA and prints. Blood had soaked into the side of the mattress closest to the balcony and formed a map of France. More blood on the floor, and the wall above the dressing table. Clement pictured the woman being punched back into the wall, then being pulled or staggering forward, collapsing to the floor or onto the bed. The blood on the floor could have come from when she tried to get off the bed and make her way outside. Women's clothes, jeans, shoes, a top, a bra were twisted in a pile on the floor. Clement probed pockets for something that might give an ID, aware that the techs would want things as undisturbed as possible. Keeble was on her way. She'd said her team needed a break, but she'd do the work herself.

'Can't sleep anyway.'

Clement wondered if the cause of her insomnia was the oppressive humidity or the psychological trauma of the break-up of a long-term relationship. He cast his eye over the bed, realised what was troubling him.

'The sheet you covered the girl with. Was that from here?'

'Yeah. I just grabbed the first thing I could.'

He couldn't blame her, but she'd contaminated important evidence. He saw Earle, who was on the other side of the double bed, bend down and pick up a phone.

'Pin-protected,' he said.

A task for Manners the station IT guy.

'Fingerprint or face ID?'

Earle checked, nodded. Good, options to open it.

Clement said, 'Get the uniforms to go and ask that lot over there if they saw or heard anything.' No point issuing more detailed instructions, Earle would be across everything.

'Want me to interview the couple too?'

Exactly what he wanted him to do. 'Yeah. Do you know the couple who found her and what room they are in?' Back on the manager. Clement clutching for her name, Christy, or Kirsty.

'Hammond. Room ten.'

He turned back to Earle. 'And could you check any bins outside for bloodstained clothing. The attacker had to be covered.'

Earle left to get started.

'Now, these blokes who rented ...'

'It was a Quickbeds booking under the name James Matar. Double with a single.' She spelled Matar for him.

'You get their rego?'

'Nah, sorry.' No, she'd not seen what car they drove, or even if they drove one, but she assumed they did.

'What about photo ID?'

'Didn't bother. He just walked in and said, "Room for Matar."' As if defending an oversight, she added, 'I mean a restaurant doesn't ask for photo ID.'

'They must have paid a deposit or bond.'

'Of course. That'll be on the computer.'

'Do you have cameras anywhere?'

She said there was a camera above the office door that dumped images onto a hard drive.

'I'll need that off you. Phone number of the blokes in fourteen?'

'It'll be on the computer too.'

'When did they check in?'

'Last night.'

Given it was now Saturday morning, he had to get specific. 'Friday?'

'Yes. I shut the office at six, and it was just before.'

They had booked till Sunday. Clement doubted they would be using the rest of their stay.

'Was the girl with them?'

'Didn't see. Just this big bloke who came for the key.'

She had no idea whether that was Matar, but she had glimpsed the big fellow and a much smaller man in the carpark. She'd not seen them since. Clement moved into the bathroom. No hairbrush, no shampoo, no toothbrush. His supposition: the girl had not been with the guys when they'd arrived in Broome. They had picked her up somewhere.

Clement walked back through the bedroom to the balcony to see Keeble's van arriving. He asked the manager to open her office.

—

By the time he reached the ground floor, the uniforms were interviewing rubberneckers and Earle had stopped to help Keeble lift the heavier cases from her van. The manager went to retrieve her keys from her unit, the slow slap of her rubber thongs stoking Clement's irritation.

Earle said, 'The Hammonds couldn't tell me anything. Only arrived this afternoon, hadn't seen the girl, didn't know who was in the room. They said the girl was unresponsive but was breathing. At first, they thought she might have been dead. The ambos told Crossthwaite and Noble the girl was unconscious.'

Presumably Crossthwaite and Noble were the uniforms. A month back Clement would have been across the newbies' names, but Lena had soaked up a lot of his attention. He glanced at his phone, saw he'd missed a text from Risely: **Josh looking okay re brain damage. Heading home.** Clement passed that on to Earle and Keeble, who was lurking, checking her gear.

Earle said he'd checked the large bins but there was no sign of bloodstains around the bin, or bloodstained clothes in the bin. Out the corner of his eye Clement saw the manager emerge from her unit and lock it methodically. Apparently, a bunch of police wasn't enough to deter potential thieves. At least not so far as she was concerned.

'How are you doing?' he asked Keeble.

'Permanently intermittently fatigued,' she cracked. He could relate. 'That's good about Josh, though.'

'Thanks for doing this one personally,' he said, and meant to place no onus on her to respond. She didn't bother. No point. Nobody was more conscientious than Keeble. She'd want to get whoever did this to the girl off the street as quick as possible. Earle said he would help Keeble get her gear upstairs.

'Manager says she has a camera dumping to a hard drive. If you could grab that before you go? Leave it with the Picador stuff on Manners' desk.'

Keeble saluted.

—

Clement headed for the open office door. The manager had retrieved the booking. James Matar. A Halls Creek address followed, and a phone number, landline. Clement dialled it.

Voice message. 'You have reached the office of Valhalla Mining. We are closed right now. Business hours are nine to four-thirty. Please call back then or leave a message after the tone, thank you.'

Clement didn't bother with a message. He would be onto Halls Creek police and have them chase this down. 'You get a credit card number for the booking?'

'Like I said. It was all done via Quickbeds. We just get a confirmation and the payment minus their percentage.' She checked her screen. 'They used PayPal.'

'You have the details?'

'Quickbeds would have those. All I have is "Paid in full by PayPal". I can give you the booking number, and Quickbeds can give you the specifics.'

'Please.' He was growing weary. Why couldn't it be simple. The printer sputtered. Clement took the paper with the booking number. 'You have a number you can call twenty-four seven?'

'No. After nine p.m. till eight a.m., you are on your own with that lot.'

Something else that would have to wait.

—

Earle read his face as Clement left the office.

'No joy?'

'Eventually, we'll get an address.' Clement explained.

Earle said, 'Keeble will get prints from the room for sure but, unfortunately, she doesn't know if any of those she lifted from the Picador crime scene belong to the attackers.'

This was true. Even if it was the same person or people who bashed Shep, Keeble might as yet have no comparison prints. But at least they could run them for ID. With assaults like this there was a big chance the offenders were in the system. Of course, they'd have to consider legacy prints in the room that could have been there days, but the cans and rubbish would yield fresh prints and that was a big start. He wondered if di Rivi was faring any better than them, and dialled the station.

'Don't really have anything useful. I've only been able to check a couple of videos and there are plenty of Landcruisers on those. What's the story with the Hartog?'

She would have learned the basics from Gimmy Moore. As briefly as possible he told her about the Hartog assault.

'Could be the same people. Listen, I want you to run a check on James Matar.' He spelled the surname. 'Let me know if there's any criminal history. At the same time do a rego check for any vehicle registered to a Matar in Halls Creek, or anywhere in the Kimberley for that matter. Then expand your search.'

'Will do.'

He ended the call. Getting Matar's phone number would help. And they could check social media. So much to do, and being this late didn't help.

'What now?' asked Earle.

Clement wondered if Lena had rolled over and gone to sleep. An image of her naked body flung itself at him. Not tonight, Daniel.

'The hospital.'

—

It was almost three a.m. by the time they made the hospital. There is nothing good about a hospital visit, thought Clement. At least at this hour in the short time it took to traverse the low-lit lawn en route to the glowing building, there was a pocket of momentary calm. Four hours at full tilt, this the first respite. Too brief. The moment the door slid open and Clement stepped inside, it was as if the shiny linoleum corridors were thin sheets of ice separating life from death.

There were three people in the triage area. A man in his thirties in a blue work singlet was nursing a shoulder or arm, his face a picture of pain. The others were an older couple, hard to say what the problem was but the man was coughing plenty.

On the way to the triage desk, a nurse emerged from a doorway, cutting across their path.

Earle said, 'Hi Gabrielle.'

She stopped, smiled brightly. 'Hello, Mr Earle. You looking for the policeman who was brought in?'

From the greeting Clement guessed Earle had likely known her from when she was a youngster.

'Yes. And the young woman brought in not long ago.'

'The policeman didn't require surgery. He's in a room. The woman they brought in went to surgery. If you wait here, I'll see if I can get an update on her status.'

She disappeared down a different corridor to the one from which she had emerged.

'Used to coach the school softball team,' explained Earle.

—

Clement turned his attention to the snack-food machine. No reason he should be hungry, and yet as if he was one of Pavlov's dogs that machine got him thinking about food. He fought that urge, but it was instantly replaced by an image of Lena.

'Good news about Shep.' Earle was suitably hushed.

Yes, it was. Before Clement managed a rejoinder, a diminutive doctor materialised and spoke her name so quickly, Clement missed it. Maybe 'Sue' or 'Tsieu'.

—

The gist was simple. They had put the young woman bashing victim into an induced coma. At this point they could not judge cognitive impairment. The bleeding had been from the nose and mouth. They could offer no opinion as to whether she had been raped, vaginally or anally.

'So far, the signs are good, but she's only just out of theatre.'

She couldn't offer any suggestion as to when the swelling of the brain might reduce. They asked her about Shepherd.

'He's regained consciousness, but he is on painkillers. We're monitoring him closely.'

They asked might they see him.

'For a short time, but he's going to be very groggy and disoriented, and I doubt he will be able to talk. His jaw doesn't appear to be broken though.'

—

They had given Shepherd a room to himself. No doubt Scott Risely had pulled strings. Which reminded Clement, he must let Risely know about the possible linked assault at the Hartog. That he'd leave for the present. Risely had only left within the last hour and there was no point disturbing him right now.

Entering the room, Clement was prepared for a shock. If anything, he was buoyed by what he saw. Shepherd's face was battered and swollen. If his jaw wasn't broken, that was almost miraculous. However, his nose seemed intact, his eyes weren't black and his head was not swathed in bandages. His bare torso already showed signs of bruising, hard to be sure in the soft light. It might have been so much worse. There was the constant pip of what Clement assumed was the opioid being dispensed via a tube. Other catheters for urine or nourishment were attached.

'Hey, mate,' ventured Clement. Shepherd's eyes fluttered, seemed to take a second to focus, and the very slightest hint of a smile appeared near one side of his mouth which made it lopsided. Clement prayed that was temporary. Shepherd tried to raise a hand.

'It's okay, Josh,' said Earle, 'we know you can't talk at the moment.'

It looked like Shepherd managed a slight nod.

'That'll teach you to go drinking at the Picador,' added Earle.

Shepherd's eyes were cloudy. Clement wasn't sure how long he'd be able to focus.

'We're trying to find who did this. Was it two men? Blink for yes.'

He managed a blink.

'You get a good look?'

He tried to blink but this time sleep took over and his eyes didn't reopen. Shepherd's breathing though was audible and even, so there was no cause for alarm. He hadn't been able to tell them much, but that single blink had at least confirmed their suspicions.

—

On the way back out from the hospital Clement dialled Keeble. She was still doing the room at the Hartog. He told her about Shepherd, and she was clearly relieved.

'I'm going to convene the team at seven,' he said, 'but if you sleep in, it's fine, just get the prints and that CCTV in train.'

'Will do,' she said. Next, he rang Jo di Rivi. She had news.

'So far, no criminal record for any James Matar. Not in WA anyway. No vehicle registrations under the name Matar except in Perth and Great Southern. None for a Landcruiser. There's not many anyway. I could chase them up now.'

Clement debated the value of disturbing people at this time. Had there been one for a Landcruiser he would have rolled that dice but … no, it was better to wait a few hours. He told her to hold off. She asked for news on Josh, and he told her what he knew as he cruised to the kerb outside Graeme Earle's house.

'Listen, go home, and grab a few hours' sleep. Graeme and I will be in the station at six but so long as you're there by seven.' He looked at Earle when he spoke, and Earle nodded.

'Keeble is going to bring the hard drive back and we'll get Manners onto that and the phone, but right now we'll achieve more by sleep.'

Di Rivi said she would finish up and be in at seven.

Earle waited for the phone to click off.

'See you in there at six,' he said and ambled up the short path to his front door. Two hours' sleep, tops.

Seven or eight years back Clement could have kept going easily, but not these days. Derby was out of the question. It would have to be his flat above the chandler. He thought about calling Halls Creek now but decided it could wait. If Matar lived in Halls Creek and was heading back by car, they wouldn't have arrived yet. At this time of night all Clement could expect would be a young cop likely still learning the ropes. He'd call in the morning and get somebody from the Halls Creek station to run down Valhalla Mining and see if they could get details on Matar. In the meantime, he would pray there were no further assaults.

—

As he drove the deserted streets to the wharf, he tried to calculate how to divvy up the work. With Shepherd out of action, that left only Charmain Dunstan plus the three of them already in the thick of it, in his detective pool. Dunstan was inexperienced. Best to put her with Jo di Rivi on the assault of the woman. It wasn't that big a handicap. Up here Clement had always used those uniforms he deemed competent to supplement his detectives on important investigations. He believed that it benefited all concerned. By now the likes of Lalor and Hagan were well drilled in what was expected of them.

It took less than ten minutes to reach the wharf. By the time fifteen was up he had brushed his teeth, stripped off and collapsed into bed. The ceiling fan was nowhere near adequate with the atmosphere pressing down on him like Hulk Hogan, so he'd bought a smaller fan that he perched on the dresser. Even before the build-up had started a week or two back, it had been hopeless with Lena and him trying to share his single bed. That had only happened a few times.

—

Lena had loved the Derby house and had moved in right away. After three weeks of sightseeing and touring on her motorcycle she had got a job at the health centre. She drove people, she pushed wheelchairs, she cleaned bathrooms if she had to. And she said she found it satisfying.

'Better than working in a bar.'

Now and again after work, Clement drove to Derby where he'd spend the night, then drive back to Broome and the station next morning. The two-hour journey was a breeze. Other times he would spend the night in Derby with Lena, and the day on any cases in Derby that needed him. That was something he'd always done, but not so frequently.

If Lena wanted to spend time in Broome, she'd ride her motorcycle, and they would stay here. It had only been since Lena that he realised how pathetic his routine had been these last few years. Life was too valuable a gift to squander on takeaway curry for one, regret and nostalgia, no matter how evocative the soundtrack.

He was tired, overtired really, yet sleep sidestepped, made him wallow, all sackcloth and ashes. Even this small flat, his refuge, seemed like a deep empty well now that he was alone.

You've been a fool to allow yourself to be chained this long to the past. The thought was like the repetitive beat of a dragon-boat drum as the blanket of sleep hovered and then was pulled away. Hadn't it been clear, years back, that Marilyn had moved on from him? Yes, he had tried with relationships the last couple of years, but this little space here had remained his grotto, the panic room into which no prospective partner would be granted entrance. Until Lena. And now he saw it for what it was, a cramped hidey-hole perfect for the single man who would not face the reality of where he stood in life.

With that confession made, sleep took him in a single gulp.

5

By ten minutes past six Saturday morning, Clement was at his desk. Keeble, bless her, had set the fingerprints running in the system before she'd finally gone home, her post-it note indicating it had been 4.30 a.m. The prints she had lifted she'd noted were 'excellent'. If there were any matches on the national crime database., Clement was hopeful he would have them by nightfall.

Criminal histories were still a state-by-state thing. Just because di Rivi's search for a criminal record for James Matar had been fruitless, didn't mean he was without an interstate record. The fingerprint database was national, so they had a fair chance of getting a hit. Of course, the name could be an alias. The manager at the Hartog had not viewed a driver's licence to confirm the person who made the booking was the person checking in. These days it was assumed that the online booking requirements would take care of those kinds of details. That was wishful thinking. Even if Matar was the real name of one of the men, though, and he was clean, his associate might not be, and could still show up on the fingerprint database. Similarly with the woman. If she showed up that would give them her identity. From there they could look at partners, family, work colleagues. The ball would be rolling. Clement dialled Manners. The IT man had been given enough time to sleep.

The phone rang a long while before being answered. Manners had recently become engaged, but his accountant fiancée was only rarely visible to the rest of the team.

'Um, what's up?' Clearly Manners, summarily wrenched from sleep understood the significance of an early weekend call.

'Josh got bashed badly last night at the Picador.' Clement detailed Shepherd's last known condition and the Hartog incident. 'Keeble brought in the hard drive from the motel CCTV camera. We have a good idea when to look for one of our suspects. The hard drives from the Picador are here too.'

'Alright, I'll be in soon. Just need to explain to Pip. We were supposed to be out on the water today.'

Clement hated himself for making judgements on people's character but he'd worked with Manners for eight years now, and somehow the idea of the techy nerd being 'out on the water' seemed all wrong. Perched over a boardgame, or wearing a headset while watching his avatar dash through a combat zone, yeah sure, that he could picture.

—

Graeme Earle entered halfway through the conversation. When Clement rang off Earle said, 'Bet you haven't had breakfast.'

'No.'

Earle's big fist dumped a square greaseproof-paper parcel on Clement's desk. The smell screamed bacon and egg.

'You know the way to a man's heart.'

'Bolted mine down on the way over. What do you want me to do?'

'Call Hall's Creek. See if they know Matar or can rouse anybody from Valhalla Mining who might have his details. We'll work from the main room.'

As Earle went off, Clement debated phoning Lena. It would be better than later in public, but it was early. To hell with it, she could drop back to sleep if she wanted. She didn't take as long to answer as Manners had, and she sounded brighter.

'I'm at work,' said Clement. 'Chances are I'll be here all weekend, or all day at least.' She asked after Josh, and Clement explained the situation.

'So you don't know who did it?'

'No direct witnesses and then there was another assault, possible rape that could be by the same guys. So, you know, be careful. We don't know if these guys are meth-heads on a rampage or what.'

She asked him to keep her posted. 'I wish you were here with me.'
He imagined her pout when she said it.

'Me too.'

—

As he climbed out of his seat, his phone rang again. Mal Gross, the
most senior of the station's desk people and the longest serving of
anybody there.

'Scott rang me last night to fill me in about Josh. You want me to
come in?'

'Graeme and I are here now. Of course I'd love you in, but I know
Sunday is golf.'

'I'll have a slice of toast and a coffee. Give me twenty. Any news
how he's doing?'

'We saw him a few hours ago, crap beaten out of him, but no skull
fracture.'

'Thicker than the hull of a submarine.'

Clement explained he thought Shepherd's jaw might have been
broken but it seemed it wasn't, although he couldn't really talk.

'That's one blessing,' cracked Gross. Mal was half a generation
ahead of Clement, and those kind of seeming put-downs were just a
wall to hide a deep affection. Although, frankly, no one would dispute
that Shepherd talked a lot of shit. Clement told Mal about the Hartog
assault. He held off on any detail. Mal would be there soon enough.

—

By a quarter to seven, di Rivi and Charmain Dunstan who was rostered
on anyway had arrived along with Mal Gross, who announced that
Manners was newly arrived in the carpark. Graeme Earle had made
contact with Halls Creek. They were now trying to rouse somebody
from Valhalla Mining. Manners arrived and headed to the kitchen for
a coffee. When the small espresso machine had been purchased the
old plunger pot had been shuffled to the back of a cupboard behind
the Brasso and WD40. Just over a month in, the espresso machine
was buggered because people were too lazy to top up the water, so the
indestructible plunger had been reinstated.

Mal Gross said, 'I know a bloke who was on the board of Valhalla.

Not sure if he still is, but let me chase him up. Chances are the head office is in Perth and they'll have details of all the employees.'

Clement asked di Rivi if she had a list of those Matar phone numbers she'd got when checking vehicles registered to men of that name. She had them on her phone.

'Message them to Mal.' He asked Gross to call the numbers and see if he could establish if any of them might be their person of interest, or at least related to him. Mal was an old hand. Clement had no doubt that he'd sniff out any lead.

Gross said, 'I'll get onto the telcos, see if they have a James Matar of Halls Creek.' Clement had been about to suggest the same thing. Even if the phone numbers didn't match any of the registered owners of the vehicles, they might still obtain Matar's phone number. Australia had a limited number of telcos, so this wasn't that difficult a job. Internet, or pulling data, was a different kettle of fish.

Once they had Matar's phone number, even if he didn't answer, they could check calls in and out. That might lead them to the girl's identity, the other fellow, or both. And they could also try to ping the phone for its current location.

'And something more for you,' added Clement. 'This mob, Quickbeds, took the booking via PayPal. There's a reference number.'

'If it's PayPal, whoever paid will have an email address,' said Gross. 'I'll get Carmel to chase this down while I do the phone.'

Carmel Young was rostered duty sergeant. It would mean they could work with much more speed. Between phone, email and CCTV they should close on Matar rapidly. Gross left for his domain, the front office.

'Right.' Clement felt a surge of adrenalin, food, coffee, action. 'Jo and Charmain, I want you on the Hartog case. If our victim comes to, and let's pray she does, I think she will prefer having female officers. Meantime we need to try to establish her identity, as that could lead us straight to her attackers. There's a chance her prints might be in the system. The uniforms there last night ...' he'd already lost their names. Earle came to his rescue. 'Crossthwaite and Noble.' Clement made an effort to commit them to memory even as he ran on,

'… interviewed a few people but the place is full and there are loads more who might be able to provide significant information. Manners is setting up the CCTV hard drive from the Hartog for us.' Manners waved in acknowledgement and headed for his IT room.

'Is she on the video, do we know?'

'The manager didn't think so, but one of the men is as he checked in. As we know, most likely the vehicle is a white, cream or beige Landcruiser. Graeme and I will look for it from the Picador end, you see if you can grab any footage from the motel or nearby premises that might have a camera. There's nothing in the carpark itself. Whatever you get, you can pass on to Manners while you do the face-to-face interviews. Now, we may be wrong in assuming that these attacks are by the same men. It could be coincidence, don't forget that. We have what we think is her phone. Pin-protected. It has been printed. If she is out of danger in the ICU, I think your first course of action might be to take the phone and use her thumbprint.' Getting open a pin-protected phone could be an absolute nightmare. Sometimes you never cracked it. And trying to get the likes of an international company like Apple involved was a complication he didn't need. At this stage, where they had not much more than suspicions, it would be a waste of time even trying.

Di Rivi said, 'Do we have a photo of the victim?'

'No. The ambos needed to get her to hospital urgently. So I suggest you also get photos of her. They might be confronting, but you may need to use the headshot to get confirmation of an identity. An identity is a priority. But you can also follow up on the Picador. See if the staff and the patrons whose numbers we have think the woman in hospital may be the same woman as was at the Picador.'

Mal Gross had returned and was waiting patiently. Now Clement directed his gaze to him.

Gross said, 'My Valhalla contact is getting onto the head office. He'll get somebody in there asap to check employment records. Carmel is also looking for any James Matar on social media.'

'That's a good idea.' Clement turned back to di Rivi. 'You never know, when you see what she looks like, you might recognise her as the Facebook or Insta friend of one of the James Matars. We might be able to identify both of them that way.' Clement's phone was buzzing. It was Risely.

'Yes, boss.'

'Hospital rang. Josh is conscious but they said to give them another hour to run more checks.'

'Will do, thanks. There's a potential linked crime.' He filled Risely in. Risely cursed under his breath. Nobody wanted a crime spree. Normally, Risely could have expected to have the Regional Commander tap dancing in his ear but as he was about to take up that role himself, he would be spared. For now. Eventually the Assistant Commissioner would find out. Hopefully by then they would have this done and dusted. They ended the call with mutual promises of updates.

Clement passed the news on to the team. He took a large bite of his roll, colder now but he savoured it all the same. Normally this time on a Saturday he'd be cooking for Lena.

'What about the bikies?' asked Earle.

Clement had forgotten all about the idea of approaching them. While they might know something, it was problematic whether they would spill. 'Backburner for now. Let's take a look at the CCTV.' Clement suggested to di Rivi that while she checked on the victim's condition, he and Earle would see what Manners might have found.

She said, 'I'll get Charmain checking reports for missing persons too. Perhaps the Hartog victim has been reported.'

Clement was on the verge of suggesting that it was likely too early for that but held his tongue. He wanted to encourage his team to think of every angle, and who knew, maybe they would get lucky?

—

Manners' office was adorned with Harry Potter, Batman and Marvel paraphernalia. Under the watchful eye of the Joker were two monitors. A post-it note was stuck on one: *Picador Main Door*. On the other was *Hartog*.

'Ready to go,' said Manners.

Earle took the Picador, Clement the Hartog. They knew fairly accurately what time Shepherd had left the bar, and also what time the big fellow from room fourteen had called in to the Hartog office on Friday, so this ought to be time efficient.

There was the usual slightly blurry image you got off these cameras, although the Hartog's was far better than most, definitely clearer than the Picador's.

'Yours is practically hi-def,' joked Earle. Di Rivi had made a note of the time sequence when the trio had left the Picador, and Earle was first to reach the critical juncture.

'This will be them.'

The shot was only of the trio's backs, but it was obvious that one of the men was around one hundred and ninety-three centimetres, at least three centimetres taller than Clement, and by the look of him not a kilo shy of Earle. Unlike Earle, the weight wasn't carried on the gut, arse and hips. This bloke was powerful. The other fellow was much shorter with a solid build. He probably had a centimetre or two on the girl. After taking screenshots, Earle began searching for earlier vision that might show the three entering the pub.

About five minutes after the first success, it was Clement's turn. His screen showed a very big man approaching and entering the Hartog office. Clement froze the frame and screenshotted him. The guy had a moustache, looked late thirties, ethnicity indeterminate. There was a partial image of a vehicle, likely a Landcruiser, moving through the shot in the background, but nothing to identify the vehicle.

Di Rivi entered. 'The hospital says she's still in an induced coma, but we may try and open her phone using facial recognition or thumb.'

'Be quicker than this,' said Manners.

'And I think I may have her photo.' It was Earle hunched over his monitor. 'If she's the same woman from the Picador.' Earle pointed at his monitor which was frozen with the time stamp 19.41. Blurry image and hard to give an estimate of age, other than under fifty. Slightly chubby, non-descript hair of medium length. It looked dark in the photo. In company with the same big man as from the Hartog office, and a smaller man. Closest to the camera, his chin slightly elevated, he was the one captured in most detail.

'Mid-twenties?' proposed Clement.

'I reckon,' said di Rivi.

'Can you sharpen that?' asked Clement of Manners.

'I can give it a go.'

'Separate shots, if possible, too,' requested Clement. 'Then send them to our phones.'

Manners said he would get that done.

'We all agree that bloke is the same as the Hartog?' Clement tapped the big man visible in both images.

'Absolutely,' said Earle.

Di Rivi announced she would leave for the hospital right away.

'We'll see you there,' said Clement to her back. They could spend more time here looking for better shots of the three at the bar, but Clement's instinct was to get moving. Apart from anything else, once they had that phone open, he reckoned there was a good chance there would be clear shots of what were, now, three persons of great interest. Before heading to the car, Clement went out to the front desk.

Mal Gross was on the phone. 'Thanks, appreciate it.' He ended the call. 'That was the Valhalla person in Perth. They're just about to enter the office. Now, good news. From the numbers associated with car regos under the name Matar, I phoned and got a young woman in Perth, Heba Matar. She has a cousin, James, who she says works in mining up north. Says he's never been in trouble.'

That would tally with there being no obvious criminal record.

'He's twenty-four. She's looking for a photo for me. She describes him as average height or just under and stocky.'

The small guy. 'When Manners has sharpened that image, send it to Heba and see if she confirms it's her cousin.'

Clement was ninety-seven percent sure it would be, but better to make that one hundred. 'Did she have a phone number on him?'

'No, but she's given me the phone number for the parents in Sydney. I tried it, but it went through to a voice message. I've left a message to contact us urgently. I'm waiting for the telcos to get back to me. Heba didn't know if her cousin was on Facebook or other social media but she's going to try to find him for me. She doesn't know of any friends he might have up this way.'

Clement was further buoyed. This was all very good news. They had likely identified at least one of the people involved in the assaults. Next, they needed an address and car registration.

'Good work. We're off to the hospital.'

—

Shepherd's eyes were no longer glazed but they didn't have the clarity or alertness that comes with being drug-free. The bruising on his bare torso was more evident with each passing second. In a day or two he would be blue enough to pass as one of the creatures from *Avatar*. No doubt Manners would know the name of the tribe. Clement recalled he had never seen the movie in the cinema. Phoebe was just a baby then. He or Marilyn would lie with her on their stomach on a big blue beanbag, trying to catch a minute or two of television. *Law and Order* or *CSI*. Maybe that was a little earlier, the years swirled together, mist on a distant horizon. Shepherd himself would have been a kid then.

'Did these guys attack you in the carpark?' asked Clement.

Shepherd was working hard to focus. He tried to say 'yeah' but it came out as a hoarse whisper, so he nodded and sipped the water from the cup beside him.

'Was there a woman with them?'

A nod.

'Did she look like she was scared? Did she say anything?'

'No.' An easier word to manage, though pretty much a grunt.

'Did she join in?'

Shepherd shook his head.

'How about names? You hear any names?'

A mouthed 'no'.

'Did you see their car?' Earle again.

Shepherd nodded.

'Landcruiser?' asked Earle.

Another nod. So perhaps it was the big guy or the woman who owned the Landcruiser, seeing as nothing had tripped for 'Matar'. Clement asked if it was white. Shepherd indicated a 'maybe' with a shrug, gestured writing. Clement gave him his pad and pen.

'You get the numberplate?' Clement's hope running ahead, he knew.

Shepherd took the pen and very slowly and deliberately, like a kindergarten child who has just learned their first letters, made a W and a shaky Y. WY was the numberplate associated with registrations from Wyndham, Halls Creek and Kununurra. So that worked.

'Great job, mate,' said Earle.

'We'll get them,' said Clement.

Shepherd offered a thumbs up.

Clement's phone vibrated. A text from Mal Gross: **Heba confirms photo is her cousin**

—

When they emerged back into hospital reception di Rivi was waiting.

'Shep's looking better,' announced Clement. 'But they beat the shit out of him.'

Di Rivi wasted no time. 'She's still in an induced coma but her thumbprint unlocked the phone. She had a vaccination certificate stored. Her name is Heather Dawson, twenty-two. There were text messages from her housemate Dee. We rang her. They both work at Woolies. Heather went for a drink at the Roey last night, about six-thirty. Dee went to the Sun for a movie with a girlfriend and didn't hear from Heather. They're not super close, just share the house. Heather has a boyfriend, Anthony, but he's working on a tourist pearling lugger. Would have been off the coast last night and isn't due back until midday. Dee didn't know any James Matar and didn't have any idea who the two men might be. She hinted that Heather might have gone with the guys for drinks or drugs. Only got a bit worried this morning when she still hadn't showed up. They're supposed to be working today.'

A comprehensive run down. 'Family?'

'Heather is from Carnarvon but Dee didn't have details. Best news though …' di Rivi shoved the phone in Clement's face. A clear shot of the two suspects, James Matar, and the unknown big guy who looked late twenties to thirty. 'This is from Heather's phone. She snapped them yesterday.'

Clement thinking the background looked like the beer garden at the Roebuck. 'Charmain is in the car calling Heather's family. What do you want us to do?'

'Heather doesn't have a car?'

'Doesn't have a licence according to Dee.'

So, the Landcruiser by process of elimination belongs to the big guy, or maybe has been hired, stolen or borrowed. Clement shuffled the courses of action.

'What we really need now is a name for the big guy. If Heather's family can't shed any light, try the Roebuck, see if they used a credit card or if anybody happens to know them. We might get lucky. Check the cameras in case you get a glimpse of the Landcruiser.'

Things were coming together fast.

—

More progress came via Mal Gross the minute they entered the station. James Matar was indeed employed by Valhalla Mining and their people had supplied a Halls Creek address on him. Gross had arranged for the local Halls Creek cops to bring Matar and whoever he might be with into custody. Clement did a mental calculation. The drive from Broome to Halls Creek would take around seven to eight hours. The two men had left the Hartog at likely around midnight. So they could be in Halls Creek now, or quite soon. On the other hand, they might try and throw police by heading elsewhere. It would be better to wait before he and Earle hared off to Halls Creek. Maybe the telcos could get a ping off the phone? Graeme Earle was waiting on his thoughts.

'We'll wait till Halls Creek grabs them or somebody else spots them. Update the BOLO. We're looking for a Landcruiser with Wyndham plates. And can you get them watching the road into and out of Halls Creek?'

It was a Saturday, and Halls Creek might well be understaffed, but it was the best he could think of for now. A full roadblock would be hard to justify but if they had eyes in and out, it would be as effective. 'What about the telcos?'

'Matar's dad rang from Sydney. He'd tried his son's phone but there was no answer.'

'You got the number?'

Of course he had. Gross handed it over on a piece of paper. Clement dialled. The phone rang. And rang. Gross kept talking.

'Matar is with Vodafone. They're trying to ping the phone and will let me know. Also trying to find the last phone tower.'

Clement gave a thumbs up and ended the unanswered call. Matar could run but he couldn't hide.

—

Eventually, they would get a hit on the prints, or the Landcruiser would turn up on video or Matar would arrive back in Halls Creek. Or those two would get themselves into more trouble. But Clement never liked to settle for 'eventually'. For the time being, as there was nothing to do except wait, he told Earle, who had been stifling yawns the last five minutes, to grab more zeds. Though fatigue had dug trenches all around Clement he was determined to maintain a vigil. Once they had the two men in custody it would be different. At least he was able to savour the prospect of calling Lena.

Clement retreated to his office and was about to dial when he was assaulted by the image of Mathias, her uncle. Though they had never met personally, they had once or twice in the early days communicated via Skype.

'Only old people use Skype,' Lena had laughed. He supposed that was true. In more recent times they hadn't bothered. A phone call was just as easy, and Mathias had joked that he could run to the toilet for a pee and keep talking. Clement had been postponing the inevitable confession to Mathias. He checked the time, half-nine. Just the wrong time to call Hamburg. It would be bleak early morning there.

But I have to do it soon, he told himself. It will only get harder. He was readying to call Lena when professionalism got the better of him. He had promised Scott Risely he would keep him updated. His call caught Risely gardening.

'I have to do the garden now. Later in the day is going to be impossible. I'm already frying.'

As it turned out, Risely had been informed directly by the hospital on the condition of Shepherd and Heather Dawson, but he was pleased to learn of the developments with Matar and Dawson's phone.

'Listen, Dan, I've been meaning to have a word to you. You should apply for my job, you really should. I think you'd be a cert.'

Back in the days before Lena, the idea had grazed the extremity of Clement's thoughts but, since then, had vanished. It was burdensome to contemplate so much change. His personal commitment to Lena was increasing. He was becoming more needy, he knew it. Maybe that was not a good thing. Maybe he would scare her off. At the same time a change of job with more responsibility might mean less time on his hands for spending with Lena. And wasn't that the opposite of what he wanted?

What would happen if he applied for the job and then Lena gave him an ultimatum to come on the next stage of her life's adventure with her? This concern had been loitering for weeks but as if it were Medusa, he had steadfastly refused to look it in the eye.

'I don't know ...'

'What's holding you back?'

Lena, of course.

'Is it confidence?'

'I wouldn't want to step out of the field.' This was a part-truth.

'It's not like there are that many cases worthy of you. If you want field action, you should think about going back to Perth. They'd take you in a heartbeat.'

Risely was absolutely correct about seeking more investigative challenges in Perth. If that's what Clement really wanted.

'I'll think about it,' said Clement.

'See that you do, and ...' Risely hovered, 'don't take too long. If it's not in within a fortnight, you'll be too late to be considered.'

'Appreciate that.' Clement ended the call. He needed to speak to Lena about these things, but worried he might scare her off. So many things he must confront. He leaned back in his chair and closed his eyes.

6

She wasn't sure who was with her but there were at least two people back there in the darkness. Ahead was almost as bad; 'think dappled but deep on the grey scale' she reckoned is what she'd say if she ever had to explain this to anyone. Though why she would have to, she had no idea. It was a long corridor stretching way ahead of her, the walls in close on each side were stone, and mouldy, you could smell them, the ceiling clear of her head but not by that much. The light was like dim moonlight but how could a moon shine through the concrete above her? There were no torches fixed to the walls, and she didn't seem to be carrying one either. Maybe one of those behind her had a torch. A bunker, that's what this seemed like. The corridor was endless.

—

But no sooner had that thought jumped from her than the corridor expanded and transformed into her childhood lounge room. On the shelf above the sofa, she recognised the ornaments her mum used to dust when visitors were expected. Characters from Christopher Robin, a little windmill from Greece, a London taxi in miniature. Without warning that house was gone and now she was in bush ... but not Australian bush, more like jungle.

'I'm scared,' came from behind her and she recognised the voice now. It was Jess, one of her old schoolfriends. Why was Jess here? Jess sounded the same as when they were fifteen.

'Don't be pathetic.' A voice she'd heard before but couldn't place. A young guy. 'What are you waiting for?'

It was the guy again, a smart-arse, a dude, you could just tell.

Why had she stopped? It was dangerous here, crocodiles. Dangerous up ahead. Safer to go nowhere.

'This is far enough,' she heard herself saying but couldn't be sure if it was to the others or herself ...

—

Her eyes flick open. She realises she has been dreaming. She is lying on a groundsheet. She feels something coiling around her body, pinning her arms, a thick rope. No, not a rope ... She tries to scream but the python has already wrapped itself around her neck and is crushing her windpipe. It is rolling, tightening, crushing her chest. Its skin seems shiny, it is all motion. Her breathing is shallow and fast. And gets faster. Shallower. She is losing consciousness, panting. She struggles to call out to make any sound, but the force is overwhelming ...

—

Like a U-boat breaking the surface, transitioning quickly from its vague outline below the water to a solid object, she woke this time for real. Her forehead was wet with sweat, her pillow damp, the singlet, the only item of clothing on her body, soaked. The dream slipped away like seawater off the submarine's deck. Light was streaming in through the cane blind that was the border of her open-air boudoir. Her dwelling was not much more than a bush hut, her bed a thin mattress over an old iron single-frame whose legs camped on a synthetic mat thrown on flat dirt. The hut's interior consisted of a living room cum kitchen cum bedroom, plus a bathroom with a toilet that fed into a septic tank. Even with the door and windows open, in summer she found it too hard to sleep inside. The old bushie she'd bought the place off along with an acre of land had given her the heads-up: when the build-up starts, you're better off outside.

She checked her watch. God, 9.30 already.

'Scrounger!' she called. She heard the old bitch lift her body from her favourite spot on the sofa inside, heard her waddle out, a slow tail wag, drooling. A sign the day had begun, and the dark hours could be left behind.

It had been like this for years now, struggling to sleep at night until, exhausted, she succumbed in the early hours. Often, like last night, the pattern could be that she would be able to sleep initially, catching about two good hours of shut-eye. But then she would wake knowing the rest of the long dark night stretched ahead of her, a near endless tunnel, and that there was no remedy but exhaustion. She might read, listen to music or, most often, play her guitar. She didn't play very well but she found it relaxing. That was the one positive weapon she had developed since her problems had begun.

Eight years back.

A pity she had only discovered guitar three years ago. When she'd eaten her way through the heart of the night she would, at least on good nights, start to feel drowsy. With dawn breathing down night's neck she'd finally fall asleep, managing to get another two or three good solid sleeping hours into her. It wouldn't have done for a nine-to-five job, but she had more latitude, and thankfully, when she was in her professional mode as a guide, it was easier. By the time she'd tidied up the camp sites, made sure fires were out or contained and the vehicle was ready for an early start, she would often be able to sleep for three, sometimes four more hours. Which was fine. When she roused her clients, it would be with breakfast already on the go. They would be ignorant she'd already been up a couple of hours.

Thankfully, demand for her services had been very strong this year. Even this late in the season, November, when a lot of the tourist accommodation had closed, there were still people desiring to experience one of the world's most ancient and unblemished lands. She'd just got back from three days up by the Mitchell Plateau with a family, and now had a male client good to go in forty-eight hours. Her friends marvelled at her taking on male clients all on her own.

Many times it would be three or four men comprising the party she was guiding, but it was the one-on-ones that most of her girlfriends were surprised about. Sure, occasionally the men might get flirty, a little fresh with her, but none of them had ever tried anything inappropriate. Occasionally she wondered if it was because she was just too plain, but there were always plenty of dudes at the pub willing to chat her up. Most of her clients were women, two or three, occasionally a woman on her own. They were much more comfortable with a female guide. And families too. The reality was, out there in the bush you were almost certain to see each other naked sometime. No changerooms here, toilet walls were a bush if you were lucky, stings and bites in private places that needed ointment, or just the plain old joy of skinny dipping.

'We're not at war with nature,' she would say in her readiness talk, 'but often it just doesn't like visitors.'

—

While she hadn't retained her entire dream, she'd preserved morsels. She'd been in a cellar, or basement, somewhere underground. And two people had been with her. At some point it had seemed like Jess, but she had a sense that earlier in the dream it had been someone else. That part of the dream was gone to God. It really didn't matter what the setting, however; the general sense of unease was all too familiar. All her sleep problems had started around the same time. Sleep was scary. Sleep itself was the jungle. If she did dream, it usually had an air of foreboding. You didn't have to be Freud to work out why. She had never seen a therapist. Why bother? She knew what ailed her, and nothing, certainly no therapist, was going to exorcise those demons.

That thought connected her swiftly to another.

As she stretched, enjoying the sense of the muscles in her shoulders and neck throwing off night-chains, she tried to remember what it had been like before all her problems had started. Life hadn't been perfect, far from it. She'd busted up with Jacob, or more correctly he'd broken it off with her. But she'd come to realise that relationships were secondary. The person you really needed to live with was yourself. She had managed that, and if that meant living your life in a mental compound then that was a price she was prepared to pay.

Oh, but the sleep ... simple, selfish sleep, that was the thing denied her. How she would love to be able to once more drain it like a vampire draining blood.

She had resigned herself. Things could be a whole lot worse. She looked up at the sky as if that might tell her what lay in store. Pointless, because she already knew. It would be hot and sultry. Nothing was going to get better for a while yet.

7

A light knock on the door brought Clement up out of his sleep. He took a moment to realise he was in the chair in his office. Mal Gross stood at the door waiting patiently. Clement checked his watch. 10.15!

'Shit.' He'd been out to it for close on an hour.

'There was no point waking you till now,' said Gross. 'Halls Creek picked up James Matar ten minutes ago.'

Clement sat upright. His back was stiff, his legs numb. He gave himself a face massage that approximated rubbing his eyes but was more about stretching the skin down.

'The other bloke?'

'No sign.'

The disappointment yanked him down. Clement got to his feet, unsteadily.

'Made you a fresh coffee,' said Mal Gross.

'Lifesaver,' managed Clement. He roused Graeme Earle who was stretched out on the bed in the rarely used sick bay. Five minutes later, with a mug of coffee in his mitt, Clement was on the phone to Steve Eaton, the ranking officer at Halls Creek.

—

James Matar had been picked up at a roadblock on the Great Northern Highway on the outskirts of Halls Creek. It appeared Matar had hitched a ride in a ute. According to its driver, Matar had approached him at a Derby service station, asking for a lift north and offering fifty bucks for petrol. There had been no sign of the unidentified big man assumed to be Matar's accomplice in the ute, and the driver had sworn blind he had only given a lift to Matar, who had appeared to be on his own.

If Matar and the accomplice had split up in Derby then the other fellow could have taken the Gibb River Road – the famous, in many stretches unsealed artery that ran east then north from Derby. It was not the route you would take if looking for a quick getaway. Perhaps Matar and his mate had split up knowing the police would be looking for two men. Then again, they may not have realised the police would be onto them so quickly. If they had split up in Broome, then the big bloke could still be here in town.

'What have you told Matar so far?'

As requested, Eaton had merely told Matar that he was required to accompany police for questioning in relation to two assaults in Broome.

'What do you want me to do with him?' asked Eaton. Clement's brain was a flea circus. He needed to speak with Matar as soon as possible. Eaton could arrest him on suspicion of the Shepherd assault and hold him for six hours with extensions. Even if they could grab a light aircraft now it would be the best part of two-and-a-half hours to fly to Halls Creek. Seven-and-a-half hours if they drove. Clement wondered how police in Manhattan or London would react if they had to cover that kind of distance.

'Print him and get a DNA sample. Get his shoes and clothes as evidence. Was he travelling with luggage?'

'He had a backpack with him.'

'Any bloodstains on the pack or clothes, or shoes?'

'Nothing to the naked eye.'

A thought hit Clement. 'Why don't we do a Zoom interview?'

Such an interview might not be admissible for court, he was unsure, but that was a secondary concern. Right now, he needed information.

'I suppose we could.'

Fingerprints taken by Keeble would surely establish Matar had been in room fourteen of the Hartog. DNA would likely be necessary in relation to the assaults.

'I'll call you back in ten minutes.'

—

He roused Earle, who looked as untidy as he did. 'I needed that sleep,' Earle said.

Clement laid out the news. I must make sure my head is clear, he told himself. It was amazing how often a careless decision made when weary or fatigued could cost many hours in investigative time. Leaving Earle to get himself together, Clement went to the bathroom, washed up, studied the mirror. The deepening ruts below his eyes said he was kidding himself if he reckoned Lena would still find him desirable a year or two from now.

Of course, I shouldn't be thinking of my own personal shit, he thought. But trying to eliminate those concerns was like trying to eradicate weeds. They sprouted anywhere, anytime, even in the thick of the hunt. He wiped those thoughts as he wiped his hands. There was simply no point indulging himself. But he allowed one last thought: was Lena making him feel younger or older?

He left the bathroom and popped his head in to Manners. The fingerprint database was still churning, and Manners methodically searching traffic cameras. Manners spoke without invitation.

'The sarge and I are liaising with the telcos,' he said. 'If we get any phone numbers, we can progress things.'

—

Clement and Earle set themselves up in the main room and made the Zoom call to Halls Creek. The screen lit up, close on the florid face of Eaton. Around Clement's age, he carried an extra kilo or two but essentially looked healthy. Especially his face. His skin, observed Clement, florid or not, looks more youthful than mine. Maybe he was younger, maybe he was one of those blokes who just had a young face. Or maybe the years were filching a heftier tax from Clement. Such thoughts had rarely bullied him before Lena.

'Good to go,' said Eaton and as he stepped away revealed James Matar sitting on a chair facing the camera. Eaton took up a position behind him, to the side. Matar hadn't shaved and his hair was greasy and unkempt. He had been sweating too. He was of solid build. His low forehead could have you reaching for stereotypes. In this case 'not bright', but Clement knew no judgement could be formed from sight alone. The bloke had probably been travelling for hours in a ute, it was sweltering, and he could have any amount of drugs in his system. All of which would contribute to the glazed veneer.

'I'm Detective Inspector Daniel Clement of the Broome police. This is Detective Sergeant Graeme Earle. Could you state your name please?'

'James Matar.'

Clement wasn't worried about the formalities yet. Matar hadn't been charged with anything.

'James, we know you were in Broome last night at the Picador in company with another man and Ms Heather Lawson. A policeman was badly assaulted in the carpark, and he has identified you as one of the people who assaulted him.'

'That's bullshit.'

'You're denying you assaulted Detective Sergeant Shepherd last night.'

'Never assaulted anyone.'

He shifted in his chair, an obvious tell.

'You booked a room at the Hartog Motel.'

'That's right, there a law against that?'

'You booked through to Sunday but left early.'

'I got homesick.'

Earle spoke for the first time. 'Sure it wasn't because you bashed Heather Lawson senseless?'

Matar's mouth dropped open, his eyes darting. 'What? No. That's bullshit!' He almost leapt out of the chair.

Clement remained steady. 'Heather Lawson is in a coma in hospital. Can you see this, James?' Selecting the photos of Lawson unconscious in hospital that Clement now had on his phone, he held it to the computer lens. 'She's barely recognisable but that's her.'

'We never did that. When we left her, she was fine.'

'Who's we?' asked Earle. 'We need your mate's name.'

Matar seemed to consider acting dumb. 'Me and Nick.'

'Nick who?' asked Earle.

'I dunno his second name. Nick, that's all I know.'

So, it was going to be like that, thought Clement, who was suddenly feeling charged.

'Where is Nick now?'

'No idea.'

Earle, gruff. 'Listen, mate, don't mess us around. We're giving you a chance. Where's your buddy?'

Matar was getting jumpy. 'He's not my buddy. I told you I don't know where he is.'

'What's his phone number?' Clement demanding.

'I don't know. I never got his phone number.'

'It's not in your phone?'

'No!'

Clement said, 'Listen, James, you haven't been charged with anything yet but if you have his phone number and aren't giving it, you are hindering a police investigation.'

Matar maintained ignorance.

'Sergeant Eaton, could you get Mr Matar's phone and have him search through it while you watch.'

Matar protested it was a waste of time. However, Eaton, using gloves, passed the phone to Matar and watched as he trawled through.

'See, no Nick. I told you.'

Eaton took the phone back. Clement was inclined to believe Matar. He asked when Matar last saw Nick.

'At the motel.'

Earle playing the heavy. 'You raped the young woman, you bashed her, and you both decided you had a better chance if you split up.'

'No!' Matar almost screaming it. 'You're trying to fit me up.'

'When exactly did you last see Nick?' Clement keeping it neutral.

'I dunno ...' his head bobbled, '... I suppose it was about half-twelve.'

'Before? After? Exactly?'

'Before, a bit before.' Moistening his lips.

'So, you decided you'd had enough of Broome, and you left the Hartog, splitting up with Nick, even though you didn't have a ride to get to Halls Creek.'

A moment while Matar searched that to see if there was a hidden trap. 'Yeah.'

'And Heather Lawson was asleep in the room when you left? Uninjured?'

'Yeah. She was fine.'

'So you just left the room with Heather asleep inside?'

'That's right.'

'See, this is what I find hard to grasp, James. That at one in the morning, you just quit a motel that you'd already paid an extra night for.'

Matar was agitated, sweating up. He broke.

'Nick was a bit crazy. I didn't want to hang around with him any longer.'

First step.

'What did he do that made you think he was crazy?'

Matar seemed unsure whether to answer or not.

'Did he hurt Heather?'

'No. I told you.'

He hadn't of course told them anything really. Clement changed tack.

'Are you and Nick good friends?'

'I don't even know his second name!'

'So why don't you tell us all about how you two met.'

There wasn't much to tell. The previous Thursday night he'd met Nick in the pub at Halls Creek. Nick said he was from Kununurra, that he had a few days off work and was driving towards Broome without any specific plan.

'He said he was from Kununurra?'

'That's right.'

'Did he say where he worked? If he was married ...?'

'Think he said he worked at the council.'

Clement's look was enough. Earle left the room. Either he would call Kununurra or more likely leave that to Mal Gross. They would send through the photos they had. Kununurra was small, there was a good chance somebody would recognise the bloke, especially if he worked for the council.

'So you met him in the pub?' Clement steering the conversation.

Matar took it up. They got on well. They had a heap to drink, and he invited Nick to crash at his place. Clement suggested they might have consumed drugs.

'Just a bit of pot,' Matar said. Clement didn't believe him but let the story continue. Nick had suggested Matar join him in Broome for the weekend. As Matar had Friday through Sunday off anyway, he agreed and booked a room.

They had left Friday morning, driven to Broome, and checked in at the Hartog. Then gone to a few pubs, smoked a few joints. They picked up Heather Lawson at the Roebuck. She seemed up for 'a bit of a party'.

Earle returned and silently resumed his seat, hearing how Nick had scored meth from a bloke that Heather knew about. They had a smoke. Matar only indulged 'to be social'. They then went to the Picador for a drink.

Leaving the Picador, Matar claimed he went to the gents while the other two carried on to the carpark. When he came out into the carpark, Nick was 'standing over some bloke on the ground, kicking him'. Matar pulled him away and they drove to the Hartog where he and Nick had sex with Lawson.

'She was absolutely up for it.'

After sex, Nick and Lawson smoked more meth. Matar claimed he had seen too many meth casualties, so he stuck to a joint.

'The girl curled up on the bed and went to sleep.'

However, according to Matar, Nick seemed 'wired' and Matar decided he didn't want to spend any more time with him. It wasn't his idea of fun, hanging about in a motel room. When he said he was going to leave, Nick said he would go too. He was worried about cops after the fight in the carpark. They both left the motel. Nick tried to convince Matar to head back with him, but Matar reckoned the trip back with Nick would be too dangerous for all sorts of reasons, so he refused.

'What are the reasons it would have been too dangerous?' Clement was sure Matar was withholding.

'He had a rifle in the back.'

That elevated the threat.

'Did he use it or threaten anybody with this rifle?'

'No. But I didn't want to be alone with him. He was losing it a bit.'

'By raping and beating up Heather Lawson.' Earle interjecting.

'I never said that.'

But you were scared, thought Clement. Yes, you were.

'Were you worried what he'd do when he found out you wanted to split up?'

'Not really. It was more ... him calling me a bunch of names. Weak cunt, stuff like that.'

'And you weren't scared, even though he had a rifle.'

'Not then I wasn't, but I didn't want to spend another seven or eight hours with him.'

When Matar left, he said he didn't even look around at Nick, just jogged off. Luckily for Matar almost right away he'd scored a lift to Derby.

Clement noted details of the people who allegedly gave him a lift to Derby: three Indigenous boys in an old Commodore. No names or number plate.

'So it's possible that Nick went back up to the room after you left.'

'S'pose. But he had all his shit with him.'

Clement was certain Matar wasn't telling the whole truth. But the part about the Hartog fitted his body language.

'You said you didn't attack Sergeant Shepherd.'

'That's right. I didn't see anything. Nick said the bloke had a go at him.'

Clement looked at his partner. Earle pulled a face. Would Matar attack Shepherd? Shepherd was a big bloke. It was more likely Nick would be the aggressor. That didn't mean Matar hadn't joined in. And naturally Matar was going to paint himself the innocent. Josh Shepherd had fingered them both. However, it was fair to say he wasn't absolutely alert when doing so. He'd been bashed and was sedated. When Shepherd was recovered, he would be able to give a precise account.

'We're going to keep you in custody for now, James. When we pick up Nick, which we will, he's going to have his story. If it differs from yours, and my guess is it will, you could be in the shit. So I think if there's anything you would like to say or add, this would be the time. And if you have any idea where we can find Nick, now would be the time to tell us.'

'All I know is he said he lived in Kununurra. I got no idea where he is.'

'Did he mention how long he'd been there, or where he was from?'

Matar shifted. 'Nah, I can't remember. I don't know where he was born or anything, but he talked about Darwin a bit.'

'How do you mean?' asked Earle.

'Just, you know, pubs and good places to hang out. He's obviously spent a bit of time there, but I dunno when.'

Clement let it go at that.

'Now, I presume you will have no objection to giving us a blood sample to confirm you have only a low dose of methamphetamine in your system? Supporting what you told us, that you barely indulged. And it can help us clear you for the assaults.'

This was stretching it. Matar seemed genuinely panicked.

'I dunno.'

'Well, it's going to work in your favour when we confirm there's not much in your system. Especially if Nick's is high like you're saying.'

Clement's main intent was to gauge how honest Matar had been. Judging from his reaction, it was safe to say, not completely.

Eventually he caved. 'Yeah, okay.'

'That's great. Thank you. Alright James, Sergeant Eaton will look after you until we either clear you or arrest you. But if you know anything you haven't mentioned, or remember something, you get the officers there to call me, okay?'

Matar blinked, managed to nod.

'Thanks, Sergeant.'

As soon as the computer image vanished, Earle told Clement that Mal Gross was 'onto Kununurra'.

Good, things were moving. Clement asked Earle his thoughts on Matar.

'Shep could have been unsure who was doing what to him, but it seems bloody convenient that Matar is having a pee when it all went down.'

Clement agreed. 'We'll be able to check his shoes, maybe see if they were used to kick Shep. What about Heather Lawson?'

'He seemed genuinely shocked.'

Again, Clement agreed.

Earle said, 'Maybe he was so out to it he didn't know what he did. But then he'd be soaked in blood and the quickest reaction is to get rid of the clothes. They weren't at the motel.'

'We need to check the surrounding streets. See if there are any clothes like that. Mind you, if he's lying about getting the lift from Broome to Derby, and went that far with Nick, say, they could have dumped their clothes anywhere.'

Under that scenario, the car would surely have blood in it. They needed that Landcruiser.

'Maybe Matar passed out, came to, found the girl unconscious, and Nick gone,' offered Earle. 'If he was on the single bed and he was careful, he could have stepped around the blood.'

Clement argued, 'But then he wouldn't have been surprised when he heard Lawson had been bashed.'

As always, by the process of elimination you were drawn to the most logical conclusion that would fit the admittedly incomplete facts they had.

'However, it would be possible,' said Clement, 'things went just as Matar said. He was worried about Nick's behaviour, bashing a bloke in the carpark. He wanted to get away. He left. Nick, angry, went back up to the room and whatever happened with Heather Lawson took place then.'

Mal Gross appeared, wearing a broad smile.

'Name is Nicholas Cooper, works for the council at Kununurra, mainly on roads. Hasn't been in any trouble there, no record here in WA.'

Earle said, 'He mentioned Darwin, apparently. Might be worth checking with NT.'

Gross acknowledged with a nod.

Clement said, 'Let's say Matar is telling the truth and he left about twelve-thirty. Cooper goes back up to the motel, rapes or bashes Heather Lawson and leaves, when ... one? One-thirty?'

Shrugs of agreement.

'If he heads back to Kununurra direct via Halls Creek, he'd get to Halls Creek ...'

'Say eight hours,' said Earle.

'Nine-thirty,' said Gross.

And now it was a little after eleven a.m. Clement calculated.

'It's possible he got through Halls Creek before we alerted them.'

'In which case,' said Gross, 'he'd be halfway to Kununurra now.'

'Unless he's still here or took the Gibb River Road or headed north or south!' Earle threw his hands up.

Too many options. Clement tried to place himself in Cooper's shoes. Meth-head, in trouble. Would he peel off to parts unknown or head to the familiar? Would he be prepared to take a slower journey along the Gibb River Road?

'My gut tells me he'll head back home to Kununurra as quick as he can, hope we're a few steps behind him. If he's going to run, I reckon he will grab what he needs, maybe head back to the Territory.'

But his gut could be wrong. He made his decision.

'Mal, I want you to check with the telcos and see who Cooper's provider is. We need to ping that phone. Then I want you to alert all the roadhouses along the Gibb River Road just in case. I want whoever we can get on the Great Northern looking for that Landcruiser. And warn everyone he is likely armed.' His eyes met Earle's. 'We are going to Kununurra.'

8

As much as she had enjoyed her time as a primary-school teacher, Sarah Larkin's passion had always been art, and that she now had the opportunity to indulge herself in this was more than enough compensation for the loss of income. Even after the unexpected development that she had been carrying not one child but two, and the subsequent birth of the twin girls, Rob's wage had so far proven sufficient. Perhaps as they grew older, or another child entered the picture, the economics might become more difficult. For now, however, she was determined to enjoy every minute she could painting. Getting to spend so much time with the girls, now going on for four, was an additional bonus. Naturally, with them in tow she couldn't have the same single-minded focus on her art as she would if it were just her out here. She liked to find unusual and exotic places to render in watercolours, but it was impossible to hike far with the girls. The gorges were magnificent but for now she needed to paint such terrain from a distance. For this reason, she tended to stick more to easily negotiated bush, or the water.

Of course, it was never the same as if it were just her on her own. Water could prove treacherous. She had debated bringing them today to a remote spot near Ivanhoe Crossing. That wasn't too long a boat trip from the town at Kununurra, though a fair bit longer than the fifteen minutes it would take if she drove. Margaret, her elderly neighbour, wouldn't have minded being on twins-duty, yet the truth was, Sarah loved having them with her. But you were always on guard having two little ones in crocodile territory. That awareness became keener when you had launched the tinny with the girls strapped into their lifejackets. It wasn't drowning that scared you shitless. It was coming up against some monster salty. Especially when there had been talk of a big one east of here. She wasn't planning on going that far east. Still, up here, you never knew.

A few years before she and Rob had moved here from quaint and cold Manjimup, a tourist had been taken by a crocodile. In recent times some of the locals had had narrow escapes. All this flowed through her mind as the gentle breeze made by the bow splitting the water ruffled her hair. Not much more than a waft, it was still welcome. The sunlight crackled. The outboard was not powerful, but it had enough guts to push the boat to safety quickly if she needed. The girls were well behaved and sat quietly. They had been well drilled that they were not to move about, fight, or even put their hands in the water. They had seen crocs from a distance and had a sensible level of fear.

Sarah alternated a steady watch on the water ahead, with close examination of the muddy bank to starboard. She could put the boat into the bank if needed, so long as there was no sign of any crocodiles about; however, she had a better plan. Not far from here were the remnants of an old jetty. They reminded her of a skeleton from one of those archaeological sites on TV, where they try to reconstruct a whole animal using a few remaining bones. The deepest part of the jetty had crumbled; only a few wooden vertical pylons were left. However, the first couple of metres close to the bank remained intact. The planks were wobbly but stable enough. The kids could climb up onto that and she could tie the runabout there while she painted. A little path ran back into the bush from where it would be safe enough for the kids to explore and picnic.

The runabout rounded the bend in the river, offering a view of the jetty's carcass. She drew closer, the mum part of her brain thinking it might be best to feed the girls first. It was 12.30; the girls, who normally ate lunch at midday, would be hungry. They would settle better if she fed them soon. She slowed the tinny in preparation for a stop.

'What's that, Mummy?'

It was Anastacia, the more talkative of the twins. At first, Sarah couldn't see what she was pointing at. Then she realised it was one of the closest stumps to them, furthest out in the water.

'It's part of the old jetty.'

'But there.'

Now she saw where Anastacia was pointing. It was just above the waterline and more to the back side of the post. As her eyes zeroed in, she at first told herself she was imagining things, it was a plastic bag or something that had been caught.

But now she was only two metres away and she had no doubt what was lashed tight to the post.

It was part of a human forearm and hand.

—

On approach to Kununurra Clement found himself, as always, stunned by the landscape: ochre dirt, patches of tropical vegetation, a long silver streak of water with green trim, humps of rock like the backs of ancient bison. I am the sheriff of all I behold, thought Clement, and half-smiled at the truth of it. He doubted that any other law enforcement officer in the world had a jurisdiction as big as his. I must bring Lena up here, he thought. She hadn't made it this far yet on her motorcycle tours. The Police Air Wing out of Karratha had requisitioned a Cessna for them. Had Clement identified Cooper earlier, he and Earle might have been able to take the commercial flight from Broome, but it was too long to wait for the next.

Graeme Earle sat beside him, paying no attention at all to the surrounds that tourists came from the other side of the planet to see. He had Wordle.

They had been in the air around two hours. Clement checked his watch. Just after one-thirty now. If he had guessed right and Cooper was heading back to Kununurra, the cops could be intercepting him right now. If he had guessed wrong, then they had a long way to go yet, and Scott Risely could pass the problem of the budget related to this trip onto his successor. Possibly Clement himself. They had warrants in train and when they came through, they could search Cooper's house and car. His car at this stage being probably more pertinent. If any of Heather Lawson's blood was found in there, Cooper would be up the creek.

—

Simone Livesy, as was often the case, had been designated to meet them. The sergeant was waiting for them on the other side of the tarmac heat-haze, a bottle of water for each. She drew them from her hip, gunslinger-style.

'Have they picked Cooper up?' asked Clement, thanking her for the water.

'Not yet.'

Even after that short walk they both drank greedily. Clement guessed it would officially be around thirty-seven degrees Celsius. On the tarmac it was likely forty-plus. Clement checked his phone, hoping there might be new information from Mal Gross, Manners or di Rivi. Nothing.

Livesy shot a thumb at the Kluger just the other side of the wire fence. 'This will be your car. You just need to drop me back to the station.'

'You can walk, can't you?' joked Earle.

'Watch it, you.' Livesy made a gun out of her finger and pointed it at Earle. 'You're booked at your usual.' That would be the Oxford, a good solid hotel. Clement made enough trips here each year for it to be familiar. 'Just booked for one night so far, but I've asked for a hold.'

She handed Clement the car keys. They walked through the gate and climbed into the Kluger. Clement and Earle had each brought a small backpack. Clement's case contained t-shirts, shorts, socks, jocks, a toilet bag and a battery charger. If things ran on, he'd buy what he needed.

Clement asked if she'd come in to work especially for them.

'Well, for Josh, really.' Most of the police in the Kimberley knew one another. 'I took a drive by Cooper's house on the way here but there was no vehicle present.'

Livesy eased herself into the back seat. She was mid-thirties, but the sun had extracted taxes from her skin.

'What about the warrants?' asked Clement.

'On their way. Your man Mal is a dynamo.'

He sure was. The station was only a short drive, but long enough to establish that Nicholas Cooper had been no problem since living in Kununurra.

'We got onto the town clerk. Cooper's been here ten months.' Kununurra was a small town, two main streets. Most everybody knew one another. 'My husband's mate is a bigwig at the council. Cooper hasn't ruffled any feathers.'

So maybe it was a drug-fuelled rampage? They were becoming all too common in the Kimberley. Clement found himself wishing for the good old days of pot, heroin even, when users curled up 'on the nod'. Meth was a bulldozer ploughing down everyone in its way.

—

The warrants were waiting for them at the station, along with Callum Nelson, the sergeant who, though twenty years younger, filled the same role here as Mal Gross in Broome. Like Gross and Livesy had done, Nelson had given up his Saturday. Clement had worked with him before and had found him very competent.

'Still no sign of him, but he could have taken a break. I've got a patrol car heading west keeping an eye out. The house is rented. Cooper is sole occupant. I've spoken to the owner. He lives up the same street. If Cooper isn't there, give me a call and I'll get him to open up for you. I've got Davis and Fernandez to back you up.' He nodded at two uniformed cops in their twenties. They reminded Clement of Shepherd with their short, styled haircuts and muscles honed from hours in the gym. This injected him with emotion he never realised he'd feel on behalf of Shepherd, the poor kid lying there blue as the jokes from a buck's-night comedian.

Clement thanked Nelson, introduced himself and Earle to the constables, took the warrants and left. Davis and Fernandez followed the Kluger in a paddy wagon. Thankfully the air-conditioning was strong and quickly kicked in. Clement felt his phone vibrate, saw it was di Rivi.

'Yes, Sergeant.'

She asked how it was going and Clement told her. 'Hope I haven't pulled the wrong rein.'

'Charmain just got back from interviewing Anthony Edmonds, Heather Lawson's boyfriend, at the hospital. Pretty devastated, as you'd expect. He had no idea who she was meeting at the pub. He'd left first thing Friday on the boat. Dropped in to see her at Woolies soon as he got back, and the housemate Dee told him what had happened. He said they didn't use drugs apart from a bit of pot. Didn't recognise the photo of Cooper or Matar.'

'How did he react?' Last thing Clement needed was a vigilante.

'Hold on.' He heard di Rivi checking with Dunstan. 'Very calm, teary.'

Hopefully one less thing to worry about. 'And how is her condition?'

'Her vitals are good, there is some reduction in the swelling of her brain, but they are being cautious.'

'You know if Mal has had any luck with Cooper's record or phone number?'

'I think they've got the telco and they are trying to ping the phone but nothing yet. Nothing on his record.'

He thanked her for keeping him updated and ended the call as they swung into Cooper's street.

—

It was on the outer edge of town, the house as basic as you could get, dark brick with aluminium sliding windows. No lawn, just a gravel patch out front of a low, cement porch with a couple of poles. The adjoining carport was vacant. A palm threw scant shade. No semblance of pot plant or garden.

'I'll check,' said Clement and forced himself out into the heat. It was like walking through a wall of soggy cardboard. He went to the door and knocked, just in case. When there was no answer, he dialled Nelson and asked him to call the owner.

Earle showed solidarity, switching off the engine and abandoning the air-con to join his partner in the shade of the carport. It made about one degree difference, but at least future skin cancers would be less likely. Clement thought of dismissing the uniforms but decided it was better to keep them in case Cooper suddenly materialised.

—

Thankfully the owner didn't waste any time. A figure emerged from a house further up the street and began walking their way. As he got closer Clement saw he was a man of about sixty in a chain-store ersatz Hawaiian shirt, shorts and thongs. He was three-quarters bald and without a cap. Clement couldn't fathom that in this climate.

'George Antinovic,' said the man as he arrived.

More introductions. Antinovic had big rough hands. Clement guessed builder or miner in his past. While Antinovic sorted through a key ring, Clement asked him how long Cooper had been living here.

'About six months. There was another bloke here to start with and Nick took the second room off him. Then the other fella left, and Nick took over the lease. That was about a month ago but he's still on his own.'

Antinovic opened the door then stepped back to allow them to enter. It was stifling inside.

'There's an air cooler.'

He fiddled around and the cooler rumbled. You could paint a battleship with a toothbrush in the time it would take this place to cool.

'Any problems from Cooper? Complaints?'

'Nope.'

'Alright, well, we'll take it from here,' said Clement. 'We can drop the key back to you.'

'Number seven,' said Antinovic. His thongs slapped their way back up the street.

'You may as well tell our backup we'll be okay,' said Clement to Earle, who went off to comply.

There was no point opening windows because the air outside was so heavy it wasn't shifting. Blinds were drawn. That cut out a few rays at least. The living room was a dump but Clement had seen far worse. He was sweating already as he walked into the adjoining kitchen, donning latex gloves. You didn't want to leave Cooper any escape hatch where he could claim evidence had been planted. Dishes were still soaking in a sink, tumblers with the remnants of what smelled like bourbon and Coke had been herded onto the edge of the sink and left.

He heard Earle return.

'Living the high life,' he said.

Clement checked the fridge. It was running. Eggs, butter and a solitary can of beer. Half a bottle of Coke.

'There's a computer.' Earle's voice floated in. 'Fuck, it's hot in here.'

Clement stepped back into the living room, had a sense that the cooler was achieving something. Not much though. Earle was in the bedroom where the lingering smell of marijuana had nowhere to flee. The bed hadn't been made, an opened jar of Vaseline with a pubic hair curled in it was on the dresser. The laptop was an Acer and was sitting on a small desk. Clement pressed the on button, hopeful. The screen took a while to fire up. Password-protected. To be expected.

He was melting in here. There was a desk fan. Clement put it on, copped a blast of hot air. That wasn't going to help much. Still at the dresser, Earle hooked a biro under the handle of the top drawer and pulled it open.

'Bingo.'

Clement walked back and looked over his partner's shoulder, saw an ice pipe. Earle photographed it, pulled the next drawer, empty apart from a few socks, jocks and underneath them, an external hard drive. That was promising: often they were not password-protected.

'Let's grab these and get back to the station. I'm dying.' The interior had barely improved by the time they switched off the air cooler.

—

After dropping the key back to Antinovic with a request he notify them as soon as he heard from or saw Cooper, Clement drove to the nearest supermart. The car air-conditioning was a blessed relief but hadn't hit its peak, and the water Livesy had given them was already hot.

'Let's hydrate.' His shirt was soaked.

In the cool of the little store, Earle grabbed a non-alcoholic ginger beer, Clement went for some tropical fruit combo. He fought the urge to stick his head in the fridge. They guzzled most of their drinks before they'd made it back to the Kluger. Clement's phone rang. It was Mal Gross.

'At last.' He sounded as frustrated as Clement himself. 'At eight-oh-six this morning there was a ping on Cooper's phone at Halls Creek. Nothing since.'

So, the good news was that to have reached Halls Creek by then, he must have taken the Great Northern Highway, likely to come back to here. The bad news was that he hadn't yet turned up, and there was no further indication of the phone's current location. Maybe he'd discarded it in the vast pockets of no-signal you found up here. Possibly he had pulled off into the bush to take a nap. However, it couldn't be ruled out that he had headed south down the Tanami or even due east along Duncan Road from where he could head onto the Buntine Highway or continue north on Duncan. The fact he had reached Halls Creek before expected meant he was either driving super-fast or he'd left Broome earlier than they'd calculated. It was frustrating that things couldn't be nailed down further, but it was what it was. This was a massive area to police, and even though the escape routes were few it was no easy task to man them.

'Let's get eyes on the Tanami for a start. Call everybody we can and keep a lookout for the vehicle. Same for Duncan Road in case he tries to get back to the Territory direct.' The border to the Northern Territory was just beyond the Bungle Bungles. Cooper would be loath to abandon everything in Kununurra, reasoned Clement, but nothing could be left to chance. He could call for air surveillance but how long would it take to set that up? Clement thanked Mal and asked him to keep him informed of any developments at all.

—

At the station Livesy volunteered her office and computer. Clement didn't want her to lose a day of rest for what might amount to thumb-twiddling. 'We can manage this. You and the sergeant should enjoy your day while you can.'

She protested but Clement assured them they could handle things from here.

'Go and enjoy the pool,' said Earle. Eventually she agreed, Nelson too.

'But I'll be on standby,' Nelson assured them.

On a long shot, Clement called Cooper's phone number that Vodafone had provided Mal Gross. No signal. Nothing. For now, Earle and Clement were marking time. They turned their attention to the external hard drive and ran it off Livesy's computer. The hope that there might be something in there that would lead them to him was a faint one.

It had one folder: Photos. They opened it and were flooded with images of naked women. The photos were not professional. This was Cooper's personal stash, that much was obvious from the snippets of background beyond the gynaecological close-ups. A reflection or two of Cooper himself nailed it. Despite there being well over a hundred photos and a dozen videos, Clement and Earle could identify only four separate women, and two of them had facial features partially obscured. They were pretty certain Heather Dawson wasn't among the four.

'Look at this,' Graeme Earle tapped the screen. The still image showed a naked young woman, her arms and legs tied down, it seemed, to the legs of the bed. She could have been laughing. But maybe not. The sixth video turned out to be the video of that session. To start with it was a shot across the bed, the camera having been left on the dresser probably. It caught Cooper's hands fastening one of her legs.

'You're going to love this,' Cooper could be heard saying as he tied her down.

'Not too tight,' she said.

'How's that?'

'Yeah, that's okay.'

There was a momentary shot of Cooper, naked torso, heading back to scoop up the camera. The camera shot flipped and zigzagged. Clunking, breathing. Then the camera panned the length of the naked body. He must have held the camera one-handed because it focused on a feather trawling across the girl's face, eyes, nose, cheek. The feather travelled down her neck, swirled around her right breast, tickled her nipple. The faintest of moans.

'That good?'

'Mmm.'

Then the other breast. Then down her chest to her navel, along her leg, the outside first. When it got to her feet, the feather reversed, and Cooper used the sharp end to tickle the soles of her feet. She giggled.

'Stop it.'

Clement's gut tightened as the sharp end of the quill started to draw up the inside of the woman's leg. At this point she was completely vulnerable. But just as it got to her labia, the feather reversed again. Clement released his breath, realised how tense he had become. The feather tickled and probed. The woman's breathing became faster and deeper.

'Come on, do it now,' she whispered.

'You sure?'

'Yeah, come on.'

It sounded like Cooper slipped off his shorts, then he climbed on top of her, and they had sex.

—

Surprisingly, while he kept filming the whole time, it was only of her face. This wasn't Cooper showing any decorum. The five videos before this one had all been explicit. Different camera angles, different positions. The six following were much the same. The most recent one showed Cooper doing his feather trick again on a young woman who was bound to his bed, just like the earlier one. She was one whose face was obscured by her hair, but she was clearly a different person from the previous bondage young woman.

'What do you reckon?' asked Clement when they'd finished watching the lot.

'I have to invest in a feather,' said Earle.

There was nothing in there that could be construed as violent. Just that tense moment when the girl had been restrained and Cooper had scraped the sharp quill over her body.

'Nothing we can get him on there,' summarised Clement. The women all seemed more than willing participants.

'Ice changes everything,' said Earle, and Clement knew he was right. A meth-head could quickly turn violent.

Clement became aware of raised and excited voices in the main room. When there was a knock on the office door, he drew the obvious conclusion: Cooper had been apprehended. He pulled the door open to find the uniform Fernandez there.

'Sorry, sir, but we just got news and Sergeant Nelson said to tell you.'

'You got Cooper?'

'No. A local mum out in her boat with her kids up near Ivanhoe.' He gingerly lifted the phone screen to Clement's eye level. 'She found this.'

Clement blinked twice in case his imagination was playing tricks, but the image remained. A human hand and part of an arm knotted to a post in the river.

9

The young mum who had taken the picture was waiting in the kitchen having a cold drink. Sarah Larkin couldn't have been more than thirty-three. Clement's money would have been on late twenties. Brown hair hung loose around her shoulders, a sombrero-style straw hat was parked on the laminex beside her glass. No doubt her mechanism of choice to protect herself from the sun. That told him she was sensible, a good start with a witness. She wore shorts and a long-sleeved light cotton blouse. Clement and Earle entered, and Clement introduced them both.

'I'm sorry if I was supposed to wait but I had my twins with me, and I didn't want to be hanging around. Also, once that tide goes out it's all mud flat around there.'

'Where are the twins now?'

'I dropped them off to a friend before I came here.'

'Not a very pleasant experience for you?'

She took another gulp of water and fanned her hand as if the vapours had her. 'Oh my God, awful.'

'This place is near Ivanhoe Crossing?'

'About four or five k further east. By water I mean. Don't ask me if you're going cross-country. We use a tinny. I paint. Watercolours. There's an old jetty there.'

Clement pulled up a chair at the table and Earle joined him. Clement asked her to begin at the beginning. So she did. Yes, there might be a lot of superfluous information in such an account but better too much than too little.

After about ten minutes, Clement was confident he had the gist of what had happened.

'And you didn't see any other body parts?'

'I wasn't looking.'

He allowed himself a half smile.

'I reckon it was a croc took them, but you saw the hand ...'

He had indeed and he knew what was troubling her most. That rope.

'Is there any chance you could come with us to show us the exact location?' asked Clement. She said she was happy to oblige.

'Their dad can collect the girls and make them dinner.'

Clement thanked her. Callum Nelson entered, explaining that he'd come as soon as he heard.

'And Livesy is on standby,' he added.

Clement suggested they get people to the scene as soon as possible. 'I'll call Keeble,' he said, 'get her up here.'

'What about the other matter?' asked Nelson, not wanting to be specific in front of a member of the general public. Graeme Earle took the cue, guiding Sarah Larkin out to the car.

Clement said, 'I'm sure Livesy can handle Cooper, but definitely keep the roadblock into town in place.'

As he filled up his water bottle for the trip, he couldn't help but reflect on the fact that bad things always came in a bunch. First it had been Josh, then Heather Lawson, and now this.

—

It was nearly an hour later by the time they approached the crime scene in two shallow draft boats. The tide was lower than it had been when the photo of the hand had been taken.

'Before, the waterline was right up to where the rope is,' said Sarah Larkin, who had assured them she could cope with going back.

Nobody was looking forward to the retrieval. Apart from the gruesome reality of a severed human arm, there was personal danger. They were all sure a crocodile had taken the body and there was every good chance it would be lurking. The banks near the jetty were muddy, giving onto tall grass leading up into scrubby bush and then taller trees. From what Clement could see from here, they were at least clear of crocs. But it wasn't just big saltwater crocodiles that might take you in the water up here. There were also sharks.

—

Clement, Eaton, Earle and Sarah Larkin travelled in the lead boat with a policewoman skipper. The boat had a temporary canvas lid rigged for shade extending from the permanent but shallow cockpit. Four more police plus another skipper travelled in the boat behind. The rest of the station's complement were manning roadblocks or on standby in case Cooper showed. Nelson had explained that while the location could be reached cross-country by car, boat would be quicker. Keeble would be well on her way to Kununurra by now. As Clement had done, she was flying in a light aircraft. Clement's discussion with her had been primarily about whether to leave the crime scene till she got there. She had told him it was too big a risk with the carrion up there. They were lucky they had what they did. They needed the hand.

'Take photographs, be as careful as you can, especially with any knots. But you already know that.'

Which of course, he did. Whether knots were tied, how they were tied, the material used, all were important potential idiosyncrasies that might identify the killer.

—

The skippers cut their engines. Everybody had their eyes peeled for crocodiles on land or in the water. The plan was for the second boat to get into the shore and for the police in that boat to suit up and sweep the area for anything relevant: cans, bottles, cartons, cigarette stubs.

It was odd, Clement knew, to feel a sense of relief that the hand was still clearly visible as they drew close. Nonetheless, that's exactly how he felt, for any minute some bird could rip at it.

'Can you get us close to that post?' Clement asked the skipper. They had been introduced but he'd lost her name. She cut the engines completely and Graeme Earle, an experienced boatie, pulled the outboard up. Where the sun streamed down free of tree branches, the bottom of the river was indicated but only as indefinite silty smoke. Clement felt as much as heard the underside of the boat nudge gently into the muck. He could almost reach out and touch the post from here. It was not much more than a metre away. Clement, who had swapped out of trousers for shorts, began to pull on waders to protect his feet. Collecting this evidence not a job that could be delegated.

'What's that?' It was Earle.

Clement's stomach clenched. He swivelled, expecting to see the outline of a crocodile, but immediately realised Earle was not so much alarmed as curious, pointing at a small shape close to the bottom of the post just visible above the water.

'It's a boot,' said Nelson.

'Oh my God!' Larkin's hand flew to her mouth.

Clement understood why. It was a boot of some kind, but with a foot and part of a leg still in it.

'I'm going over,' said Clement. He pulled on thick rubber gloves, hoisted his arse up onto the gunwale, buried the idea of a monster crocodile gliding towards him, and dropped into the water which was instantly refreshing. People did swim in the river, even this far up. To Clement that was inconceivable. He waded to the boot, where skin and bone was visible above the encased ankle. Attempting to pull it up he was taken completely by surprise. The boot was literally as heavy as lead. It took effort to lift the thing up out of the water. Now he could see why it was so heavy.

It was a diving boot, the kind that went with those old-fashioned diving suits.

As he handed it across carefully to be put in the evidence esky his mind was already contemplating just how planned and horrendous this killing had been. Somebody had lashed their victim to a post in a section of river known to be inhabited by saltwater crocodiles. Additionally, they had strapped the victim's feet into diving boots, all the better to anchor them.

The murder was planned and cruel, that much was apparent. What was unknown was whether this was the end of it, or only the beginning.

10

The morgue at Kununurra District Hospital was at least air-conditioned. Flanked by Lisa Keeble and Graeme Earle, Clement stood looking over his grisly haul. It had taken only about ten minutes to find the second boot.

Each and every one of those minutes had hung over him like a guillotine, admitted Clement, if only to himself. It didn't matter how many eyes were on the lookout, you couldn't shake that fear. That guillotine simile he realised probably came to him because of these severed body parts. There had only been the one hand, the left one found. Callum Nelson had a team seeking to locate any other body parts, but the locals were not optimistic. Crocodiles often had defined territories, but in that stretch apparently there was no dominant one. It was a free-for-all.

—

Though a scientist not a doctor, Keeble had done numerous courses on causes of death, attended many post-mortems and coronial inquests. She was a true professional. Almost as important, she was positive and pleasant. I'm getting too old to deal with cranky, thought Clement. Or maybe just too cranky to deal with cranky? Whatever, Keeble made his job so much easier. Her quest for the truth took in all kinds of evidence sifting, scientific testing, medical know-how and gut instinct.

The victim's two feet were still encased in their boots, so far barely infiltrated by marine bugs. Samples of the few that were present had been collected and would be sent soon as possible to Clement's entomologist mate, Rhino David, in Perth.

'You have to assume she hadn't been there long,' Keeble was scrutinising the body parts. 'Forty-eight hours, maybe sixty. Otherwise, I'm sure these would have been more infested.'

'She?' said Earle.

Keeble pointed. 'Nail polish on the fingernails. I think she was tied to the pole, hands behind her back. I reckon the croc took most of her in one go. Head, torso, most of her legs. Probably stashed that, then came back and got the right arm, maybe the knots were a bit looser that side.' She stood posing as she imagined the victim must have been with hands tied behind her back.

'The croc probably struck from front on.'

With extreme care, she picked up the hand and fingerprinted it.

'The prints will still be useable?' It was Earle who asked the question, but Clement had been thinking the same thing.

'Oh yes. They were out of the water a lot of the time, remember.'

'What about the rope?' asked Clement.

'Nothing special on the knots. They are what you or I might do. The rope also seems standard, but if we get a suspect with rope on them or access to rope, Rhino might be able to make a DNA match. How do you think the killer got her on the pole?' Keeble's concentration didn't waver as she printed each finger.

Clement had considered this. 'I think the killer might have taken her out there at low tide. It would be difficult from a boat.' Clement avoided 'he' even though he suspected a man was involved. 'The killer could have used a boat or come cross-country. I got a text from Nelson to say there are vehicle tracks.'

Earle said, 'Can we tell if she was alive when she was tied up?'

From what they had to go on, Keeble couldn't offer an opinion.

'For her sake, I hope not.' Earle sighed, hands jammed into his pockets.

Keeble, who was yet to see the site, said she would head out there right after this. Having printed the hand, she placed it in a small cooler. She had set up a camera on a tripod and now she clicked that on.

'Okay, let's take a look at these feet.'

Very carefully, Keeble undid the laces and studded straps of both diving boots. Then she removed the laces entirely and bagged them.

'We might get more information from the interior of these boots than we will from the exterior,' she cautioned. She spread the aperture of the boot as much as she could. Then she had to seize the stump of what remained of the leg and pull. Reluctantly the boot gave up an ankle, and the right foot. Keeble followed the same procedure for the left foot.

'Almost definitely a woman, painted toenails, plus the small size. I'd say young, looking at the skin, under thirty.'

Clement envisaged her tied to the post by her hands, her feet encased in the boots. She was crocodile bait. And the croc took it. Literally everything that wasn't tied down. Keeble shook her head, no less affected than him. But instantly he blotted out every emotion because as Keeble removed her hand it revealed part of a tattoo on the victim's leg.

The tattoo started above the ankle but most of it had gone with the leg.

'Shame there isn't more of the tattoo,' said Earle.

'It might be enough,' said Keeble hopefully.

'Is the same tattoo above the other ankle?' asked Clement.

'Yes.' Keeble moved the ankle to demonstrate.

The fact the tattoo was also on the other ankle clinched it for Clement.

'They were wings,' said Clement, 'like with Achilles.'

Keeble's mouth formed an O.

Clement said to Earle, 'Remember that last sex video on the hard drive. It showed a girl with those tattoos. We need to get a warrant for Nicholas Cooper's arrest. For murder. Then we need to pick him up, and quick.'

11

Her next booking wasn't till Monday, but she liked to provide the small comforts that ensure clients have such a good time they will recommend you. Most of her work these days came from word of mouth. She didn't bother so much with ads anymore, didn't need to. She was good friends with most of the hotel reception staff in town and they would often advise tourists that rather than hire a car themselves they would be better off hiring her as their guide. And lately there had been a shortage of hire cars so often people had no alternative than to look for a tour.

She strolled through the supermart double-checking her list: tinned tuna, baked beans, eggs, sausages. You didn't have to be fancy. Every meal cooked in the open seemed to taste better, and after four or five hours of hiking, a client would swear the icy Coke or beer she supplied was the best ever. She was reaching for soft drinks in the fridge when a voice behind her said, 'Hello, Bella.'

Even before she turned, she recognised that nasal, slightly high voice forever burned in her memory.

And there he was with that same infuriating half-smile.

'What are you doing here?' She shot those words out like a flamethrower.

'You really have to ask me that?'

She was feeling prickly, embarrassed. 'Listen, Jarrad, I don't have anything to say to you.'

He stood there nodding sombrely. 'I understand. But you really don't have a choice. For your own sake, not for mine. I would have written to you, but I didn't know how to find you.'

She started moving down the aisle. He followed.

'Hey, I don't blame you. The old Jarrad was contemptible, but I have changed so much.'

She tried to shut her ears.

'I know it's kind of a cliché, but I found God, I truly did. So, I am here ...'

She swung around the bottom of the aisle. Momentary freedom.

'... for atonement, I suppose. And that's something you could—'

She spun and hissed in his face. 'Get the fuck away from me. I want nothing to do with you.'

She turned back, took two more paces and stopped. Glancing over her shoulder, she was surprised to see he hadn't followed her, but neither had he retreated.

She headed towards the checkout, grabbing a handful of torch batteries en route. Flustered, she handed over the wrong card at first.

—

When she stepped out of the shop, it seemed she had rid herself of him, but as she bent to untie Scrounger, he emerged from where he must have been standing under a tree. Scrounger detected him or her misgivings or both, and gave a threatening growl. That halted him.

Out in the clear light she could make a better assessment of him. The same slim body that for a man reeked of immaturity, although the stupid moustache had gone. Long pants, not shorts, that was different, and he was wearing a plain, light-blue shirt. She only remembered him in those 'hip' music tees: the Ramones, Nick Cave. As if that bit of printed cotton stretched across his chest guaranteed him a seat at the table of the uber-cool. Too dumb to comprehend that anybody who had to proclaim that was already the antithesis of their heroes.

'Please.' He started shuffling after her, Scrounger turning back on the lead to ward him off. She was tempted to let go. 'Since you knew me, Bella, I've had a transformation. I got cancer.'

'I'm sorry to hear that.' She was almost at her car now.

'I despaired. But when I repented, when I repudiated my past and acknowledged my wrongs, everything changed. The cancer went.

I survived, and I knew I had a mission.'

'I'm pleased for you, but I don't want anything to do with you.'

'You really need to listen to me.'

'No, I really don't.'

As if following the conversation, Scrounger growled another warning as he closed. He stopped, went to hold out his hand for her to sniff.

'Nice boy.'

'It's a she, and I wouldn't do that.'

She took pleasure in seeing him retract his hand. The dog wouldn't attack him unless she sensed real danger, but it was pleasing that it looked likely she may.

'We could have a coffee ...'

She ignored him, climbed into her 2016 model Nissan Patrol, Scrounger bounding in and proprietarily sitting up against her thigh.

He came around to the front of her car, still talking, but she couldn't hear him now because she had fired up the radio and then the engine. He was lips through a windscreen, that was all. She drove straight at him, swinging right at the last minute. In her rear-vision mirror, she saw him still gesturing desperately as he grew smaller.

12

The sun was a drunk sliding down the bar to the floor. Up here, darkness came swiftly. Clement stood looking out the station window, the electric lights in the station brighter by the second. Like his frustration. There was still no sign of Cooper. Patrol cars had been running up and down the highway between Halls Creek and Kununurra, and along the road north to Kalumburu, without finding any trace of him. The same story on the Tanami and over at the Buntine.

There was no record of any calls to or from Cooper's phone since the night before. The odds remained he was somewhere in the bush, but that twine was slimming strand by strand, leaving Clement dangling over a ravine. Perhaps he should have called for air surveillance after all.

Tomorrow, Risely could get fixed-wing aircraft and helicopters doing aerial sweeps, but for now that would be pointless. The dark fear lying in the silt of Clement's stomach was that Cooper had slipped through Kununurra before they had the roadblocks in place. He would only have had maybe a twenty- to thirty-minute window, but that was enough. He could be in Darwin by now. Or maybe he was a Bourne devotee and had played a few shrewd tricks, dropped his phone in the back of a truck heading east while he turned around and headed south.

Doubling Clement's frustration was lack of a clearly identifiable headshot of the young woman and presumed victim, in Cooper's sex video. Cooper's photography hadn't been concerned with the woman's face. Lying on her back with the camera focusing on her naked body, her reddish hair fanned across her face, leaving only an eye or nostril and cheek visible. Fortunately, Livesy had already identified one of the other young women as a local, Shauna. Perhaps Shauna could ID the victim. Trouble was, they didn't have a phone number on Shauna, who was itinerant. Livesy had asked all the station cops to keep an eye out for her.

—

Clement had managed to speak over the phone with Oscar, one of Cooper's workmates at the council. According to Oscar, Cooper was a 'good dude' although he could get a bit tetchy.

'You just give him space, then he settles.'

Oscar was evasive on whether Cooper might be a meth-head.

'I never seen him take any.'

Clement had already constructed a vision of Oscar: Warwick Capper hair, tatts, shallow beard. Clement didn't bother to reassure Oscar that no matter what he confided, he wouldn't be targeted. Raising that might make him more defensive, so he let the evasion slide. The pipe they'd found at Cooper's was suggestive enough. Besides, it was immaterial whether Cooper was a regular user or his Broome episode was a one-off. Matar's testimony was clear enough. Keeble had photographed, measured and weighed the boots. She had samples of the rope used to fasten the hand, and she had the victim's DNA. Hopefully they would not need to track with urgency where the boots and ropes were purchased because Cooper would be caught and confess. However, in court they might have to prove that Cooper bought those boots and that rope. Keeble, he knew, would begin that angle of the investigation as soon as she could. Right now, apart from finding Cooper, the priority was establishing the victim's identity. Keeble had already made sure the prints were being spun through the database.

—

The sun finally gave up the ghost and collapsed. Clement sighed. This might have been over, resolved successfully, if he'd been a bit quicker, a bit smarter, a bit luckier. If experience had taught Clement one lesson though, it was that you couldn't beat yourself up over things now out of your control. Perhaps he should have got roadblocks in place earlier. The thing was he hadn't. Yes, it would have been easier if the crocodile hadn't taken the victim's head with it. Or if she'd had short hair that didn't cover her face in that video. Accept it, that's all you could do, hang in there, play with the cards dealt.

Clement's phone pinged, and hope leapt like a striker in the penalty area, but no, Cooper hadn't been located. However, there was some consolation in Manners' message: **Prints Match: Nicholas Cooper.** Finally, a match to Cooper's prints from the Broome motel room. The fingerprint database had turned Cooper up, and with his photo, his record.

Attached was a screenshot. Earle's phone had pinged at the same time. He sidled over, no doubt studying the same info.

Nicholas Cooper, age twenty-eight. Five years earlier in Darwin, Cooper had been convicted of a vicious assault that had left a hotel patron with a broken jaw. Three years before that in Darwin he had been convicted of a sexual assault against a nineteen-year-old woman.

'He's certainly got the form,' observed Earle.

Assault and sexual assault. Cooper might as well have been climbing a staircase that arrived at a landing under a sign: 'Long Prison Sentence'. You take a bloke who already had demonstrated lack of respect for his fellow humans, then put him on meth, you knew the only kind of outcome you were going to get.

There was no point waiting around here with his thumb up his backside. Clement said, 'Let's go to the pub, try and ID this victim.'

—

A little after 6.30 and the pub was already crowded. Two big doormen stood by a steel grille that led from the beer garden to the street. A good place to start. Though they'd dispensed with suitcoats and long-sleeved shirts, Clement guessed he and Earle stood out as cops. Apart from a couple of Hawaiian shirts, it was all tees and singlets in the large beer garden. The doormen were the only ones dressed like them. Earle and Clement introduced themselves and asked if they knew of a young woman with tattoos of wings on her ankles and calves.

'Red-brown hair, probably late twenties, thirty?'

They didn't recall her, doubted she was local.

'This the croc victim?' one of them asked as the logic must have snaked its way to the summit.

'Yes, it is.' No point lying. Word would be all over town.

'Speak to Lucy,' said the same doorman and pointed to a small young woman in singlet and shorts who was holding court at the table closest to the stage where karaoke was being tooled up. 'She knows everyone.'

Clement said he'd try Lucy and directed Earle to interview the bar staff.

Clement approached, didn't wait for Lucy who was waving her cigarette animatedly to finish telling her story to the half-dozen men and women at her table.

'Hey Lucy, sorry to interrupt.' She swung his way, curious. The others in the group waited for her cue. Clement explained they were detectives trying to identify a young woman.

'She had wings tattooed on her ankles and calves, red-brown hair.'

Lucy's mouth was open. 'Shit, yeah, I know her. What was her name?' Pitching it to the others but really asking herself. 'Rain! That's right. Rain. She was up dancing and I jumped up and joined her for a bit. You remember. You said she was skanky.' Pointing at one of her girlfriends, who was forced to say, 'She kinda was. She was okay though.'

'I thought she was cool,' announced Lucy.

'When was this?'

A quick confab.

'Wednesday night. I think she said something about getting into town the day before. She was going on about how the place had changed. Said she was here years ago.'

According to Lucy and her crew, Rain was definitely Australian.

'Any of you get any photos?'

No, they hadn't.

'She sang "Bad Romance". I told her she should do "Hard Rain's Gonna Fall" but she never knew that one. I think she mentioned meeting up with her ex or something.'

That could fit with Cooper.

'Do you know where she was from or where she was staying?'

Lucy, little goldmine that she was, believed she'd said she was staying at a caravan park.

'You know which one?' There were at least four possibilities.

'I'm guessing the Wide River. I could be wrong though.'

The Wide River was the cheapest. Clement reckoned Lucy was likely right.

'This ex, did she give a name?'

Lucy shrugged.

'Was Rain from Darwin by any chance?'

'Dunno if she said where she was from. I think Sydney but she had that look, like from everywhere and nowhere. You know what I mean?'

—

From time to time it happened that Clement felt the presence of somebody watching him. He doubted that it was innate, and he was sure it wasn't paranoia manifesting, but it was a real awareness, just as other people might sense a temperature shift, or smell smoke from a long-off bushfire. He felt it now and reflexively turned to look behind him. A man about thirty, slim, intense had been lurking among a group of other drinkers but Clement was sure eavesdropping. Caught out, he swiftly turned his head back to the group he was with. It was, Clement supposed, to be expected that two cops showing up asking questions about a missing young woman was going to neatly tie in with gossip about a headless croc victim having been found. All the same, he marked the face. Over the next day or so he expected they would wind up interviewing most of the people currently here.

'Do you or your friends know Nick Cooper?'

He had Cooper's photo ready to flash but didn't need to. Both Lucy and her female friend knew him.

'Would you have seen him with Rain?'

Lucy only remembered Rain dancing by herself. 'That was maybe early in the last set of karaoke, because she did her Gaga song early in the last set. I remember because I was down for "Dancing Queen" about two songs after.'

Nobody had seen her leave.

Clement took Lucy's name and phone number and thanked her. Karaoke was getting underway. He met Earle in the quieter lounge bar.

'Got a name, Rain. Don't know how it's spelled, and it sounds like a nickname but it's a start. They think she was staying in the Wide River.'

Earle said, 'The glassy knows Cooper. Reckons Wednesday arvo Cooper and a girl with red-brown hair he hadn't seen before were here having a drink.'

'Rain said she came here to meet up with her ex.'

'Sounds like Cooper.'

'It does. Possible though he was an interlude.' Whichever way they cut it though, Cooper was the perfect fit. Violent past, sexual assault. If Heather Lawson died, he might well have two deaths to answer for.

'Excuse me.'

The young woman was short with a perkiness about her that reminded Clement of Reese Witherspoon. She wore a pretty dress, white with strawberries, that was out of place amid the frayed denim and tattoos. Her hair looked freshly washed. He imagined her sitting on the deck of a yacht club. 'You're the police.' The statement was meant as a question.

'Yes. Detectives Clement and Earle. Have you seen a young woman with tattoos of wings on her calves?'

'No. Is she the victim?'

Clement held his tongue. She relented, smiled.

'Bek Dyson, like the hairdryer.'

Clement had no idea what she was talking about but nodded.

'I'm a journalist.'

She looked too young for that. Mind you. Clement was getting older; everybody looked younger to him. And perhaps up here they got their start fresh out of uni.

'For who?' asked Earle.

'Whom,' she corrected with a smile. 'BoomBox. We're an online news hub.'

Whatever that might mean, thought Clement.

'We have no comment for the time being,' he said.

'But the victim of the crocodile attack was a young woman with Achilles tattoos on her ankles and calves?'

'We never mentioned a crocodile attack,' said Earle.

'Everybody's talking about it,' beamed the girl who apparently shared her name with a hairdryer.

'Not us,' said Clement and signalled Earle to go.

She would just be the start. A crocodile victim was media gold. When the circumstances leaked, this town would be Fort Knox.

'I'm at the Brolga Motel, room eight if you'd like to ...'

Letting the words fall like silent dandruff behind him, Clement stepped out of the pub and checked his phone. No update. Next stop, the caravan park.

—

Though the Wide River was the cheapest of the caravan parks, it wasn't too bad. Those without caravans could hire chalets or erected tents or pitch their own tents. The night was growing steamier. Ever the optimist, Graeme Earle surmised they would get a storm in the next few days. Caravan parks were familiar territory to Clement. His parents had owned one in Broome way back when nobody visited the north-west except for a few hippies, absconding debtors and single men inspired by the Leyland brothers.

The managers of Wide River were a familiar type: a couple in their fifties, the husband a smoker and candidate for diabetes, the wife a non-smoker in shorts, sandals, polo top, with a perm straight out of the 70s. They were relaxing on the low porch out front of their chalet, the smell of chops drifting from the kitchen through the flywire door.

'Rain?' the husband pulled a face, managed to shake his head. His director chair creaked.

His wife ignored him. 'Yeah, we've got a redhead. Haven't seen her today. Nor yesterday come to think of it.' She hauled herself out of her chair and bade them follow. 'Quicker than me firing up the computer.' She stopped outside of one of their own pre-erected tents. It was a good size, zipped up, a sure sign nobody was in. You were marooned here; you wanted the breeze the way Crusoe wanted rescue.

'Anyone in?' she called. No response.

The tent would have been hot even with the flaps open.

'We'll take it from here. Thanks.'

When Clement unzipped the tent, hot air rushed out. Earle shone the small torch he always carried. It revealed a blow-up mattress, no sheets, and beside it a kitbag and a toilet bag. There was a small plastic sealable bag containing crackers too. A bar fridge clearly came with the tent. Inside the fridge was a half-full large bottle of mineral water, a tin of sardines and a small block of cheese. Frugal.

Scrawled in biro on a plastic name tag on the kitbag was 'Lorraine Miller'. 'Rain' was not a hippie name, just a bit of typical Aussie shortening. What was important was evidence the kitbag wasn't second-hand or stolen. Clement felt not the slightest ripple of triumph that now he almost certainly had a name to match the body parts left by the crocodile.

13

Ever since being confronted by Jarrad, she had felt anxious and on edge. She'd come back to camp, tried to busy herself with preparations to take her mind off it but the unease persisted. She turned her attention to Scrounger, hoping a distraction might work. Too old to rumble now, Scrounger did her best to participate but they knew one another too well to pretend it was anything but an attempted diversion. She'd first come across the dog more than four years ago now. Part cattle-dog, part whatever, it had been scrounging around the bins at the rear of the servo. The mangy dog had snarled when she'd tried to offer it water. Two days later it had been more relaxed to see her. She had taken pity on the dog. The next day she'd slipped a rope halter over it and led it, stopping at each station of mince she'd pre-emptively dropped Hansel-and-Gretel–like on the way from her car.

The bond came quick and fierce. God knew how old the dog was. For a year or two she'd taken Scrounger everywhere, even her tours. The dog would snarl like a tiger if she sensed an intruder but was obedient and, for all the show, did not bite people, although Bella had little doubt she would protect her with all she had if she sensed Bella was in danger. It soon became obvious it was best to keep her clear of most other dogs. She didn't bring Scrounger when she was guiding families. For one, there wasn't enough room in the vehicle, but you also couldn't be sure that children wouldn't provoke the dog. Nowadays, apart from trips into town or a special outing, Scrounger stayed here. Hippie Dave her neighbour made sure there was food and drink for Scrounger and that she hadn't died of snakebite. Not much you could do about that, dogs will be dogs. Fortunately, these days Scrounger preferred the comfort of the lounge rather than hunting in the bush.

Aware at some level that the tug-o-war and ball chasing of the last few minutes were less than genuine, Scrounger broke off and headed for the couch.

And Bella had nowhere to turn but back to her thoughts.

As long as she could remember from those first family holidays to Rottnest Island, she had wanted to live and work in the outdoors. Not a naturally academic kid, she'd applied herself at school, and then uni, even if it was only for a year before she heeded the calling that was dragging her to a different adventure. There were sacrifices to follow her vocation. Boyfriends and friends. She became the outlier of her siblings, as tends to happen with the one furthest from the family nest. They got shouted the overseas holidays. She missed out.

Yet it had been worth it. Until that booking.

She had cooked herself an omelette, washed up, put away the dishes. She never drank. Not any longer, although she could use a drink right now. She stood on the threshold of her little hut staring out into pitch dark. Tonight, whatever lay out there, seemed malevolent.

Who even cared if Jarrad had found God? He was a jerk. And she didn't trust him. Plus, he was the sort of person that if he 'found God', it would be all about him, his change, his redemption. She couldn't see Jarrad helping old people across the road or scrubbing dishes in a soup kitchen. She climbed onto her bed and turned out the light.

—

Despite the turmoil of her thoughts, she had eventually fallen asleep, but now awoke suddenly. Something wasn't as it should be. It was too quiet. Scrounger's snoring was absent. She slid off the mattress and crept into the hut. The old couch did not display the familiar outline of a canine lump.

'Scrounger?'

A bark came from outside. And a low growl. Although licensed for a gun, she did not own one. But she did keep a crossbow here just in case, and would take that on her tours for show. She could use it alright, but only for target practice, never against an animal.

However, she'd noted its appeal to men as if connecting them in an unbroken line to a noble predecessor. They wallowed in self-deceit that forsaking a gun, with which they were not proficient enough anyway, they would somehow do better with the more technically challenging crossbow. She only let them fire it at trees.

With the bow loaded she walked back outside. She had not turned on any lights, she simply followed the low growl to the right ten metres in. There she could make out Scrounger, rigid, facing the bush.

'Who's there?'

Returned by silence but that did not fool her. Whoever or whatever it was must still be there for Scrounger had not relaxed.

'Is that you, Jarrad?' How would he know she lived here, she wondered? And answered swiftly: not that hard. He could ask around. He knew her vehicle. Somebody at the servo—

Scrounger barked again, suddenly and loud as if whoever it was had taken a step closer.

If you are threatened, you must remove that threat. She crouched and aimed. It was literally a shot in the dark. She pulled the trigger. The arrow left with a whoosh.

No cry of pain, no low moan. The tension in her body if anything increased as she waited. She loaded another arrow.

'If that didn't get you, maybe the next one will.' Trying to keep the fear out of her voice, mostly succeeding. Scrounger relaxed, indicating the threat had retreated though she hadn't heard anything herself.

For three, maybe four minutes Bella held her position, listening. Clearly satisfied the threat had removed itself, Scrounger looked up wagging her tail hopefully.

'Good girl.'

Only after placing the bow carefully on the ground did she lavish affection on the dog. Then she picked up the bow again, leaving it loaded, and returned to the hut. She switched on a torch to check her intruder hadn't circled around. The hut was clear. She didn't bother firing up the generator.

Disappointingly, Scrounger resumed her spot on the couch.

Tonight, she would have liked her company on the bed, despite the heat and the irritation of the dog's coarse hair. She placed the bow on the ground within reach and lay there listening to the sounds of her own body. Her thoughts wandered all over, Jarrad and Lorraine of course, a first boyfriend, Cameron, met at Rottnest when she was fourteen. Bike rides, the smell of sea salt and sunscreen on his warm body as they awkwardly pressed into one another side-by-side on the top of a bluff, both lots of parents sleeping. It has lasted the school holidays. Texts, a couple of nervous phone calls. Wouldn't it be weirdly wonderful, she thought, if one day Cameron turned up here as a client, booked by chance. Or better, not by chance, like he had chosen her. What might he be doing now? His parents were better off than hers. Dalkeith or one of those expensive suburbs. She had hoped their paths might have crossed at uni but he probably went to UWA. That would have been closer to where he lived.

Her thoughts insisted on returning to Pentecost River. She should have refused their request to go there, though as she was working for the tour company then that really wasn't her prerogative. Like all tourists, they had wanted to look at crocodiles. She'd told them over and over, you can't get too close to the river. We need a good distance …

Mud, the smell of rotting leaves, the itch of insect bites. A humidity that was a living thing, a fetid breath …

For hours she lay there, her thoughts washing over her. Dawn and sleep were still some way off.

***

It was a good thing he had shifted after the dog barked. He heard something fizz through the air just centimetres from him in the line where he had been. He kept edging away.

Because he had already walked the route, he did not need a torch until well into his retreat. He felt good about himself. He knew where she lived, he knew about the dog and the bow. It wouldn't be long now.

14

Fresh fruit and a piece of toast did Clement for breakfast. Graeme Earle added croissants. There was only one other table occupied in the Oxford's dining area, a tourist couple in their sixties. It was an unpleasant time of year up here, the reverse of those coastal destinations that became ghost towns in winter. It was going to get relentlessly hotter and nastier. Pretty much the only staff were backpackers. They didn't know better. Yet. To give his feet a rest after their arduous day yesterday, Clement was in thongs. Even on the short journey from the room to the dining room the heat from the pavers had scorched up through the rubber soles. He'd almost had to skip. It was only just past seven a.m. Earle was wearing more substantial sandals, shorts, and a colourful tent of a shirt.

No fresh information had come to light on Lorraine Miller. She had been a roll-up at the Wide River caravan park, paying cash in advance for three nights. She did not have a driver's licence but had given a postal address in Benalla in country Victoria. Mal Gross, finally packing up when Clement's call had reached him about 9.30 last night, had promised to get onto that first thing this morning. It would have been after midnight in Benalla then and it was really all about confirming the victim was Lorraine Miller and letting the family know. The phone number Miller had given to the caravan park people as her own contact was dead when Clement tried it last night. He tried again, with the same result. The phone itself was neither in the tent nor anywhere near the jetty.

The killer had taken it with him, reasoned Clement, destroyed it.

Physically, Clement felt much better than he had when he retired to bed at midnight, the long day and scant progress sitting in his stomach like an undigested meal. Although they had identified Cooper, he remained at large. The life of a police detective, Clement reflected, is full of such partial victories, and uncertain outcomes. You may know who you are after, but not where to find them. You might find them, yet still not convict them. And no matter how hard you tried not to, you stored all the disappointments and failures: I could have done better. I should have done better.

The antidote was hearing Lena's voice.

He had debated whether to call her. She was not one to go to bed early, and he doubted she would care even if he'd woken her. However, in his relationship with Marilyn it had been easy to let his frustration at a case spill over and poison their own clear water. Time after time he would later be found reprimanding himself: I shouldn't have called. It would have been better not to have spoken.

The residue of those times had left its mark. However, in the end he had convinced himself: Lena is not Marilyn, and I am a whole lot smarter now. Lena had been awake, hoping he would call, she'd said. They had talked a little of the case, mainly of inconsequential things, the heat, what they'd eaten. She sounded normal, enthusiastic even, and that quelled the anxiety that ever since he first dated girls had ridden sidecar whenever he called a lover long-distance.

—

It had started with Barbara when he was sixteen. She was a Perth girl holidaying at the caravan park with her parents. Barbara and he had kissed. Not the first kiss he'd had with a girl but the first with a city girl. She was fifteen or sixteen. She'd pushed his wandering hands away. He hadn't cared, a feel of her breast through her singlet and bra would have been too much to expect. The kiss alone was more than he might have dreamed of just a few months earlier. When Barbara's family had left Broome to continue their holiday, he had been dejected. A giant sinkhole had opened in his life, and it could no longer be filled by a fishing trip with his dad, or by bowling at three stumps, or by developing the perfect outswinger, or by raiding the stash of *Penthouse* magazines he'd found the previous summer in one of the site caravans and hidden at the bottom of his cricket trunk.

He and Barbara had promised to call one another. This was well before mobile phones, 1990 or thereabouts. He'd had to sneak into the office, avoiding the prying eyes of his sister, to make his phone calls. The first one had been typically teenage awkward, especially with her father answering, but overall it had been positive. He'd gone to bed with aching loins, buried his face into his pillow imagining it was her. But a few days later when he next got the opportunity to call, he'd sensed a cooling in her. Nothing he could put his finger on, but the call left him edgy. His appetite abandoned him. The third call he'd struggled through a snowdrift of reluctant discourse from her before eventually being told, 'Look, I like you, Dan, as a friend, but there's no point calling me again.'

He was shattered. The experience set the template for a number of such calls over the years. He'd learned a harsh lesson back then: if Daniel Clement was out of sight he was also definitely out of mind. The telephone line was an umbilical cord through which, within the first dozen words, he could unerringly gauge the emotional state of his soon-to-be former lover. It never surprised to the upside.

Until Marilyn. Her ardour had been undiminished even after marriage. For a few years. And then he'd begun to sense the problems, the things unsaid, the chill.

—

Like a neurologist checking over an MRI to make sure nothing sinister had been missed, so deeply had Clement been analysing last night's Lena call that when his phone buzzed his first instinct was that she was ringing to say she didn't love him after all. His next and more logical response was that it was news that Cooper had been located.

In fact, it was Scott Risely responding to Clement. Last night Clement had texted to let his superior know they might have identified the victim.

'Good work on the ID,' said Risely without preamble. 'I've got a Cessna going out of Halls Creek to see what it can spot off the road.'

'Nelson says one of the fellows here has a helicopter licence. If we can sweet-talk one of the stations into loaning us a chopper, he could check all around Chamberlain and Emma Gorges.'

Helicopters were great in a confined search area but with the vast tracts of land up here they could be a low-return investment unless you had solid intel. One advantage, however, was that because they were used so regularly by the big stations, Cooper might not suspect their purpose.

'Okay, I'll speak to Callum and get that in train. The shit fight has started. Got Marshall and Robard ringing me every ten minutes' – they were assistant commissioners – 'and now the phone is already running hot from media. They've got wind of a fatal crocodile attack near Kununurra and want a confirm or deny. Is there any point in keeping quiet?'

In some investigations there might be, but Clement knew from the reaction at the pub last night it must already be the talk of the town.

'We can confirm a fatal attack but as yet, the family doesn't know. I need to check with Mal on that. Nobody except the witness who found the body parts, the station here, and us, know the circumstances. Let's keep it that way if we can.' There would be panic if people heard there was a psycho killer on the loose. 'The assaults in Broome give us a good cover story to push why we're looking for the Landcruiser. Let's see if somebody out there can give us Cooper's current whereabouts.'

Risely thought it a good plan. 'See, mate, you could do my job standing on your head. Speak later.'

—

Though a desk job was looking more attractive by the minute, Clement's desire to get Cooper was growing faster. Keeble entered the dining room, grabbed herself a juice and a pastry and joined them. Clement had caught up with her late after she had returned from the site of the body recovery. She'd said she was heading back out there this morning.

'I'll be leaving soon,' she announced.

'That all you going to eat?' Earle nodded at the pastry.

'I snacked late.'

Clement filled her in on Risely's media warning.

'At least the site isn't easy to get to,' she said.

'You get a chance to print any of that stuff they collected?' asked Clement. Callum Nelson's people had collected a few cans and wrappers from near the site.

'Don't get your hopes up. There was an empty bourbon and Coke can that yielded up a print.' She had told him last night that there had been tyre tracks that looked promising. 'Those tyre tracks weren't much to go on, but I reckon if we get a bit further back in the bush there might be a better sample.'

If they could match tyre tracks to Cooper's vehicle it would be nirvana. But as of now they had no Cooper, and the tyre tracks were iffy. He watched Keeble break her pastry with precision.

'Have you called Rhino yet?' she asked. She popped a piece of pastry in her mouth without shedding a single flake. Across from her, Earle's polo shirt looked like a breadboard.

'Just about to.' He dialled. A world-class specialist in forensics, especially in DNA, Rhino could tell fake barramundi from the real thing, he could nominate which mine had produced the gold for a piece of jewellery and, he liked to boast, which make of breast implant certain Hollywood starlets had under their oh-so-transparent frocks.

'So long as I can do that by touch,' he'd laugh, always trying to get a rise out of those colleagues he considered wowsers. If he succeeded, it wasn't with Keeble. He'd never so much as scored a point. It was a schoolboy taking on Federer.

'Probably the same implant you use,' she'd said when he tried his shtick with her. The jousting concealed mutual professional respect.

The phone picked up. Clement put it on speaker.

'I'm on my way in now,' said Rhino. 'Just had a quick row on the Swan.'

An early row across the glassy surface of the river was a Rhino ritual.

'Everything arrived?'

'Apparently. Body parts and marine grubs, right?'

'Did you get those photos I sent?' asked Keeble after another delicate swallow.

'That Lisa? Yeah, I had a look. Because there's nothing much there, I reckon sixty hours, around there, from time of death. Did you get in your bikini to distract the croc?'

'No, they have a larger brain than you, Rhino.'

Banter was a feature of any conversation between the two.

'Come on, Lisa, I'm a man, I don't have a brain, only that other thing.'

'And not much of that either from what I've heard.'

Rhino cackled. Clement was back calculating. The body parts were found Saturday about midday. So from Wednesday midnight to Thursday midday might be the window. That put Cooper right in it.

'The samples from the victim at the Hartog?' prompted Clement.

'They are in train. You want to see if they match any DNA I can get off the body parts, right?'

Clement said that was exactly what he wanted. He explained they had also found a can.

Rhino said, 'The hand you found tied to the post is a chance. If the victim put up a fight, we could get DNA from under the nails but otherwise, unless there is blood, it will be tough; with the sun up that way, your erection lasts longer than any sample.'

'Leave you to it,' said Clement and ended the call.

'I'm gone,' said Keeble and with that she was. Not a trace of her was left, not a crumb even on her plate.

Earle had also done the calculations on time of death. 'If Cooper can't tell us where he was Wednesday night, Thursday morning, he's in even deeper shit.'

Clement wondered how Mal Gross was doing with Benalla. He called.

'Was just about to ring you,' said Gross. 'Benalla just got back to me. The house was an address where Lorraine Miller rented for a month about three months back. The landlady had another address for Miller in Bega, south-coast of New South Wales. She thinks that might be the parents. I'm about to call Bega now.'

Clement saw he had another call coming in so thanked Gross and took the incoming. It was Steve Eaton at Halls Creek.

'We may have something,' said Eaton. 'One of the vehicles we stopped near the Doon Doon Roadhouse was a Landcruiser. The car fitted the description, but it was a family. They told my officer they had seen a Landcruiser just like theirs with a single fella in it, off the road near Home Valley Station. It had Wyndham plates. He showed them a photo of Cooper and they said it looked a lot like the man. A big man, they said.'

Nothing definitive. Up this way there could be any number of blokes on their own in light-coloured Landcruisers, a big percentage of them with Wyndham plates.

Clement kicked doubt aside. He was already moving. 'We'll get a helicopter up in the air. You maintain a watch on the roads. I'll call Wyndham.'

—

An hour had elapsed since the phone call. Around ten minutes earlier Clement's helicopter had reached the search area a hundred kilometres west of Kununurra. On Clement's instructions, it was flying over the densest bush. Clement believed that was where a fugitive might hide. Graeme Earle tapped him on the shoulder and pointed below, where a telltale glint had caught his eye. Clement instructed the pilot to wheel around.

On the next pass from the north, they got a better view. The vehicle, at ground level camouflaged by trees, was indeed a light-coloured Landcruiser. Clement couldn't tell if anybody was inside. With Cooper armed, Clement did not want to provoke him into panicked flight so, having recorded the coordinates, he instructed the pilot to head back to the border of the station where, courtesy of the station foreman, a vehicle would be waiting for them.

There was many an acre of space to put down. The pilot got them within fifty metres of the waiting vehicle, a well-seasoned Ford. Once landed, while Earle loaded their kitbag containing vests, restraints and tasers into the vehicle, Clement thanked the station foreman, Mark.

'I'm not sure how long we'll be,' he told Mark, who was slim, with muscles in his arms like cables.

'No worries. I brought a bike.' He nodded to where a trailbike sat in the shade.

Clement told the pilot to wait there, he'd radio him if he needed him back up in the air. On a map he showed Mark where they had spotted the vehicle parked.

'Can you tell me the best way there?'

'There's a track runs off here,' he pointed to the main feeder road. 'He probably came that way. From here you can cut through the bush to that track. It's not that bad. Want me to show you?'

Clement said he would be very grateful. 'Just close enough so I can see the track. This man has a rifle.'

That didn't seem to worry Mark. Earle and Clement familiarised themselves with the Ford. It had bashed out many a bush kilometre, but it would serve their purpose. Earle radioed the Wyndham police to tell them to stand by on the northern side of where Cooper, if it was him, might exit.

'Nice and slow,' Clement requested of their guide.

—

The car pulled to the right, and the rubber on the pedals was worn but, overall, the beast moved okay. Ahead, Mark wound his way easily through the brush. Earle drove, following cautiously. A little over ten minutes, the bike halted, and Mark pointed.

'That's your track.'

Not much more than flattened scrub and dirt.

They thanked him and turned left.

The track ran parallel to the water, probably a kilometre in. From what Clement could tell, the Landcruiser had been parked off the track about fifty metres further inland. Hopefully that lessened the probability of an ambush. Clement stopped about forty metres short of where he thought would have been a direct line to the Landcruiser. They got out of the car, donned their jackets, and checked their weapons.

Clement made one last radio call to Callum Nelson to confirm Cooper had not been seen elsewhere.

'No. Yours is the only likely sighting.'

Clement announced they were going to approach the vehicle. Nelson said they had a medical team standing by, just in case, and wished them luck.

—

It was hot and humid. With the vest on it was like being in an old-fashioned phone-box, thought Clement, idly wondering when they had disappeared from his life and deciding it was probably before Marilyn had. Life changes around you and you don't even notice. As fast as they gulped water, they sweated. Earle plotted a diagonal that should take them towards the vehicle. The ground was mostly grassy, low scrub but about five minutes in they spotted the thicket of bush that must be where the car was. From there they took it very carefully. Clement was all too aware that Cooper could be sitting in the distance with Clement's head in his sights, so he diverted to lines that offered intermittent cover. The snap of dry leaves under their feet seemed so loud that they must have been heard back in Kununurra. He felt himself tensing as they drew closer.

Now they could see tyres through a gap between a gum trunk and denser bush. As always in these situations, an image of Phoebe jammed its way into his head. Then Lena. Now they were only metres from the car. There was no sound. Clement edged to the right and Earle went with him. They drew their pistols at the same time. They came around to a patch where the bush fell away, revealing the back of the Landcruiser. Clement signalled Earle wait. He checked the numberplate carefully. It matched Cooper's vehicle.

He listened. Silence.

Surely if Cooper had a position to ambush them, he would have done so by now. But Clement couldn't see directly into the vehicle. Perhaps Cooper had abandoned it? He signalled Earle move to get a bead on the passenger side to their left while he took a similar forty-five-degree angle to the right allowing him to aim for the driver door. Both doors were closed. That was unusual in this heat. But he could see the driver's window was down.

'Nicholas Cooper, this is Detective Inspector Daniel Clement of Broome Police. Could you open the door please and step out.'

His heart was thunder. It didn't matter he'd been through this kind of situation before.

'Nicholas, open your door please.'

Still no response. He nodded to Earle, and they advanced in unison, guns ready. He reached an angle where he could see a man's head. His heartrate quickened even further. He stopped; his breathing had grown progressively shallower.

'Nicholas?'

Nothing. He covered the ground as quickly as he could, reaching the driver door in three heart-thumping seconds.

Nicholas Cooper was sitting in the car, his head lolling back. Blood spatter from where the bullet had exited the back of his head. The rifle must have slipped after he'd pulled the trigger, for it was between his legs, the barrel resting against his left inner thigh, the butt on the floor against his right foot.

They could stop looking.

15

Scott Risely had driven out to the airstrip personally to pick them up. It was a bit after eight Sunday night. Risely was in shorts and a Mambo shirt. It was cooler here than in Kununurra but no less oppressive. Despite his protests they'd just dropped Graeme Earle off at his house. Clement had assured his partner he could handle the paperwork, even if that might have stretched the truth. It had been a long day and the last thing he wanted to consider was writing a draft report. However, it was always better to do it while details were fresh.

'The wonderful sound of a silent phone.' Risely turned and beamed Clement's way. 'The commissioner is happy. The media is happy. My wife is happy. Everybody's happy.'

Clement lifted an eyebrow.

'Cooper's family?'

A suddenly sober Risely nodded. 'A mother in Queensland and a sister. I spoke to the mum briefly. She said he'd been troubled mentally for years.'

A familiar story. We ascribe so much evil to people. I'm especially guilty of that, surmised Clement.

'I doubt Keeble is very happy either,' he said, picturing her ankle-deep in evidence bags.

Earle and Clement had waited with the corpse, securing the crime scene till Keeble and her contingent could get there. When Clement and Earle had left, Keeble, who had flown in ahead of most of her team who would travel by road, was just beginning the long task of running the scene.

Risely nodded. 'Yeah, she hasn't stopped. How's she going?'

Clement of course had wondered the same thing. 'Doesn't seem to be affecting her work.'

'She's quite close to Beth.' That was Risely's wife. 'Boyfriend was playing away apparently.'

So, for once Shepherd might have been on the money. In one way it didn't surprise Clement. If a couple like that break up, infidelity has to be high up there on the cause list. On the other hand, it was a shock. He could recall no signs their love had been on the wane. Risely rode over his silence.

'There was no suicide note?'

Clement explained they found nothing written. Nothing in Cooper's pockets, on the dash, in the glovebox.

'He could have been sitting on it,' explained Clement. 'We didn't want to disturb the body too much.' But if that were the case Keeble would have found it and for sure been in touch by now.

'Why do you think he killed himself?'

We rarely know the answer to that question, thought Clement, taking a stab regardless. 'You know what spree killers can be like. They've made up their mind how it's going to end before it starts. Using ice screwed with his brain I suppose. Maybe he was horrified at what he'd done, couldn't take it. Or maybe he'd achieved what he'd set out to do.'

'Was he in a relationship with Lorraine Miller?'

Clement had wondered the same thing. 'I don't know. I honestly have to say, it is confusing. Her death seems more planned, the diving boots for a start. And then he's just lost it.'

'Station or home?' asked Risely, meaning where would he like to be dropped.

'Station.' Make a start on those reports. Take the pain now, bank future free time. 'Did we get onto Lorraine Miller's family, do you know?'

He felt awful that concern for them had slipped by him.

'I think Mal said he hadn't been able to locate them yet.'

While another police officer might give them the tragic news, Clement would make a point of calling them to discuss what had happened. Families of victims, no matter how devastated, welcomed closure. Plus, it was just the right thing to do.

His mind drifted again to procedure.

'Keeble will do a GSR.' Clement was certain the gunshot residue test would confirm Cooper fired the rifle.

'Did you have her check you guys?'

'Yes. She also sighted and examined our weapons, neither of which had been fired.'

Couldn't be too careful these days. The hierarchy was always hammering into the serving police that the public needed to be assured about the conduct of the police. Lot of good it did though. Somebody was sure to suggest they'd killed Cooper by forcing his own hand to pull the trigger on his weapon. Maybe Clement was getting too old for this. Maybe he was just tired. It had been a long couple of days.

—

They swung into the entrance at the back of the station. At least tonight when he finished up, he could drive to Derby and sleep in tomorrow. He'd write up the initial report now and then he'd take the day off, spend it with Lena, while forensics ran their tests. Poor Keeble would get no such break. She had data from four crime scenes on the go.

Risely pulled up by the back door. 'Call me if you need me.'

Clement entered the station. The night shift would be on, but he doubted that any of his team would be found here. Manners likely had gone by now. He made his way to the kitchen and boiled the kettle for a green tea. His blood pressure had been creeping up over the last year or so, but now with Lena's healthy eating regime he expected it would have at least stabilised. This time of night he didn't want coffee anyway.

He made his tea, took the mug and went to his office. Beside his computer he found a note from Mal Gross. **Miller parents and sister overseas for holiday. Trying to find out where.**

An overseas holiday. One of those highlights of your life. Clement couldn't think of a worse situation to receive the news any parent dreads.

He had texted Lena earlier to say he was safe and that they had found the suspect dead. Now he called her. Any anxiety he had felt that first time had receded.

'It's good to hear your voice,' he told her when she answered, and he meant it.

'Yours too. I made a risotto.'

He had forgotten what it was like to have somebody prepare a meal you could enjoy after work. Women had cooked for him on dates. The Earles had invited him to dinner often, but it would have to have been the early days with Marilyn when that had actually been a thing: a waiting meal after a long day. And no, of course he had not appreciated the effort made. But you learn.

Clearly Lena had made an effort, and he did not want to disappoint her. He explained he had a bit to do yet.

'But I'll drive there tonight. I'm sure the risotto will taste even better tomorrow.'

They talked but Clement kept it brief. The sooner he was done here, the sooner he could see her.

He began drafting his report the instant he was off the phone. There was one wrinkle, minor, but it still bugged him: how did Cooper make it that quickly to Kununurra from Broome? Yes, he could have driven foot to the floor, but even then, it was a stretch. Most likely Matar had been wrong about what time he had left Broome. If he had left, say, forty minutes earlier than he thought, then the numbers worked. The other possibility was Matar had out-and-out lied about the time because he had been involved in the Lawson assault. At the time, Clement had been pretty darn sure Matar was confused and shocked by the news of the assault on Lawson. But if Matar were involved then, even with Cooper dead, Matar could be prosecuted. Clement made a note to follow up. He was back into the report in his office when Keeble rang. She explained she was calling from the station homestead. Mobile reception at the scene would be a no-go.

'You must be exhausted,' he said.

'I'm too tired to be tired,' she answered. She explained that the GSR test on Cooper was positive. 'He shot himself. Cooper's body is being flown to Perth. Rhino reckons the forty-eight- to sixty-hour window on time of death of Lorraine Miller stands.'

Clement well knew her habit of making dot points on all the outstanding issues and could picture her reading from her notes as she continued.

'James Matar's tox screen was positive to meth. Cooper's suicide has made it difficult to test for Heather Lawson's blood in the vehicle, at least for the time being.'

He told her she had done well, and she should call it a night.

'I'm taking tomorrow off.' It felt like a guilty confession as he said it. He knew how hard she had worked.

'I should be so lucky,' she said and rang off.

Should I have said something comforting about her break-up? he asked himself. He didn't want to overstep the mark. She might find it embarrassing to know work colleagues were talking about it, speculating. But people were. And if we don't reach out to our colleagues when we suspect they're having a hard time of it, what sort of friends are we?

Clement heard a noise in the main room and poked his head out of his office to see di Rivi dressed in civvies. She congratulated him on solving the case. He accepted it but wished Cooper had been captured alive. He nodded at her clothes.

'Night out?'

'Went for Chinese,' she said. 'Heather Lawson is conscious, and they said I can interview her tonight.' Di Rivi explained the hospital had called early in the morning, but she had decided not to bother Clement with the news. 'Not with everything else that was going down.'

He reassured her that was a good call. 'You know what you're doing,' he said.

'I'm heading out there now if you want to come. I mean I can handle it. You must be whacked.'

'Is Josh still in hospital?' He felt guilty he had not spared a thought for him all day.

'Yes. They are letting him out tomorrow. He was calling me every ten minutes for news. I told him not to harass you guys.'

Clement grabbed his keys. 'Let's go.'

—

While the police had been given permission by Lawson's medical team to interview Lawson, her boyfriend and flatmate would not be allowed to visit until the next day. When di Rivi and Clement arrived, a nurse was in with Heather Lawson writing up charts, so Clement excused himself.

'I'll pop in on Josh, come back.'

Shepherd was sitting in his chair in pyjama shorts, watching TV.

'Hey!' he managed. His face was still bruised. 'Was this guy a psycho, a meth-head or what?'

Clement explained as succinctly as he could what they knew about Cooper and how the day had unfolded. 'How are you feeling?'

'Sore when I move. Hurts like shit when I cough but I'm not pissing blood anymore. It's hard getting out of the chair.'

'One thing I wanted to check. The second man, James Matar, the smaller one. Did he join in the assault?'

'Shit, yeah. The big bloke, Cooper? He did all the damage, but when I was on the ground the other wanker kicked me a few times. I'd just about passed out by then anyway. Is he trying to get out of it?'

'Said he was in the gents.'

'Lying prick. He was there when I came out. The three of them. How's the girl?'

Clement explained he was going to check but that she was conscious and able to be interviewed.

'You want any chocolate?' Even though it pained him, Shepherd leaned over and pulled out the bedside drawer. 'The station chipped in. The footy blokes have promised me a carton. And the Picador are offering me a free dinner for six. Not that I want to go back there.'

Clement declined the chocolate, explained he was taking a day off in Derby while the forensics and data got collected. Everything had to be packaged up for Homicide down in Perth.

'Graeme and I will come and see you at your place.'

'The bloke topped himself?'

'Yeah.'

'Bugger. Would have liked a proper go with him.'

—

When Clement entered Lawson's room it was clear di Rivi had not long had her interview underway. She would have introduced herself first and explained she was the investigating detective. At the point Clement entered, she was establishing that Heather Lawson knew her own name. Compared to Lawson, Shepherd was unblemished. Heather Lawson's face was one swollen bruise. Clement felt sick in the pit of his stomach, torn between wanting to cry out and cry. Part of him was glad of how things had ended for Cooper. Perhaps that was wrong, but it was also human. He admired that di Rivi, who could not possibly be feeling less sickened than he was, maintained a friendly, professional manner. She was seated in the only available chair beside the bed. They had been told that, amazingly, Lawson's jaw, like Shepherd's, had not been broken although there was a lower tooth missing in her mouth. Whether that was as a result of the assault he did not know.

'This is Detective Inspector Clement.'

'Good evening, Heather. Thank you for seeing us. You're a brave woman.'

'Inspector Clement has been involved in tracking down these men: Nicholas Cooper and James Matar.' Di Rivi produced photos of them and showed her. Lawson's eyes were slits in puffy purple. 'Can you see those okay? You can just nod if it's easier, or give a thumbs up.'

Lawson managed a thumbs up.

'Now, last Friday these two men spent time with you. Do you recall going to the Picador Hotel?'

Lawson's thumb went up.

'And when you left the hotel, did these men attack another man in the carpark?'

'Mainly ...' Lawson managed a whispered grunt as she pointed at Cooper.

'Mainly Nick, right? But the other man, James, also attacked the man. Is that right?'

Lawson's thumb went up. Clement couldn't fault di Rivi so far.

'You're doing really well, Heather, thank you. Now, after the Picador you went to room fourteen at the Hartog Motel with these men.'

She seemed unsure. Clement decided to help out, 'The Hartog Motel. You might not remember the room number, that's okay.'

Lawson's thumb went up.

'You were found very badly beaten, and we don't know yet exactly what happened, so please if you can help us.'

Almost done, thought Clement. They would soon be able to leave Heather Lawson in peace.

'Did these men assault you?'

Clement's gaze went to the thumb, but this time it did not rise.

Di Rivi said, 'It's okay, Heather, the men are already in custody, they can't hurt you. Did they assault you?'

Lawson mouthed, 'No.'

Di Rivi and Clement swapped looks. What was going on?

Clement said, 'Those men are not in any position to harm you. You can tell us. Did they do this to you?'

She managed to shake her head.

'Then who?' asked di Rivi.

To answer took effort. 'Tony'.

Di Rivi said, 'Your boyfriend, Tony Edmonds, did this to you?'

This time the thumb went up.

16

'Where is the boyfriend?' Lena was watching him eat. By the time he made Derby it was a quarter to two in the morning, but she had been waiting for him. He hadn't realised how hungry he was. When he'd arrived, he had been overcome by a surge of passion he regarded as not lost, but unable to be found: a CD missing from its case, something you resigned yourself to as gone to God, but hoped might turn up in an unexpected location. Not since Marilyn had he felt this. He was barely into the room when he seized Lena and kissed and squeezed her and clumsily tried to drag her to the bedroom.

'Eat first,' she'd said, pushing back, her always-handy baton magically appearing like a finger in his chest. 'Believe me, I know how to use this.'

He had no doubt she did.

She waited patiently for him to swallow the risotto. Then he answered her question about Tony Edmonds' whereabouts.

'Di Rivi's trying to find him. He wasn't at their flat. The flatmate hadn't seen him since this morning.'

'Who fucked up?'

Clement supposed that was the way most people would view it.

'Nobody really. Dunstan's inexperienced and to be fair, the boat the boyfriend works on should have been out. It was only that they had engine trouble and turned back early. So we didn't realise Edmonds was in Broome when she was attacked. When he presented at the hospital, he put on the grieving act. Or maybe he regretted what he'd done. Dunstan hadn't checked when he actually got back. Normally di Rivi might have made sure that had been done, but it's been frantic with the murder.'

—

Clement could only surmise as to the chain of events. Edmonds might have gone looking for Heather at the pub and then tracked her down via word of mouth. That, or one of his mates had spied Heather out and about with Cooper and Matar and called him. It was a lot easier for people close to the scene than for cops. When you were a cop, nobody wanted to share what they knew. At least it explained Clement's nagging doubt about Cooper.

'I couldn't work out how he got through Kununurra so quickly. But he must have left Broome right away, just like Matar thought. Lawson was asleep where they left her. Edmondson came to the motel. The door was open. He found Heather, knew she'd been partying with these blokes, and bang.'

'So the dude who shot himself didn't bash her?'

'No. But here's the awful irony: if Edmondson hadn't attacked his girlfriend, a psycho would still be out there. We wouldn't have got to Cooper that quickly otherwise. We wouldn't have got there via the assault on Shepherd. It was that motel booking that gave us the lead we needed.'

This balance and counterbalance of good and evil was a characteristic of the job, yet never ceased to amaze him. So often the bad guys come undone not from their big crime but from some stupid, petty act: they litter, or get a parking fine, or play music too loud. The biggest cases are often cracked years later, not by hard work but a fluke.

If any good was to come from what had happened to Heather Lawson, perhaps identifying Cooper was it. Somebody who lashed a person to a post in crocodile waters and weighed them down with lead boots was not somebody you wanted around.

***

He lay on the bed naked under the fan. Alone. Hotels and motels, what were they except ghost ships? No, that wasn't quite right. There were staff here. In a way hotels are forerunners to hospitals, he considered. A training ground for those last days most of us will endure when we are incapable of acting for ourselves, when free will has been stolen from us, when our bodies have disintegrated. Rooms like this one, in every little city or town, were really repositories of loneliness. Like those *Alien* movies where everybody climbs into their own perspex pod. Oh yes, you could be persuaded to think of a hotel as a hub of life: the bridal parties, honeymoons, all futile sabre rattling against the inevitable isolation and abandonment. The sports teams celebrating the body, the excellence of physicality, the heaped breakfast plates. But given time, every one of those elite sportspeople will find themselves mired in the same mud, tangled in the same sheets as everybody else. Feeble, and dependent.

Businesspeople sense the futility, the flying from city to city, the desperate clamour for taxis, the glancing friendships that will be swamped by the lava of time. Despite the rush from that closed deal, that approved merger, they know in their blood that the freshly laundered towels and straight bedspreads are no more than a theatre set.

We all find ourselves in this position at some point. Under a whirring fan with a whirling brain, alone. But at least most people are granted a little respite, some brief time of partnership, oneness with another. That melding of flesh and blood that is humanity's closest approximation to the divine. He should have had that. They should have been together. They would have been together. Probably married in a simple ceremony under a clear blue sky.

But it had been stolen from him.

What he had done was brutal but necessary and therefore he felt no guilt. It was pointless to doubt one's actions after the event. Though we have no control over happiness, as humans we can at least ensure justice. Of course, it was meant to happen. The message had come to him, had it not? He had been tapped on the shoulder by fate and asked, 'Well, what are you going to do about it?'

If there were any doubt at all about what action he should take, it had been resolved by the location to which he had been blown. This land here was primeval. It was the furnace where God's fury could cleave mighty gorges from the earth's gut, reduce forests to ash and desert. His chosen instrument of death had appropriately been a dinosaur, a monster with no brain to reason, a reptile immobile unless warmed by sun, a creature from the beginning of creation. Also, the perfect start and end of the circle.

There was more blood yet to be spilled. He had noticed the police the other day at the pub. He was fairly certain they had not noticed him. Even if they had, what could they do?

The blades above him spun, just visible as a blur. He began to hum a childhood song. It was about gathering sticks to build a fire. That's what he was doing: gathering his sticks.

***

Clement woke at eight, admired the naked body beside him, slipped on shorts and began breakfast. He found smoked salmon in the fridge. Lena must have picked it up in Broome: he wouldn't expect to find it here. Certainly, it had never graced this fridge in his solo time here. He heard her rise and head to the bathroom, then the shower going. The timing was perfect. She arrived in a sarong, freshly showered, as he dished up.

'So, tell me all about it,' she demanded as she ate. He liked watching her eat. He liked sharing breakfast with another, and at a table rather than just unwrapping a roll on his office desk. 'Why did he kill her?'

Clement had not really had time to properly ponder what was essentially the same question Risely had asked. The last forty-eight hours he'd been chasing a speeding motorcycle trying to find out who was under the helmet.

'Maybe it was the drugs. But some people—' he corrected himself because in truth he had never come across a woman given to this kind of brutality, 'some men have a violent vein that runs just below their surface. I'm not a psychologist, I don't know what triggers them.' He told her then about the sex tape.

'Perhaps there was something sadistic in it after all,' he concluded, thinking about the vulnerability of those women.

'You've never tied someone up and fucked them?'

She sounded almost surprised. Lena's directness was one of the qualities that he most loved about her, but she could, he was reluctant to admit, shock him.

'No.' He almost didn't ask the question but made himself. 'Have you?'

She was shovelling a forkful of scrambled egg into her mouth. Its edges crinkled, the beginning of a smile.

His phone buzzed. This was to be expected. Keeble had a lot to cover, and she would make him her first port of call. There might also be questions from the press. When he saw Scott Risely's ID, he expected the latter might be the genesis of the call.

'Sorry, just swallowing a mouthful of egg,' he apologised.

Risely asked him if he had enjoyed his sleep. Clement looked over at Lena.

'Yes, I feel great,' he answered.

'Well, enjoy some respite. Just letting you know we tracked Lorraine Miller's family to Greece. We had a consular official give them the news. As per your instruction, I said you as the lead investigating officer would call as soon as possible. We will be releasing the name to the press soon.'

Risely rang off without further ado. Clement filled Lena in.

'I have to ring Mathias and tell him about us,' he said. The news he'd just received had churned that issue to the surface again.

'He won't be surprised. He knows what I'm like.'

Clement debated telling her that he had been prewarned but wavered long enough for his phone to ring again. It was only just coming on to nine. He wondered if it was Risely ringing back having forgotten something. He didn't recognise the number.

'Clement,' he answered warily.

'Inspector, it's Simone Livesy.'

At least it wasn't the press.

'Hi Simone.' He was wondering what had prompted the Kununurra cop to call.

'You remember we were trying to find that girl in the video, Shauna.'

Shauna … that's right. They had wanted to know if Cooper had been threatening.

Livesy continued, 'We located her up Kalumburu. We gave her a lift back and I spoke with her last night about Nicholas Cooper.'

'What did she say?'

'She liked him. She said he was sexy, and not violent towards her. She liked the stuff he did to her. But she said later he got very down, talked about some girl in Darwin who he'd busted up with. But this is the kicker. You think Lorraine Miller was killed Wednesday night or early Thursday morning?'

Already Clement was getting a sour taste in his mouth. 'That's the hypothesis.'

'Well, Shauna swears she was with Cooper from Wednesday afternoon at two p.m. through to ten a.m. Thursday morning when he headed off to Halls Creek.'

The disquiet spread to Clement's gut. If Shauna was telling the truth, and their timeline was right, Nicholas Cooper could not have killed Lorraine Miller.

17

Bek Dyson was a journalist. In her heart at least. To rephrase – as she knew she would if she were at a party and anybody bothered to ask what she did for a living – she would say that her intention was to become a journalist. To herself, here in private at the Kununurra library flicking through historic news articles, however, she had not the slightest doubt that she was a journalist. A piece of paper from some university was purely confirmation of what she knew to be part of her defining self. And besides, there was *BoomBox*. She wrote for that. Well, she submitted articles to that pretentious wanker Damien who ran the site from a tiny office paid for by his real-estate mogul father. It was really no more than a gossip rag for recently graduated private-schoolies who nearly all lived in the affluent Perth suburbs close to their former schools and the university campus.

He'd only run two of her articles so far. One was on a nightclub brawl where two ex-PLC girls had wrestled each other over a footballer; the other was a photo piece on the dog shelter and what determined which pooch would get rescued quickest and which would be longest in the institution. No surprise there: the cute puppies were adopted out before the article was finished, the old and the blind would be there until the end of their days.

Here, though, was her big chance.

It had been a spur of the moment thing to fly here from Broome. Jerome, her ex, was working in Broome these days and she'd allowed herself to believe the fantasy that she could engineer a meeting and things might take up where they had left off, but of course by now he had another girlfriend. One who clearly didn't mind him being stoned most days and enjoyed watching endless reruns of *Game of Thrones*. Put it down as yet another ridiculous escapade in the pantheon of such escapades that defined the life of Bek Dyson.

And then she had heard about the crocodile attack. Yes, that anyone should lose their life to a crocodile or shark attack was awful; however – and it was a very pertinent *however* – it was also newsworthy. When she heard two detectives were interviewing people at the pub, she'd hightailed it over there hoping to get information, but they hadn't taken her seriously. That was annoying. If she could have got more information, it might have been a foot in the door at one of the bigger media companies. Still, she wasn't giving up. She was on the spot and ahead of the game. She needed to strike while the iron was hot. Or the blood was fresh … maybe that was a better metaphor.

She had heard locals talking about previous attacks, in particular one fatal attack involving a female tourist eight years ago.

Regrettable as it was, when it came to getting eyeballs on your story, the fact was you would get many more eyeballs for a fatal attack on a young woman, with or without Achilles tattoos, than you would on some old local fisherman with a gut that looked like a robber's swag. This had set an idea running around her brain that if she could find a thesis for her story, some moral that ran through fatal crocodile and shark attacks in exotic lands, then she might have a decent enough article that she could have published by a real news service. Then she could tell Damien to get fucked.

She even allowed herself the fanciful idea that if the crocodile victim was an international tourist, she might get foreign eyeballs on her story. Foreign eyeballs were so much more desirable than local ones. But at the pub after speaking to the crew who she'd seen the detectives talking with, she learned that the girl they had been asking about was named Rain and was Australian. The crew there couldn't wait to talk to Bek. People love the idea their name will be in the media. The spokesperson had been a girl named Lucy.

'I remember the girl because she did "Bad Romance". That's one of Bree's songs.' She'd gestured airily at a girl over by the bar.

'What night was this?' Dyson figured she may as well follow the cops' line of questioning.

'Wednesday.'

I was here Wednesday, she thought, growing excited at the prospect she might have interacted with the girl.

'What did the girl look like?'

Lucy's description fitted half the women in the pub.

'What was she wearing?' Bek Dyson guessed Lucy might be the sort of girl who remembered that stuff really well.

'I'm pretty sure it was a short dress, blue with this little black-and-white pattern.'

Bek couldn't recall that herself, but maybe she didn't need to. Before all this, when she'd arrived from Broome, Bek had been thinking of writing a story called 'The Wild West' about Kununurra being the last town of its kind, the wild frontier. Even Broome now was bucket-list tame. Naturally she had taken lots of photos while in Kununurra, particularly those nights at the pub.

'Do you know where she was staying?' she had asked Lucy and her gang.

They thought Rain had been staying at Wide River Caravan Park.

Bingo.

—

Bek had driven over there in her hire car – the smallest and cheapest available – and seen that one of the tents was cordoned off. She had attempted to interview the managers to get more details about Rain, but the woman had told her the police had requested they say nothing for the time being. Clearly, they knew Rain's full name, but they weren't saying what it was.

She left disappointed yet still hopeful. For now, she had to bide her time on specifics, but she could at least write that the police had been to the caravan park and sealed off the tent of a young woman who 'may have been the victim'.

Back in her own motel room she had downloaded all the photos from her phone and painstakingly gone through those from Wednesday night. She almost missed it. Two drunks, one male, one female about twenty, were yahooing into the lens but behind them she saw a blue dress.

She let out a howl of excitement. There was a photo, clear enough, a young woman of average looks wearing a blue dress with a tiny black-and-white flower pattern. Rain. She was talking to somebody mostly out of shot but by the look of the hand holding the beer glass, a male. Bek checked and rechecked her other photos, but this was the only one showing that young woman. More would have been better. However, one was all she needed.

She had been about to put the photo and story on X when a warning bell went off. She only had Lucy's assertion that this was the girl the police were after, the one who had sung 'Bad Romance' at karaoke. What if that wasn't right? What if Lucy had mixed her up with another girl?

She deleted the photo from her post and replaced it with a generic one of the pub, and one of the tents now cordoned off. When the police released a photo of Rain, she would be able to see if hers matched. If so, it might well be the last photo of her alive. Now, that was precious.

A little rejig on the tweet giving the basics: Girl killed by crocodile, police at camp site. Off it went. Next thing she knew, she was getting real news organisations contacting her. It was incredibly exciting. Two already had said they would take a story. Broome was forgotten. Fuckhead Damien was history. Bek Dyson was being launched. But until the police confirmed that Rain was the victim or provided a photo, she had to bide her time on the launchpad, waiting, yet not idle. The more background on crocodile attacks up here, the better.

Hence, research in the library.

—

So far, working from most recent backwards, she had a local fisherman who had lost the lower part of his leg two years back, a couple of dogs that had been taken, and a young girl swimming near Ivanhoe Crossing who had been mauled by a shark.

Now she'd reached the big story.

Eight years earlier a young woman, a Swedish tourist, Ebba Olsson, had been taken by a croc at a remote spot on the Pentecost River. She had been part of a tour party. A successful line producer for a Danish television company, Olsson had recently been filming a series on adventurous tours around the world. The shoot had concluded the previous week in Darwin and Ms Olsson and a couple of others from the show had decided to take a week off exploring the Kimberley. Tragically, when the others had arisen in the morning there was no sign of Ms Olsson who the previous evening had announced her intention of heading to the water's edge in the morning to do yoga. The guide, Isabella Tait, had expressly warned her against this. It seemed Ms Olsson may have ignored that warning because there were clear marks of a big crocodile having been at the bank.

Dyson studied the photo accompanying the story. The guide, a very young woman, surely only twenty-one or -two, was pointing out a position on the bank to two police officers. A young man and woman, perhaps other members of the party, were comforting one another.

This is coming together, thought Dyson. And there is an international angle if she could just find a way to weave it in. She wondered if the two policemen in the photo were still around.

Her brain was ticking. This really could be big. And then she took another look at the photo and dizzying colours exploded inside her head.

18

Not yet midday, Clement was back at the station in Broome. He had just finished speaking by phone with Shauna Young to confirm for himself what Simone Livesy had told him. It was too important to be trying to do this from his own place in Derby. Shauna Young was adamant. She had met up with Cooper just after lunch, Wednesday, at the supermart in Kununurra. He'd told her he had a few days off and was going on the road. She'd been hoping he might invite her, but he didn't. However, he did invite her back to his place. First, they went for a swim by the river because it was so hot. Close to town where they swam was safe enough from big saltwater crocodiles and a bit too busy for the smaller freshwater crocs.

After that they went back to his place where they smoked a bit of weed and listened to music and had sex. 'Nothing special,' like what had been captured on the video. Shauna said she knew he'd had a girl around there either that morning or the night before.

'How did you know that?' asked Clement.

'You could smell her.'

Clement had persisted but Young said she just knew, and it didn't bother her.

Later, after sex and pot, they had meth that Cooper had scored.

'Are you sure you didn't fall asleep? That he didn't go out?' Clement had asked.

Young had laughed. She wasn't falling asleep with that gear in her system. They had finally fallen asleep in the early hours. In fact, she'd woken at about four and Cooper still hadn't moved.

'Like a goanna been squished by a truck,' was her description.

Cooper had wanted to head to Broome, and he left about ten a.m. on the Thursday, dropping her on the road out of town to Kalumburu.

—

A check back with the pub in Halls Creek where Cooper had met up with James Matar worked with this timeline. There was no way that Cooper could have killed Lorraine Miller. On Wednesday night when he was smoking dope and drinking beer with Shauna Young, Lorraine Miller was seen alive at the pub.

'We got it wrong,' Clement confessed to the main players in his team. Mal Gross, Graeme Earle who had responded to his request to come in, Jo di Rivi, Charmain Dunstan and Manners. Keeble was too busy, but he had already spoken to her. 'Actually I got it wrong. I fell into the trap of relying on probability. Cooper beat up Josh, and appeared to have assaulted Heather Lawson. So, with the victim on his video the day before she likely was murdered, everything pointed to him. But he didn't assault Lawson. He was likely mentally unstable, certainly after the drugs, maybe before. Shauna Young described how he would get very sad and depressed quite suddenly. I think Nicholas Cooper was a young man who ran off the rails and didn't know where to turn for help. Apart from beating up on Josh, he may not have committed any other violent acts throughout our timeline.'

'We have a killer still out there.' Earle voiced what they were all thinking.

'I'm afraid so.'

It was lazy, he thought. I equated Cooper's sex games with Miller's horrible demise. Looking at it objectively now, it was dumb: the knots on the rope found tied to the post near Ivanhoe weren't the same as those in the video in Cooper's sex games. The diving boots suggested planning. Nothing much else about Cooper suggested planning. Everything seemed impulsive.

He studied the faces of his people, wondered how many might be giving him the same critique as he had just given himself.

'We need to find out everything we can about Lorraine Miller. She either saw her killer at the pub or not long after. We need every photo that everybody in that crowd took. We need to check those tyre marks Keeble found, to see what we can establish.'

He looked up to see Scott Risely standing there. He wasn't sure how long he had been listening. He'd called his superior before he'd left Derby to give him the bad news.

'Any chance we can speak with Lorraine's family?' Clement asked.

'I'll try and get you onto them. There might be something else,' said Risely. 'There's a tweet with a photo allegedly showing Lorraine Miller at the pub Wednesday night.'

Damn. Some journo was already ahead of him. Risely wasn't finished.

'They also say that Lorraine Miller was a witness to the last fatal crocodile attack near Kununurra.'

***

Bek Dyson was over the moon. This was a genuine scoop. She had recognised the girl in that newspaper photo hugging the boy. It was Rain, eight years younger but for sure the same girl she herself had snapped in the background Wednesday night at the pub. Further reading had identified her as Lorraine Miller.

Bang. 'Rain' was Lorraine Miller.

No more waiting for the police. She had tweeted her photo of Miller identifying her as the believed victim and revealed that she was a witness to the fatal attack eight years earlier. Her tweet was going off. She didn't know if she was ahead of the police or not, but no way had she been prepared to sit on the story. Bek had forced the cops' hand. They were still being hush-hush about that crime scene but had just confirmed Lorraine Miller as the victim. While her tweets were great as teasers, Bek was now well into what was going to be the feature story that would break her big-time. Lorraine Miller aka 'Rain' had been around eight years earlier when a crocodile had taken the Swedish tourist Ebba Olsson over on the Pentecost. What were the odds of that? Had Lorraine Miller suicided maybe? Had there been something between Olsson and Miller? Bek hadn't been exactly sure where the Pentecost River was and had to look it up. Her next move would be to get up there. She had been writing flat out all morning and her story was quickly coming together. Her phone was running hot. Other journos from the big papers were wanting to cash in on her story but she wasn't going to do their work for them.

There was a knock on her door. She wondered if that might be the cops now. She was wearing shorts, a singlet and no shoes and her room was a mess. Earlier when the maid had poked in her head, she'd told her not to bother cleaning while she was still working. She walked over and opened the door a crack.

Sunglasses. The man smiled. And then she felt a jolt and the next thing she knew she was on the carpet. She tried to speak but no words came out. She was a sea of confusion and fear. What was happening?

The man's fist smashed into her.

***

Homicide in Perth had stayed out of the investigation up until now. Nobody had a better reputation than him, Clement knew that without any conceit. The case had seemed to be contained to the local area, but the revelation that Lorraine Miller had been at the scene of a fatal crocodile attack eight years earlier changed everything. Risely was liaising on the details with Perth, but it seemed likely that at least two more detectives would be sent to the Kimberley to help investigate. Assistant commissioners, the deputy commissioner and the main man would all be pounding fists on tables. Risely, Clement knew, would do his best to keep him at the helm of the case, though to date Clement hadn't exactly covered himself in glory. The list of people he'd disappointed continued to grow. There was no time, however, to indulge himself in navel-gazing.

—

He had told di Rivi and Dunstan to pursue Tony Edmonds, who was still at large. Just because the homicide was back on the table didn't mean everything else could be put on hold. That left just Gross, Earle, Manners and himself for now running down the Miller homicide from here. Plus Keeble's team of course. Perth would help with all the other logistics they needed. Risely still hadn't managed to get hold of the Miller family.

Mal Gross loomed in his doorway. 'I'm pulling all the press coverage from the old case: print and TV. Meantime, I don't know if you have the time for this, but I got a phone call from the ex of Nicholas Cooper in Darwin. She wanted to know if it was possible to speak with the head of the case.' He proffered a post-it on his finger. 'I didn't make any promises.'

Only a small part of Clement wanted to take that note. But that was the part that won.

'Her name is Sandy Roser. I've cleared her to make sure she's genuine.'

Clement stuck the note to his desk, dialled. The phone rang a long time before it was answered.

'Hello?' A woman's voice.

Clement explained who he was, asked, 'Is that Ms Roser?'

'Yes, thank you for calling.'

'How can I help you?'

She had heard that her ex-boyfriend Nicholas Cooper had died. She wanted to know how. Clement wondered if this was where the accusations of trigger-happy police would start.

'He shot himself.'

She was sniffing back tears. Clement asked if she was okay. Clearly, she wasn't.

'He wasn't a bad person. He was bipolar. That was hard to live with, but we managed. Then he got into ice. That was it. I told him we were done.'

Clement asked why Cooper had got into ice in the first place.

Roser admitted she didn't really know. 'But I think he always felt inadequate and maybe meth masked that, boosted him, made him think he was really somebody.'

For months after he had moved across to Western Australia from the Territory, he would pester her with calls, six or seven times a day.

'It was a relief when he stopped calling,' Roser confessed. 'I feel awful saying that now.'

I wasn't quite as bad as that with Marilyn, thought Clement, but he supposed he was a nuisance at best. Clement told Roser she should in no way blame herself.

'When we were still going out, he told me he was going to kill himself. Loads of times he said that. But, you know, he wasn't a bad person. When he was on meth, of course, he even threatened me. He'd just snap. I'm sorry, I just wanted the police to know that there was another side to Nicholas.'

When Clement had finished the call, reinforcing with Roser that she must not blame herself for any of this, he sat there for a few long minutes pondering relationships.

Why do we fuck up the very things that might save us? In Cooper's case, if he was bipolar, then that presented an extra and perhaps, as it turned out, insurmountable challenge. Yet Sandy Roser had seemed prepared to take that on. Until drugs intervened.

Clement was grateful she had taken the trouble to call the police. He could freely admit to himself that while pursuing Cooper he had conjured an image of a sexual psychopath, a brute and bully. Having one of your own bashed did not generate empathy for the aggressor. Now, though, he saw that Cooper was more lost than anything. Suicide had likely never strayed beyond a certain boundary. Sex games or not, the seed of self-destruction had continued to grow in Nick Cooper.

We are all human. No matter what the actions of the perpetrator that Clement found himself hunting, he must always remember that.

Mal Gross arrived bearing a laptop.

'Background on the Pentecost River attack is ready to go,' he said as he began running a cable from the computer to the flat-screen monitor. 'I've also called up the Coroner's file and forwarded it to you.'

—

Earle joined Clement, and Gross began his presentation, which was all web-based: links to print articles, TV news footage from the time. Ebba Olsson's death had been huge news. It had happened just before Clement had come back to the Kimberley, a period when his mind had been crammed with Perth murders, and his disintegrating marriage. It had registered peripherally, only as a shocking event. Both Graeme

Earle and Mal Gross had been in Broome when the attack occurred, and both recalled the hubbub though neither had been on the scene, nor involved in the case. That had been handled out of Kununurra.

'I remember it pretty much like those news reports.' Gross clicked the remote and the TV screen went blank. 'It was a small party. They said four on that' – he nodded at the now dead screen – 'that sounds right. They were up at the Pentecost, and everybody knows you camp well back there.'

Clement was thinking that the guide looked young. He doubted she could be older than twenty-one. Earle took up the story.

'I remember it like they said. The foreign girl – what was she, German?'

'Swedish according to that,' said Clement.

Earle continued, 'They said she must have gone down to the river.'

'Did you recognise the cops?'

'That was Mike O'Donnell. I met him a couple of times.'

Mal Gross said, 'He retired about three years ago. I don't know the other guy.'

'Would Callum or Simone Livesy know them?'

In unison Gross and Earle thought they would be too young.

'But Steve Eaton at Halls Creek almost certainly would,' added Gross.

—

Clement called Steve Eaton. He remembered the tragedy well.

'Mike O'Donnell was the senior cop. He retired to Albany.'

It was curious that many of those who'd spent a big chunk of their lives in the heat of the north headed to the far south on retirement. Eaton thought the younger cop in the photo was named Vodanovic or Vudanovic, but he didn't know what had happened to him.

It didn't take Gross long to find a number for O'Donnell.

'I'll speak with O'Donnell,' Clement told Earle. 'How about you get over to the TV station, see what they have? Maybe they have a whole bunch of stuff they never aired.'

Earle left immediately. Because he had been around so long, he had excellent contacts with the local media. And while much of the historic footage was jettisoned in the old days, the ability to store material digitally meant nowadays a whole lot more was kept. And not just the edited stories that aired.

Mulling it over, Clement was thinking that the news crew, who almost certainly had flown out from here, would have filmed a whole lot of shots that for one reason or another did not air. Given how big the story was at the time, and the international interest, there had to be at least a fifty-fifty chance that the original footage might remain.

—

He dialled O'Donnell, interrupting him pushing a shopping trolley. Clement introduced himself and told the former policeman why he was calling. O'Donnell hadn't heard the news about the most recent fatality.

'Haven't got the paper for years. Don't even bother with TV these days,' he said.

After requesting O'Donnell's discretion, Clement told him about the calculated way Lorraine Miller had been killed.

'Jesus.'

Going off the still photo of her eight years back – she hadn't been seen on the TV news reports of the time – Clement had no doubt it was the same girl. The photo of the boy, Jarrad Lester, hadn't shown much of his face, it being largely obscured by Miller in his arms. Nonetheless, he heard a distant chime of recognition in his head. I need a better photo, he'd told himself.

To O'Donnell Clement said, 'Given Miller's history, I have to at least look at the possibility that this was payback. What was your instinct at the time?'

It was one of the biggest cases O'Donnell had worked on and his recollection was clear.

'There were four of them altogether. The Swedish girl we presumed was taken by a croc. There were definite marks in the mud. The guide, Bella Tait, was young, very upset, but seemed reliable. The girl, and I think it was her boyfriend, or at least they were an item, Jarrad ...'

'Lester, according to the paper.'

'Those two were very upset.'

'Did you recover the body?'

'A few parts. We never identified the actual croc. It was thick with them at that time. Voodoo and I – that's Charlie Vudonavic; he quit and went to Thailand, about a year after – we kicked around a few ideas. Could there have been foul play: a sex triangle? It didn't seem likely. The guide, Bella Tait, was young but thorough and conscientious. The other three had all worked on the same TV show. Olsson was really keen to see more of Australia before she went back to Europe, and the three of them drove from Darwin and hired Tait to guide them.'

'What about Olsson's family? She wasn't married?'

'She had a boyfriend. I called him in Copenhagen. He was devastated, as you'd expect. We contacted her parents in Sweden. They were in shock. Everybody was in shock. You can't think of a worse way to go. And no real remains didn't help.'

'Nobody contacted you claiming there was skulduggery?'

'No. And if there had been, the only ones who would know would be those three.'

That was true.

'We looked for any sign of homicide. There was no blood on the bedding, on the tents, near the camp site, in the vehicle. There was no obvious weapon apart from knives that the guide used. We really had no choice other than to believe the account and, quite frankly, there was nothing raising any flag.'

Clement thanked O'Donnell for his time and asked if it was alright if he called again.

'No problems.'

'You miss the heat?'

'About three times a year in the middle of winter. And then I thank God I'm out of it.'

—

Clement had the air wing organise a flight to Kununurra for Earle and himself, but there were still things he wanted to progress from here. First, he called up the coronial inquiry and scanned that. There seemed no new information there not covered by what O'Donnell had told him. Next, he called Keeble, who was fighting her way through data from four different crime scenes. He explained the latest.

'You're joking. That's a big coincidence, she's on the scene of two fatal croc attacks.'

'Too big.' Clement had been considering this very point. 'But it could have been staged. If someone knew Miller had been a witness to the fatal attack years back, what better way to throw us off what might be a domestic or money dispute. Did Rhino come back with anything on possible DNA under the nails of the hand we recovered?'

'Be too soon for any results.'

Clement said he would call him. 'What about Miller's tent and belongings?'

'No trace of blood. I've lifted fingerprints, one other set at least. But I hadn't run them through the system because we thought we had Cooper. They're running now.'

'What about the litter from the Ivanhoe scene?' DNA would be days away, but he was wondering about the prints.

'I didn't see any that matched the tent site, but I've got Karla double-checking, and they are going into the system too.'

A print on a can, say, at the Ivanhoe site that matched one in the tent would indicate that it was from the person who killed Miller.

'The rope?'

'Could have come from a hundred places. The diving boots, however, are a different kettle of fish, excuse the bad-taste metaphor. My research says they are Russian made, genuine antique from the nineteen-fifties. We couldn't find anywhere that specialised in antique diving gear so they could be from anywhere.'

He told her the origin of the diving boots was now critical information.

'We can palm it off to Perth if you like.'

He knew that under normal circumstances Keeble would guard her territory like a junkyard dog, but she had an enormous amount on her plate.

'Okay, why don't you do that. They've got the boots there anyway. Leave the tyre marks with me.'

'We never found Miller's phone or computer, did we?'

'No. No indication she had a computer, but she clearly had a phone.'

He told her he'd be in touch. Then called in Manners.

'I need Lorraine Miller's phone records as soon as possible.'

'No problem.'

The phone log could be invaluable in telling them who she had been in touch with. But these days you didn't stop there.

'I need her Facebook, Instagram, TikTok et al., going back ten years if you can. Any recent posts, mark to my immediate attention. Anything that mentions the attack in twenty-sixteen, the same. If you find a Jarrad Lester on there, I want to know immediately. Meanwhile I need you to liaise with Perth and ask them if they can track down Jarrad Lester. Sounds like he was employed on the same show that Ebba Olsson was. The production company may have a contact. He'd be about thirty now. Same for the guide, Isabella Tait. I want to know where she is now.'

Manners scooted off. While the call log could give them a few persons of interest, getting data was another story. That was never easy. Who she'd been texting and taking photos of was of paramount importance but could be almost impossible to obtain.

Next, he dialled Rhino.

'I'm in the middle of a shit-storm here,' Clement said. 'It looks like our prime suspect did not kill Lorraine Miller, the crocodile victim.'

'No, the croc did that.'

He told Rhino he was not in the mood for his usual wordplay. 'Did you find anything under the nails of that hand?'

'I did. Could be somebody's skin, could be her own. You want DNA, obviously.'

'Like yesterday.'

'You got it.'

—

Clement chastised himself: I have to get organised. I'm like shotgun pellets flying all over the place. There are so many angles on this killing, and I have been guilty of wanting it nice and simple so I could get back to Lena.

He returned to the main incident room, picked up a marker and went to work on the whiteboard. Under the heading *Ivanhoe* he wrote

Rope, Hand, Tyre marks, Other. He was thinking of the litter that had been picked up. Rope was under control, DNA from the nails was to be analysed, the tyre marks were being handled by Keeble, as were prints from the litter. It occurred to Clement that while Cooper had not killed Miller, perhaps a mutual acquaintance had. He made a note to compare any stray prints found at Cooper's with those at Miller's tent and the Ivanhoe site. DNA on the litter found near Ivanhoe Crossing would take time.

Next, he wrote *Phone.* Nothing gave away more about us than our phones. People who would never have kept a diary seemed not to realise that was pretty much what their phones were. But getting data off them was difficult. Despite that, they could at least get recent phone calls in and out. Manners had that underway. They should be able to get a location on when her phone had last been pinged.

His third heading was *Last Known Movements.* Under that he wrote *Pub.* Miller had either left the pub with her killer or been picked up shortly thereafter. He was sure of that in his gut. The killer had prepared carefully. Look at the diving boots for a start. A killer who went to that trouble must have either had an arrangement to meet Miller or at some point on that Wednesday night been at the pub. If Clement's team could get their hands on every photo that had been snapped that night, he was sure that the killer would be revealed. It would be an arduous task. A good one to feed to Perth.

And he needed to know more about Lorraine Miller. Rather than call, he walked the corridor to Risely's office. The door was open.

'Any luck with Lorraine Miller's family?'

'I left a message for them to notify me when they could talk, and I'd call them back.'

Why couldn't you ever have what you needed when you wanted it? It was like it was a rule of the gods.

Returning to his own office, he pulled out his phone and dialled Callum Nelson. When Nelson answered, he went straight to it.

'I want you to get every photo you can that was snapped inside or near the pub from Tuesday to Wednesday night.'

'Most of those who were there will be back there tonight.'

'Good. Use everybody you have.'

'You want me to ask the radio to put out a call?'

Clement mulled that over. What was the downside? Was there one? Not at this point. 'Yes, good idea. And get your people asking everybody in town if they saw Miller and if so with who. Also, CCTV footage from every place in and out of town you can think of for Wednesday night from ten p.m. onwards.'

Nelson said he would do.

'The guide on that fatal trip, Isabella Tait. You wouldn't know where she is?'

'There's a Bella somebody who does personal tours up here. That might be her. I'm a newbie but Livesy or one of the others will know.'

'Good. Find her if you can. I'd like to speak with her tonight if possible.'

'Got it.'

As the phone clicked in his ear Clement sighed, studied his whiteboard again. He had people running down social media, good. The next step had to be family and friends of Miller's. He needed to speak to them, find out who was close to her. Had she called them recently, mentioned anybody?

His phone buzzed. Earle.

'There's some good vision here at the station of Miller and Lester. A few candid snippets where it looks to me like Lester is doing all the talking. He could be consoling her, or he could be directing her. I can't tell. They screenshot the best still they had of him. I just sent it.'

Clement reacted to the ping. He opened the file. The shot was no close-up, but it was clear. Jarrad Lester looked early twenties, scrawny. No sportsman, no Josh Shepherd.

But that face ... yes, Clement had seen it. And recently.

Then he snatched it out of the air like a crocodile snaring a flying bird.

It was the face he'd committed to memory at the pub Saturday night when he'd been asking after Lorraine Miller.

Jarrad Lester had been in Kununurra the day what was left of Lorraine Miller had been found.

19

He hadn't reckoned on the journalist, though he had never lost sight that there was plenty that could go wrong. It did not unduly bother him. So long as he finished what he had come here to do. He could not be derailed though. That must not be allowed to happen.

He'd been driving for nearly an hour. The middle of nowhere. There was a lot of nowhere in this enormous land, that was for sure, a lot of time to consider what might have been done better. He had contemplated calling the journalist, saying he had something special to impart about Lorraine Miller, arranging a discreet meeting. He had no guarantee, however, that she would come alone and, if she didn't, then it would just be too difficult. And he needed to act quickly.

At least he'd had the presence of mind to keep his eyes and ears open at the pub. He'd seen the police sniffing around. He'd even been questioned himself. No, he didn't remember the girl, Officer. They'd bought it. Tempting as it was to run, he'd remained and noted the police talking to that group who had been near the front of the stage on Wednesday. Then he'd got lucky hearing the journalist girl pumping that same gang for information. After which he had followed her out to the caravan park. She was sniffing around alright.

The tweet had done it. Had she seen him that night? Did she have a clear photo of him?

Now that he'd scrolled through the photos on her phone, he was fairly sure the answer was no to the photo. One instance of his fingers around a glass of beer. But she still may have recognised him. When he'd appeared at her door, she hadn't seemed to react in any way other than curiosity, but then he'd zapped her almost immediately with the taser, so he couldn't be sure. It was a risk he couldn't take.

Things were coming to a head, and he must not be stopped. This evening, he knew, Bella was leaving on a tour with a single client. That made things much easier for him. It would all be over soon. From the back of the vehicle he heard a muffled groan, a body twisting and turning. She must be hot under the tarpaulin.

This was far enough, he decided. He slowed, came to a halt, switched off the engine. There was a little shade here. He grabbed the rope from the seat beside him. And the sharp knife. Fate threw people together. Sometimes, though, people interfered in what had been decreed. That was wrong. That was what must not go unpunished.

***

Clement was literally heading out the station door to go to the airport when Risely appeared.

'Finally got the Millers. Lorraine's sister Hilary is going to call you now.'

The words no sooner out of Risely's mouth than Clement's phone chimed.

He answered, introducing himself and offering his condolences. Reading the situation, Graeme Earle slid behind the wheel, allowing Clement the opportunity to focus on the call.

Hilary Miller introduced herself and explained that her parents were still in shock. She said that Superintendent Risely had explained there were developments, and the case was moving fast. Clement confirmed that. He asked how much the family had been told.

'We know how she died,' said Hilary. That, thought Clement, was the perfect choice of phrase to circumvent the horror. Talking about that grotesque scene must be extremely painful.

'We had a person of interest. We were very sure he was responsible. However, we are now confident it was not him. Can I ask you if Lorraine had received any threats of late?'

'Unfortunately we have had very little to do with Lorraine for years. We might get a call from her around Christmas or for Mum's birthday. That's about it. If she was getting threats or anything like that, we wouldn't know.'

Earle already had them gliding out of the station exit. The airport was only minutes away.

'Was she in any kind of relationship?'

'Again, we honestly don't know. We don't know where she lived, who she was involved with. What she was involved with. Almost certainly drugs.'

Could it be that simple? Cooper had been involved in drugs. Was it through Cooper that Lorraine met her killer?

'So you have no idea where she has been living?'

'The last time we heard from her was over a year ago and she was in Albury, I think.'

Clement asked why Lorraine might have returned to Kununurra.

'I have no idea. That baffles us. That was where her life changed, that crocodile attack. I mean, she didn't witness it, but she might as well have. She was going really well before that. Had a career about to take off.'

'The guy with her at the time, Jarrad Lester ...'

'Jarrad, yeah.'

'Were they a couple?'

'I think they met on the show, and they had kind of hooked up. They didn't last that long afterwards. I think that was another thing that suffered.'

'Did you meet Jarrad Lester?'

'Yes, a few times. He was like a camera operator or something. I don't know what happened to him.'

Earle was heading for the private aviation area. You could have sizzled an egg on the bonnet. And Kununurra would be hotter still.

'Would you have a contact for him, or know where his family might be?'

'Sorry. All I know is he was from Sydney.'

'How did he strike you?'

'Do you think he might be involved?'

Clement couldn't blame her for asking that question. He did his best to deflect.

'We have to investigate every channel, and the fact that Lorraine died the way she did, we have to at least consider it could be related to the previous incident. That's why I wondered if Lorraine ever got any threats, or you know, social media hate mail.'

'If she did, she never mentioned it, and I think she would have. But, like I say, the last twelve months we've heard nothing from her.'

He prompted her again about Jarrad Lester. They were already at the airport perimeter.

'I only met him three or four times. He didn't appeal to us, a bit fake, a bit ... oh, you know, *I'm in TV*. But we didn't mind him. We didn't hate him.'

'What about other boyfriends?'

Hilary thought for a moment and mentioned names.

'Could you text those through to me?'

Hilary would be happy to. Clement was wondering what more he could ask as the wick shortened.

'What about the girl who died, Ebba Olsson? Was Lorraine good friends with her?'

'I think they had become close. Lorraine said Ebba had a boyfriend, and they were going to get married. Lorraine cried heaps. For days, weeks. Like I said, I don't think she ever recovered.'

'Did she ever contact the boyfriend?'

'She might have done.'

'Do you remember his name? Would you have a contact?' He couldn't recall seeing it in the coronial file. He should have asked O'Donnell when they had spoken earlier. He kicked himself.

'On him? No. The production company was JLT, I remember that. "Jambon, Lettuce and Tomato", Lorraine used to joke. They are Danish, based in Copenhagen.'

Earle parked, switched off and looked over at him.

'Sorry, Hilary, I need to go right now. Is there anybody who was really close to Lorraine we could contact? Someone who might know if she had threats?'

'I'll think about it and text you.'

Clement thanked her for her time. The Cessna's propellors were already spinning.

—

Just after four Monday afternoon the Cessna touched down on the molten strip at Kununurra. So much for my day of rest, thought Clement, then reprimanded himself. It was churlish, him worrying about sacrificing a day off when Lorraine Miller had lost her life. Hilary Miller had lost her sister. He wondered if the Millers felt they should have reached out more. It's insoluble, he thought. What a parent needs to do, nobody can be sure. It varies with every child, and every parent. It would tear his heart out if he lost contact with Phoebe. Had Lorraine Miller been so traumatised by the attack that took her friend that she had gone off the rails? Or was she already on her way before then?

As before, Livesy, bless her, was waiting with water for them.

'Déjà vu all over again,' she cracked.

'I'll just be a minute,' said Clement, taking himself off a few paces. There had been no time earlier and the plane was too noisy for a phone call, but now he could call Mal Gross.

'We've arrived,' he said without preamble. 'We need to speak with somebody at a Danish television production company, JLT – like BLT but with J for James – who might have been there when Ebba Olsson the crocodile victim was working there.'

'Probably best I get Perth onto that.'

'Whatever you prefer. I'd like to speak with Olsson's family if it's possible too.'

Gross said he would take care of that. Earle and Livesy were waiting in the car with the air-con on. He climbed in beside Livesy who was driving.

Earle imparted what Livesy must already have told him. 'There is a

Jarrad Lester signed in to a caravan park at Emma Gorge but there is no sign of him or his car.'

Clement realised that he was shaking his head like you do when you can't catch a break. He had to stop feeling sorry for himself.

'I do have better news about Bella Tait though.' Livesy pulled out as she spoke. 'She runs her own private tour company. She has a booking in an hour but has agreed to wait till we could speak to her. She's about twenty minutes out of town.'

'Let's go straight there,' said Clement.

—

Clement used a chunk of the driving time to make a call to di Rivi. Just because he was now chasing a sadistic murderer didn't mean he could neglect such a serious assault case as Heather Lawson's.

'There is no sign of Edmonds,' she said. 'I'm sure somebody knows where he is but they're not talking to us.'

'You've got Manners checking his phone?'

'It hasn't been active for two days. We can't find any family here. He's likely headed for Perth. He got a good start on us, but I've circulated his vehicle details.'

'How's Heather Lawson doing?'

'A little better each day. I haven't wanted to push her too hard.'

'She knows him better than anyone. Ask her for anybody she can think he'd turn to.'

'Josh poked his broken nose into the station.'

No surprise. Shepherd would hate missing out on the action. Clement apologised but said he had to go. He ended the call wondering if he should leave Dunbar running down Edmonds and pull di Rivi over onto this. He heard Graeme Earle asking Livesy to make inquiries about what vehicle Jarrad Lester might be driving.

'You could check regos too,' he suggested.

'I will. And I'll notify everybody to keep an eye out.'

'And also forward any information to Lisa Keeble.'

It was good thinking by Earle. Maybe the tyre tracks found at the jetty scene would match Lester's vehicle.

Clement had a thought himself. 'And when you speak to Keeble, ask if she can try for fingerprints at Lester's caravan park site, and run them against everything else pertinent.'

It wasn't necessary to give specific instructions to Keeble.

They turned off the main road and down a narrow dirt track. Clement had the sense they were heading towards the river as the flora was becoming progressively greener and thicker. Tall grasses lashed the car as if hazing rookies.

'I think this is the way to come, from what she told me.'

To Clement's ear, Livesy sounded far from sure.

—

The track suddenly opened, revealing a small patch of cleared ground hemmed by shrubs, grasses and a few trees. Just beyond this space was a large, wooden shack. The sheeted tin roof was relatively new, with a pitch you'd want when the rains hit, but it had no gutter. Extending on this flank some five metres was a large shade tarpaulin tethered to metal poles. A bamboo blind dropped off the edge of the tarp facing them. A big rainwater tank sat to their right at the rear of the house. Directly in front of them squatted a late-model Landcruiser with a trailer hitched. Reflected sunlight burst off the wing mirror, sharp as the blade of a light sabre.

Livesy pulled up at right angles to the Landcruiser. They got out. The sun was searing but the air wet cement. A figure appeared in the open doorway of the house, just a silhouette.

Bella Tait came towards them holding a large jerry can in each hand. Apart from her thick black hair, the first thing Clement noted about her was how corded those forearms were. Somehow the dungarees she wore, the boots, and the cut physique stretched her. She seemed taller than Livesy although, if anything, when you studied her closely, she was shorter.

—

Livesy made the running. 'Thanks so much Isabella. I'm Sergeant Simone Livesy, the one who called you.' Livesy introduced Earle and Clement. Tait finished stowing the jerry cans in the back of the car before she came over to shake their hands.

'I'm happy to help though I don't have a lot of time, as I explained.'

Despite the pressing time Clement did not like to jump in with questions. Interviews with anybody, especially potential witnesses, were productive in direct proportion to their informality. At least so Clement had found.

'Business okay even this time of the year?' He nodded at the trailer and car.

'It slows down a lot but every year more people around the world learn about the Kimberley. That's good for me.'

'How long have you been doing this?'

Clement noted her hesitation, an almost nervous lick across the lips.

'On my own, going on for five years.'

'Do you do larger parties?' Earle was giving the car the once-over. 'I've got in-laws coming over from Scotland. There'd be about seven all up.'

'Quite a few. I have a bus I hire if I need to.'

Time to get to it. Clement said, 'You know about the crocodile attack.'

'I heard.'

'It was a murder. A very violent one.'

Her brows moved. Her eyes widened. 'Murder?'

Earle gave her the details but left out the identity of the victim. Tait's initial shock melded with confusion. Questions were bunching up in her head, reckoned Clement: Why are they asking me about this? Who would do such a thing?

Clement said, 'The young woman who was killed was Lorraine Miller.'

The horror Tait registered was palpable.

'I believe you may know her.'

Her reaction was immediate. Clement identified it as pure dread.

'Yes,' she managed.

Graeme Earle said, 'Did you know she was in Kununurra?'

'No.'

'She hadn't spoken to you?'

'No. I haven't had any contact with her for eight years.'

'How about Jarrad Lester?'

'I hadn't seen him for eight years either and then he appeared in front of me in the supermart on Saturday.'

Earle asked what they had talked about.

'We didn't talk, not really. I just wanted to get away from him.' She must have read their looks. Without being asked why he had this effect, she elaborated. 'I don't know if you've had your dreams just washed away but that's what happened to me at Pentecost. It's not something you want to revisit.'

Clement could empathise. Still, the vehemence of her reaction made him curious.

'So you didn't speak? Go for a coffee?'

'I had my dog in the car.' She nodded over and for the first time Clement noticed the dog lying on what must have been on old carpet under the tarpaulin. 'I knew Jarrad for all of about five days. I didn't want to relive the worst period of my life.'

'He didn't say anything?'

'He told me he'd had cancer, and that he'd since found God. I don't have a problem with religion, but I couldn't care less. And if he really did have cancer, then I'm sorry for him, but he claimed he was over it since he'd found God.'

Her choice of those words – 'if he really did have' – was interesting. Was Lester the kind of person to exaggerate and lie? He put it to her. She took a deep breath.

'Look, I don't want to be trashing the guy. Was he a phoney? Yeah, kind of. I mean, he was always dropping names of celebrities he'd met. Maybe he had, but I don't think they were besties.'

—

Livesy had taken herself off, presumably to make the phone calls about Lester's vehicle. Now she joined them again but to her credit made herself invisible. Clement was trying to get a handle on Lester, his personality. At the same time, he had to keep an open mind about Bella Tait. Was she telling them the truth? Over years as a cop, you honed your bullshit detector. With Tait, he wasn't sure. She could be holding something back. And yet, she was being honest enough about how Olsson's death had wrecked her career. That might explain why she wanted nothing to do with Lester but, equally, many people thrust together by tragedy form a lifelong bond. That clearly wasn't the case here.

'Did Lester have a vehicle?' he asked. Right now, he needed facts.

'If he had one, I didn't see it.'

Clement's scalp felt torched. He thought, I must be breeding cancers by the second.

'Did Lester mention Lorraine being here?'

Tait pursed her lips. 'He said something about her going to be here or coming here. I was just trying to get away from him ...' She hesitated.

'What is it?'

'That night, Scrounger went very weird. Like she'd heard something out there. She went to the line of the bush and was growling. I called out. Nobody answered. Then Scrounger relaxed.'

'And you think that was Lester?'

She opened her palms. Like, I don't know.

'Could you tell us a bit about what happened to Ebba Olsson?'

'It was all in the papers and on TV.'

'We know but we'd like to hear from you.'

She ostentatiously checked her watch. 'Let's go under there.'

Thank God, thought Clement as she led them under the shadecloth. Then she started her story.

—

It had been June of 2016. Six months earlier Tait had landed her dream job, working as a guide for Breathtaking Tours. A booking for three came through, six nights and seven days. They came into the office in Kununurra.

'Ebba Olsson seemed to be their spokesperson.'

She wanted 'dangerous country', crocodiles, snakes and adventure. That was the gist anyway. Tait had the feeling that Olsson or the TV company was footing the bill and the other two were freeloading, chipping in here and there.

Clement interrupted. 'Were Miller and Lester a couple?'

'They were sleeping together from what I could see. They weren't hiding it. I sleep in the car or in my one-man. The three of them had a decent-sized tent.'

'Any kind of ménage à trois?'

Tait shook her head. 'Ebba was interested in nature. She had that northern European thing: they love the roughness out here. And if she was going to go for a fling, it wouldn't have been Jarrad. Ebba was pretty high up the food chain. Lorraine was like makeup or wardrobe, and Jarrad I think was just a helper for camera or lighting or something. Ebba was twenty-eight or -nine, they were my age. Besides, Ebba had a boyfriend, pretty much a fiancé, in Copenhagen. She was talking about them getting engaged when she got back.'

'You remember his name?'

She closed her eyes, the better to think. 'I'm pretty sure it was August. I know he was Danish. She had got out of a bad relationship. She kept saying to me, "Danes are much nicer than what I'm used to." Mind you Ebba would have been a handful for anybody.'

Clement asked what she meant by that.

'Nature up here is exciting, but you have to respect it. It was like Ebba thought she was still in the TV studio. She'd rush on ahead when we were climbing a tricky gorge. She thought she was magically protected.'

'What about the other two?' asked Earle.

'Lorraine was okay. She would do what you asked. Jarrad did too, most of the time, but he was annoying. Immature. Look, I only knew them for a few days before it happened. I'm just talking from a guide's perspective.'

Clement asked about the fateful day.

—

It had been a long day. They had been driving, hiking, getting back into the vehicle and driving some more. They'd reached a small area on the Pentecost River where they would camp overnight.

'They all wanted to swim. I said no. Too many salties up here. The other two were fine but Ebba was disappointed. She had a ritual where she would do yoga by the water's edge at sunset and just after sunrise. That night, I told her not to try that here. I deliberately set camp a good distance away. That night I cooked them a meal. We all had some wine and beer. I only had one glass to be social. Back then I used to carry an old cassette player. You couldn't get internet out there, still can't, not even radio, but with batteries, you can play music. Everybody danced. Me included. It was a really good night. I tried to get them off to bed around ten, but they were in the mood to sing and dance. I stuck it out another hour then went to the car because the tent would be too noisy still for me to sleep. I reminded them they would be up early. I put out the fire. You know, you're a guide, not their parent, but that's how you have to act. That's where I failed that night. When I got up in the morning, I assumed everybody was in their tent.'

'What time was this?' asked Earle.

'I can't remember exactly but around a quarter to six. My plan was to be moving by seven, maybe drive a little closer and see if there were any crocodiles they could examine safely. I started to make breakfast. I peeked in and saw Jarrad and Lorraine cuddled up but no sign of Ebba. I thought she must have used my single tent. But I checked that, and she wasn't there. So then I started calling her. Then I roused the others. The other two told me that when they had finally gone to bed Ebba was in the tent already asleep. They weren't sure of the time, but they thought midnight to one. Okay, I thought, she's got up early and gone to do her yoga. I had a sick feeling though about Ebba. How she'd want to be near the water, even though I warned her. There was no sign of her as I moved down there. I was wary of crocs, but I had to check. I started along the bank. About thirty metres from where I started, I found drag marks.'

'You knew they were drag marks?' It was Graeme Earle.

'I'd never seen drag marks of a human taken by a croc, but I have seen where a calf was taken. I hoped I was wrong. We searched for another half an hour. Maybe a bit longer. Then I had to go to the radio and call for help.'

An idea was churning through Clement's mind.

'That last night, you went to bed first. You didn't see Ebba go to bed?'

'No. That's what they told me.'

'Do you recall if her bed was slept in?'

'It's just an air mattress with a sheet. You probably couldn't tell, and I don't remember.'

So, thought Clement, nobody apart from Lester and Miller actually knew what happened after Tait turned in. He'd noted that point when he'd read the coronial file.

'Who usually went to bed first?'

She blew air out through her lips, like, how could she recall that?

'I tried to be the last to bed, making sure the camp site was secure. Pretty sure those first two nights I was. Out of them, Lorraine would go to bed first, I think. She was the most tired.'

'Are you a heavy sleeper?'

'Not now. Back then I could get a good night's sleep even in the car, but when you're a guide, you're still on half-alert. I'm not a mother but friends tell me about how they are always half-awake with their babies.'

'You're sure a crocodile took her?' Earle this time.

'No doubt. They found remains.'

Clement left that line for now. 'After the death, did anybody from Denmark contact you?'

'Until the inquest I didn't speak with anyone. August was in Denmark. Ebba had moved there for work. I never spoke to August or anybody from the TV company. The rest of the family lived in Sweden. Ebba and I talked about it because I'd left my family too to come work here. We had that in common. The police asked if I wanted to speak to the family if they requested but I didn't want to. I couldn't handle it. I asked the police and the tour company to deal with it. Perhaps that was wrong. I was twenty-one. I just couldn't handle it. For weeks I would just lie in bed. I didn't know if I could ever recover.'

Living out here now by herself with just a dog for company, Clement wondered if she had recovered even now. Earle asked how the inquest had gone.

'Ebba's father came over. He was the only one. Her mother I think was too affected. It was very traumatic giving evidence and I felt like I was on trial. I felt guilty. I still do. I spoke very briefly with her father. I went over to him and said how sorry I was, that I had tried to warn Ebba.'

'How did he take it?'

'Well. He kind of smiled and said, "Ebba never did what she was told."'

'August didn't come?'

'No. I'm not sure, but I think his job took him elsewhere in Europe.' She shrugged. 'I'm sorry, but I should be heading off.'

Clement looked to Earle to see if he had any other questions, but he was silent.

'Well, thank you for your time. Will we be able to reach you if we need?'

'Phone connections out here are iffy if not impossible, but I carry a sat phone too.'

She handed across a simple business card with her name, phone number and email. They thanked her and made their way back to the car.

'Where to?' asked Livesy.

'Lester's caravan,' said Clement. Ideas were forming in his head but so far, they were still just shapes draped in shadow.

—

It was after five when they got to Lester's rented caravan. He had not returned. Livesy's uniforms, Davis and Fernandez, had however done a good job of asking around about Lester. The site was thinning out and would only be open another week before closing for the season. According to witnesses, Lester was driving an old white Commodore sedan with Queensland licence plates. Nobody had the number, but it was still a big help. The last time anybody recalled seeing him was early Saturday evening. Clement texted through the information to Mal Gross who would forward it to Perth. All being well, they would get a quick result.

The warrant to search had been quickly obtained. Clement's first thought when they entered the caravan – apart from 'How does anyone not melt in here?' – was that they were going to find very little. Ten minutes later that opinion had solidified. The van was sparse. There was no computer and no personal effects, not even a bag, nothing apart from a pair of socks and jocks that had been washed and hung on the line outside.

Careful to inspect while wearing gloves, Clement and Earle checked the fridge, under the pillows, and down the side of the fixed bed. The fridge contained water, a half-block of cheese, a few tomatoes and a couple of apples.

Earle had drawn the same conclusion as Clement. 'Whatever he has is in the car with him.'

—

It was much cooler in the shade. Mal Gross had sent through a Facebook profile on Jarrad Lester. There were only four entries post-2021. All were of some type of religious nature, a photograph of a sunset or lake with Hallmark-ese wisdom such as 'And you believe this is possible without somebody greater than you?' So seemingly Christian, but neither Clement, Earle nor Livesy could make out exactly what denomination. Only twelve friends in his friendship pool. Leave it to Gross or Perth or a combination to check those profiles. With luck there would be somebody they could contact to ask about Jarrad Lester.

'I'm on my way there,' said Keeble when Clement dialled. 'I can check any prints against the can we found at the murder scene.'

He knew she'd be on the same wavelength without him prompting. 'What about the vehicle?'

'An old Commodore? Well, I don't know about the wheelbase and all of that, but looking at that terrain near the jetty, I don't see a Commodore sedan tootling over it.' Echoing Clement's initial thoughts that he'd kept to himself. Still, the murder seemed to have been planned and it wouldn't be too hard to organise a second vehicle. One like Tait's, for example.

—

Only when he'd finished speaking with Keeble did Clement properly reflect on the Isabella Tait interview. There had been nothing at all suspicious in her reactions. Maybe that was it. Usually when you're investigating there is a moment you think your interviewee could be suss, even if they aren't. The only thing that jarred was how vehemently she had reacted to Lester's name. As she said, she barely knew her clients, yet her reaction was more like that of somebody to an ex-lover or business partner. Could there have been anything between Tait and Lester? Could he have turned up here and enlisted her help, borrowed her vehicle, say? That might explain why she would react that way if she learned he was a killer and he'd implicated her. Yet her reaction of surprise at Miller being the victim had seemed genuine.

He ran his thoughts past Earle. 'Did you pick up anything I missed?'

'Nope. If she knew about the death of Miller, she's a great actress.'

'You see her as being sexually involved with Lester?'

'We don't know either of them well enough. But I suppose if she was fucking Lester, then instead of getting up early like she maintains, she could have been asleep, negligent.'

Yes, thought Clement, that would be the kind of thing that might make her angry with Lester. The record said Tait went to bed first. Was that so? Had she and Jarrad Lester got together? Told Miller to be quiet? Or Miller found out later what had gone on.

Earle interrupted his pondering. 'Maybe this Lester guy is just a jerk,' added Earle. 'Rubs everyone the wrong way.' What had Hilary Miller said? A bit full of himself. And Bella Tait had been negative about him too.

Clement's phone buzzed. Hilary Miller had emailed him with the names of three former boyfriends of Lorraine Miller. It would be useful to talk to them but right now even more useful to know if any of them could have been in Kununurra on the night she was killed. He copied the information to Gross and asked if Perth could follow up and set up contacts for potential interviews.

'You want to wait for Lisa?' asked Livesy.

She wouldn't be that long, maybe fifteen minutes. There was so much to do though, and sunset was only a step away. His thoughts drifted to the young woman journalist who had accosted them at the pub. She was the one who had first made the connection between the two cases. He wanted to speak to her. She had uncovered a photo that showed Lorraine Miller at the pub chatting to somebody, likely a man. Where had that photo come from? Was it on the night in question? Could she have taken it herself? If not, who did? And did they have more photos? Maybe one that showed who she was talking to. Was it Jarrad Lester?

'Where did that journalist say she was staying?'

Graeme Earle had amazing recall. He flicked through his mental filing cabinet. 'Brolga Motel.'

20

A black handkerchief had fallen over the town by the time Clement and Earle reached the carpark of the Brolga Motel. The trip back from Emma Gorge had been spent with both detectives on their phones while Livesy, who had since been dropped back at the station, drove. The last hour had been one big nada. No sign of Lester, no results from Keeble yet about matching fingerprints, no sign of Anthony Edmonds in Broome. Gross had sent through a number on the Danish production company but was still waiting on Perth to provide a contact on Ebba Olsson's family. The local police were making headway on getting photos from the pub uploaded to a central collection area set up by Manners. He would then allow Perth, who had far more personnel, to search for matches on Miller, and now Jarrad Lester.

Perth had been quick to turn up one of Lorraine Miller's old Sydney boyfriends and Clement had managed a conversation on the journey. A conversation that had yielded zero. He had only seen Lorraine a couple of times since they broke up. Yes, he believed she had been going out with Jarrad Lester for a time. That was the second-last time he'd seen her, and around the time of the crocodile business. The most recent time was a year ago. Lorraine had seemed out of it. He had a feeling she was on some kind of drugs or medication.

The Brolga was a mid-level motel. Nothing fancy but seemingly well kept. A sign warned the gate to the carpark would be locked from nine p.m. They caught the manager locking up for the night. She didn't need to consult her bookings.

'She's in eight,' she told them.

There was a small hire car out the front of the unit. Clement figured it was exactly what Dyson would have picked, so his hopes were high when he knocked on the door, but there was no answer.

'She's probably gone to eat,' suggested Earle.

Food wasn't a bad idea, thought Clement, then in the same breath recalled how good it had been to come home to Lena's risotto.

'Let's try the pub. She's probably there.'

—

Even on a Monday the pub was busy. Clement ordered fish and Earle a burger. Just because the bulb had been turned out didn't mean the night was cool. It was still over thirty, but at least you didn't feel your skin burning. They each did a once around but there was no sign of Dyson. Two uniformed cops, one male and one female, were diligently asking patrons if they had any photos from last Tuesday or Wednesday.

'I did that this morning,' one young bloke with tatts informed the uniforms as Clement waited at the bar for a squash. Good. The female constable approached Clement as if to interview him, then must have realised who he was.

'Don't suppose I need to ask you, Inspector.'

'Are you getting many responses?'

'We've just started but the early shift said everybody was happy to help.'

The drinks arrived and Clement excused himself and returned to where Earle sat doing Wordle. The meals came quickly. They ate fast too, sharing thoughts.

'You think Lester?' asked Earle taking a T-rex size bite from his burger.

'He's the obvious. But then I got excited about Cooper, and look what happened.'

Earle wiped his mouth with his napkin. 'If it was Lester, some lover's tiff or payback, it's very fucking elaborate.'

Clement had to agree. 'The weighted boots suggest planning. This could have been a long time coming.' Several years ago, Clement had dealt with a revenge killing up here that had gone back nearly forty years. There was no time limit on payback.

They needed a surname on Ebba Olsson's boyfriend, August. Clement checked the world clock on his phone. In Copenhagen it would be late morning, a good time to call.

—

It sounded like a young woman who answered his call down the surprisingly clear line. She answered in Danish but when he asked if she spoke English she switched immediately and asked how she might help. He explained he was a police officer from Australia. He checked the details Mal Gross had sent him.

'I'd like to speak to Mr Thor Hansen if possible.'

Clement had a feeling you weren't supposed to sound the 'h' in Thor.

'Mr Hansen is in a meeting at the moment.' That might not be a lie. From the notes it seemed Hansen was the producer, the main man. 'Would you like to speak to his assistant, Hanna?'

'Has she been there long?' There was little point speaking to anybody who hadn't been around when Ebba Olsson was working there.

'Hanna has been his assistant for a long time, yes.'

Clement said he would be grateful to speak to her. Without asking, Earle took their empty glasses to the bar for refills. Lucy, the chatty girl, entered the pub with a couple of guys.

'Hanna Lund speaking. How may I help, Inspector?'

Her English was excellent, far better, thought Clement, than you got here when you called your phone carrier about a problem that you knew would only be remedied after many such stop-start conversations. Her voice sounded mature, at least forty, he reckoned. That could also be positive.

'I'm investigating a case here in Kununurra in north-western Australia, and I need a little information on Ebba Olsson. Do you remember Ebba?'

'Of course. Ebba and I worked very closely for three years. It was terrible what happened.'

'I believe Ebba had a fiancée or boyfriend?'

'August. They were going to be married.'

'He must have been very upset.'

'We all were. You can imagine. Ebba was so full of life.'

'What was August's surname, do you remember?'

'Sorensen. I used to have to call him to tell him Ebba would be late, they were still shooting or editing. And he'd call me too.'

Hanna was proving to be an excellent source.

'Do you know how I could reach August?'

'We lost touch after a year or two. I know he moved out of their apartment after a few months. The memories were too painful. He was in banking. I think he maybe went overseas to Hong Kong ... I'm not sure.'

She couldn't recall what bank he worked for.

'I think Ebba's parents in Sweden might know. I have their old details. I never delete anything. Of course, they may no longer be there.'

Clement said he would be grateful for the details and copied them down.

'It was so tragic. August and Ebba were made for one another. When Ebba first came to us, she was single, and didn't want to date anyone full time. She had left her previous boyfriend. That didn't work out. She was lonely, I think, but she wouldn't admit it. And then she met August, and she was so happy. They were perfect together.'

If Hanna wanted to know why he was calling she was too polite to ask, but she sounded intelligent. Clement was sure she would be spinning theories with the others. Earle returned with their drinks and placed a squash before him. Clement guzzled it.

'Would you have any photos of August and Ebba?' he asked Hanna.

'I think I have but I would have to look.'

'Please, if you could. And then send them to me?'

She confirmed the best email address for him.

'Did Ebba have a large family, do you know?'

'Her mother and father were together. She had two brothers.'

'When Ebba went missing, she was with two Australians who had been on the film crew. Would you have details on them?'

She explained that regrettably they would not still have those.

'If we did have them, they would have been discarded after five years.'

A pity. He didn't think there was much more he could do at this point.

'You have been very helpful, thank you so much, Hanna.'

He finished off his squash and debated trying Ebba's family in Sweden. But he wasn't sure how long Lucy would be around and he wanted to speak with her.

—

'Hey, Lucy, how are you doing?' From what Clement could see, she looked fine. Her eyes sparkled and her skin was smooth, joyous. He recalled a time in his own life when every day had brought new promise. Yes, now he looked forward to time with Lena, but it wasn't the same thing. I've spent the second half of my life trying to claw back what ebbed away from the first half, he reflected. Envy was an unattractive vice, yet Clement couldn't help envying her youth.

Lucy said she was doing well. Earle and Clement introduced themselves to her friends.

'There's a guy we're trying to find. He's staying here. Jarrad. Wonder if any of you have seen him?'

Earle had the phone primed with the photo of Jarrad Lester. He offered it to Lucy who studied it before passing it around.

'Shit, yeah, I seen him.' Lucy's friend was wide as he was tall, with a half-afro, a moustache and a tattoo that was partially lost on his dark skin.

'Do you know when?'

He thought, shook his head slowly. 'Not today, maybe yesterday.'

Lucy now thought she had seen him too but wasn't sure exactly when, and whether it was here at the pub or in the deli where she worked.

'I know most of the people who come in here. Have a chat, you know? But I don't know him.'

'I think he was the Christian dude.' Her friend with the afro was becoming more certain now. 'Yeah, he was earbashing some chicks about hell.'

Lucy pulled a face, like she couldn't believe she had missed this. 'Really?'

'Yeah, deadset. I was getting a drink. I remember now, and this dude was going on about how the Lord had like a tracker on everyone, knew what you done, and if you didn't repay, he squashed you. I reckon it was Thursday night.'

Clement reimagined the conversation, replaced 'repay' with 'repent'. It fitted the Facebook profile, the homespun moral philosophies. The way Lorraine Miller had been killed certainly smacked of the biblical.

'Did the constables ask you if you had any photos from Tuesday and Wednesday nights?'

They had. Lucy explained that she and her friends hadn't taken many, but they had been happy to upload to the site as requested.

Clement prodded. 'That snap on social media of Lorraine Miller. You saw that?'

They had, but that wasn't one of their photos.

'The journo chick, Bek. I think that was her own one.'

Clement's ears pricked up. Earle asked how come Lucy had that impression.

'I spoke to her. She said something like "Did you see my photo?".'

Journalists became proprietorial. It may not literally have been Dyson who took the snap, but once published, it was all hers. That might be all she meant. Then again …

Clement said, 'When was this you spoke with her?'

'This morning. She came into the deli. Fact, she was supposed to be here by now. She said she was writing her story, and we would celebrate.'

Earle and Clement swapped looks. Clement sensed a faint buzzing in his ears.

'You got her number? Could you give it a call?'

Lucy obliged. Her friends had been to the bar and now returned with a drink which she sipped via a straw. Lucy pulled a face, punched on the speaker. A computerised female voice was counting numbers.

Clement took Dyson's number off her. Then they left.

—

Five minutes on, Clement and Earle were back at the Brolga. Clement had been calling the number intermittently. All he'd got was the counting robot.

The car was still out front of unit eight. When Earle's knock on the door produced no response the buzzing in Clement's head became a swarm. Earle was despatched to find somebody with a key. All kinds of worrying theories chased Clement. What if Dyson had a photo of the killer of Lorraine Miller? By publishing what she had, might she have set a target on herself?

A female cleaner arrived with Earle, brandishing a bunch of keys. She opened the door. Earle asked her to wait there.

Clicking on the light, Clement and Earle entered, calling Dyson's name. There was no response. The room was empty of humanity. The air conditioner was on. Earle ventured to the bathroom. Clement studied the scene. The mat near the door was bunched up. There was a breakfast bowl, with what might have been remnants of cornflakes and clotted milk, resting on the glass coffee table facing the TV. Beside it a scummy coffee cup. He felt it: cold, despite the furnace outside. Clement was piecing now. Maybe she had sat here. But what was wrong...

No computer.

She's a journo doing her big story. Unless she took it with her there should have been a laptop. And there was a handbag sitting by the dormant TV screen. Clement started to check the bag.

'Toothbrush and everything else is still there.' Earle reappeared in the main room.

Clement held up a purse he'd found inside the handbag, trawled through it. 'Money, credit cards, passport even.' Yet no phone or computer.

He walked back out to where the cleaner waited obediently.

'Are there any security cameras here?'

'At the gate,' she pointed.

It was possible Dyson had got a hot lead and raced off with her phone and computer to follow up. But with who? Her car was still there. They found the keys in the purse. It had to be more likely that her abductor took her computer and phone. Clement called Livesy, updated her and asked her to go through the security camera footage.

Within fifteen minutes she was set up in the motel office. Graeme

Earle meanwhile had been doorknocking every unit in the complex to see if anybody had witnessed anything. A cursory check with the five staff present revealed the last time anybody had seen Dyson was ten a.m. when she'd told the maid not to bother with her room as she was working.

Clement stood outside by the car. Had Jarrad Lester turned up, he would have been notified. The air was pleasantly scented, with what flowers Clement had no idea, but it made him think of Lena. Places always smelled better when women lived there. He hit Keeble's number, got through.

'I've finished Lester's caravan,' Keeble said, 'There wasn't much to process.'

He got no pleasure dropping the bad news. 'Good, because we might have a new crime scene back in town. The journo, Bek Dyson, has disappeared.'

'Blood, signs of a struggle …?'

Keeble, he knew, was trying to calculate the people power she'd have to allocate.

'No. It looks like she just walked out the door, but the air-con was running. Her handbag, purse, all here. Nobody here has seen her since ten this morning.'

'I can send Aditi. She'll be there pronto.'

Aditi was one of the newer techs. Clement trusted Keeble's judgement that she could handle it. In truth there wasn't much to do but print the room and the car.

'What do you think happened?'

'Either somebody called her, and she walked out into the carpark, or they knocked on her door.'

'I'm leaving now,' said Keeble, ending the call.

Clement phoned Scott Risely to bring him up to speed.

'Jesus.'

Clement could imagine Risely running fingers through his thinning hair. Fairly restrained, thought Clement. Things were spiralling out of control, and the boss could have been forgiven for more extravagance.

'Three detectives from Homicide in Perth will be arriving first flight tomorrow morning.' Clement recognised the names but none of them – one woman, two men – was known to him.

'For now we're still running the show.'

'Alright, can we invoke two-eight-seven?' Where there is an imminent threat to life the police can request a telco – in this case it would have to be Telstra as they had the coverage up here – to locate and track a phone in real time. If the phone was turned off, or the sim card had been removed, it wouldn't work. Hopefully Dyson had her phone on. And they should check Lester's too. They needed to find him, whether or not he was a killer.

Risely said, 'That's what it's for. I'll get the duty inspector of communications onto it.'

—

Clement called Manners, still at work putting in overtime. 'We need to locate Dyson's phone.' He explained they were requesting real-time tracking but, in the meantime, they still needed to see if they could ping its location. Even as he gave the number, he held little hope. A tower might have picked up a signal, but it could still have been a large distance away when it pinged. 'And we'll need all calls in and out to her phone too.'

'I'll send this through to Perth, they'll be quicker.'

Manners sounded tired, and Clement could understand why. Next to Keeble, he had the job that keeps on giving. Or taking.

'Nothing on Lester's phone location?'

'Again, that's Perth. As far as I know, nothing.'

'When we get his call log could you get somebody to check if Dyson's phone shows up on it?'

Manners said he was making a note of that right now.

Clement said, 'Go home, get some sleep. Speak tomorrow.'

Earle appeared. 'I reckon I got two-thirds of the guests. Nobody saw anything.'

Clement's phone buzzed. It was Livesy.

'Come to the office. I've got something.'

—

At eleven minutes past midday the security gate had opened, and an old white Commodore sedan had entered. The driver, wearing sunglasses and cap, looked male. Earle froze the image and tapped the numberplate.

'He's put tape across it.'

It was true. The numberplate was blacked out. The car peeled off away from the camera. At sixteen minutes past twelve the car reappeared and exited through the same gate. Like the front numberplate, the rear one was blacked out. Again, there was only the driver visible. It was impossible to see if Bek Dyson was on the floor in the rear. More likely she'd be in the boot.

It could not be ruled out that Lester had visited Dyson, or even somebody else at the motel. But this corresponded closely with the last time Dyson had been seen. And why black out the numberplates?

Livesy and Earle were waiting for him to speak. On this occasion his script had been written for him by the images on the screen.

'We have to find Jarrad Lester, and pray to God he hasn't killed her yet.'

21

At first, Bella Tait thought the reason she had woken suddenly might have been her client calling out from his tent. But as she strained to hear even a pinprick of sound, all was silent. It was therefore unlikely it was any alarm he'd raised while conscious. More likely it would have been in his sleep. Some clients carried on full conversations or, experiencing a nightmare, yelled out in alarm without realising it. It was not uncommon when city people found themselves in the vast Outback, devoid of almost every modern comfort, that the situation would play on their subconscious and fear express itself in the darkest hours.

On the other hand ...

What if Jarrad or someone was out to get her? Wouldn't you remove any potential threats?

She reached up under her pillow and pulled out the hunting knife she always carried for protection. Slowly she slid the blade from its scabbard.

All was silent. She stewed. Then got up from her bedroll and stood under the dark sky. Quietly she advanced towards Johan's tent, the sand welcome under her feet, through her toes. Near the tent opening she stopped and listened to his even breathing. She doubted now that he had made any sound. Something had woken her, but she did not think it was him. That old sixth sense.

It had been almost a relief to meet Johan and set off from Kununurra into the Outback. The police turning up like that had rattled her. Heading away from civilisation into the primitive world that surrounded it had the opposite effect on her to that felt by many city folk. Rather than bringing out a deep and hidden anxiety, it breathed air into her lungs. She belonged here.

Peering out into darkness, she sensed again a threat so real her skin prickled. Her years in the wild meant she reacted like a dingo, or lizard. Feeling the vibration through the red earth, or maybe smelling a hunter's scent with an ability she could not explain. Part of her now this animal instinct.

Are you out there, Jarrad? Is your sudden religious bent an attempt to rectify a fucked-up life?

You know a person a few days and yet you get a sense of them as a harbinger of doom. Their own and everybody they come in contact with.

She wondered if Jarrad's life had spiralled down after Ebba's death as her own had. An image came to her of three parachutists plunging earthward with failed chutes. It had taken her every ounce of self-belief, hard work and persistence to be able to start her career again. Would Lorraine and Jarrad have suffered the same fate as her? In the eyes of the public, they weren't the ones responsible. That fell on the guide. On her.

As if she had stepped through a portal, she was suddenly back on that trip. Beautiful Ebba, laughing by the campfire.

'I knit. I do!'

'You knit?' Bella couldn't imagine anybody that beautiful, and in that kind of powerful TV job, would knit.

Ebba nodding, laughing, red wine sloshing over the side of her plastic cup.

'I like this job but I will be happy to leave it behind and have children and take them on wilderness safaris. August earns plenty of money. And you know, Bella, this, what you have, you can't buy that, no matter how much money you have.'

As quickly as it had appeared, the vision vanished. Once more she was stuck with the awful unease.

If you're hunting me, Jarrad, be careful. When you come for me, I will be ready.

22

The request for live tracking of the phones had been granted but had proven fruitless. Lester was in the wind. He had not returned to the caravan park. Clement sat on the edge of the bed in his sparse hotel room, restless, frustrated. He watched the electric room clock tick over to eleven p.m., each new tick an extra lash.

We've missed him, thought Clement. He's not coming back. Manners had been in touch to say Perth was looking into Lester's social media pages and hoped to have numbers of contacts soon. They still hadn't managed to find the exact sale point of the diving boots. Likely never would. Graeme Earle was in his room catching zeds. This was the worst, this impotence.

Questions clustered along Clement's spine: What had Lester hoped to achieve by taking Dyson? Did he really think he could erase suspicion on him by killing her and taking her camera? People knew Lester had been in Kununurra at the same time as Lorraine Miller. Clearly, he would be a person of interest. *The* person of interest.

How could he be certain she'd not uploaded those photos to the cloud already? Was he too dim to consider that? Did he have an exit strategy? Was this just about him and Lorraine Miller or was there another element at play? Was he in the midst of a psychotic breakdown?

—

The conclusion that forced its way through the pack was that Jarrad Lester was an unstable psychopath. Killing an ex-girlfriend in such brutal fashion told you that much. But the abduction of Dyson showed the disorder of the man's mind. And made it even more frightening.

A killer like that on the loose, out there, innocent people who crossed his path could be slaughtered.

A spree killer. A cop's nightmare. In the end it might become suicide by cop. Lester wouldn't stop, nor care about taking strangers' lives now. However this had started, it was going to finish messy.

Clement missed Lena and badly wanted to speak with her. His finger hovered over the phone. He scrolled Contacts, hit Call.

'Daniel.' Mathias was one of the few people to call him Daniel. 'How's it going?'

'I wish you hadn't asked that. We've got a killer out there, a woman abducted by him, and we have no idea where he might be.'

'So why are you calling this old man?' The line to Germany was clear. For once Clement almost wished it wasn't. 'You can't be that short of men that you need me.'

Here goes. 'You know Lena arrived.' Clement had texted him to let him know as soon as she had made Broome. Later Lena had called him using Clement's phone.

'She's okay?'

'She's excellent.'

'I was right about her, yes?'

'You sure were. Too right.'

There was a pause, then in a different tone Mathias said, 'What do you mean? She's not in any trouble.'

'No.' No easy way to say it. 'Lena and I ...'

Laughter came rolling down the line.

'It's okay, Daniel. I know. Lena called me two weeks ago.'

Clement was as relieved as he was embarrassed. Damn Lena.

'So you know about us.'

'Of course. It's exactly what I expected. You must be good for one another. You have been a misery since you and your wife finished, and Lena needs somebody a little normal in her life.'

At least one thing that wasn't a problem. Clement exhaled slow. 'Thanks for being understanding.'

'I knew what I was doing. Didn't I warn you?' Clement heard a match flare down the line. Old habits. 'Tell me about your case.'

Clement did. In a weird way it almost relaxed him, talking through the problems, making sure there was nothing he'd missed.

'You can't locate them with their phones?'

'No. Up here there are hundreds of kilometres of nothing. It's okay if the phone is anywhere near a tower but you get a dead pocket, no chance. And I think the phones are off or disabled anyway. We'll keep trying to locate it regardless, but it will likely be a futile exercise.'

'So you have to wait for light?'

'Yes. We've got planes and helicopters to call on, and the main roads have been alerted. But I'm not sure this guy wants to get away. He might want to take as many with him as he can.'

'Then I should let you sleep. Or try to.'

Mathias knew too well what it was like.

'You should come and visit.'

'I might just do that. Give Lena my love.'

—

After Mathias rang off, Clement was still mulling over the call when there was a knock on his door. He expected it would be Graeme Earle, but it was Keeble.

'I was going to call but it looked like you were in.'

Clement stepped back and the forensic specialist entered.

'You want a tea or coffee?'

'Coffee.'

At least he had one clean mug. He clicked the kettle on.

'I can't tell you much, but I can tell you I have no match on Jarrad Lester's prints to the Lorraine Miller crime scene. Not his or hers on the can we found. No proof he was in Bek Dyson's room either. And I spoke to Rhino and we're still waiting on DNA from the skin under the nails of Lorraine's hand.'

Almost as disappointing as the sachet coffee is doomed to be, thought Clement. The kettle boiled. Clement ripped open a sachet for each of them. Hot water, long-life milk. All that could be expected, really.

Keeble took her mug, sat beside him on the bed. He was about to say, 'You look tired,' but wondered if that might sound more negative than he intended. He modified it.

'You must be looking forward to a break.'

'There's an understatement.' She sipped. 'On the positive side, this coffee is probably awful, but I'm so zonked I can't even taste it.'

'You should rest. Hopefully we'll find them tomorrow.'

'In which case, I'll have my hands full.'

They didn't need to elaborate. Neither expected a happy outcome.

Keeble nursed her cup. 'You got any idea what triggered this? Lovers' tiff?'

'Probably. I'm in the dark.' It seemed an awful long time ago that Josh had his jaw broken, and that Nicholas Cooper was a prime suspect. As if on the same wavelength, Keeble asked if di Rivi had found Tony Edmonds.

'She hasn't been in touch. I'm sure she would if she had news. Perth hasn't been able to identify where or when the diving boots were bought.'

While such evidence was important for any subsequent court hearing, Clement was fearful this would end before any lawyer got to the chance to click on their meter.

'How are you doing,' he said, dipping his toe in, adding, 'personally, I mean.'

'I'm good.' An enigmatic smile. 'I didn't figure on my being on my own. But I should have. Carlo and me, we just … happened. I don't know that I ever thought we'd be permanent but then I can't say I saw it ending.'

'With Marilyn, I couldn't let go.' Clement had no idea why he was volunteering this. Perhaps it was the weight of the case, or the possibility of a future with Lena setting him free.

'It's not like that for me. I've let go. It's done and dusted. He moved his things out. They could all fit in a car. His guitar was the only thing that took up room.'

She drained her mug, got up and sat the mug down by the TV. She headed to the door.

'We'll get him,' she said, and then she was gone.

—

He'd put off calling Lena. Fatigue was a looming wave about to break on him. Instead, he texted her – **Called Mathias. Thanks for letting me know**. He added a grumpy emoji and then, thinking better of it, added two laughing ones. And finally, a heart. Then he typed, **Need sleep, call tomorrow**. He added two hearts this time. A thought jabbed him: I'm nearly fifty and I'm as inarticulate as a millennial. I'd rather use a stupid little picture than say how I feel. Was he just another tragic middle-aged man, ready to trade in the station wagon for a sports car? He didn't care. And actually, what was wrong with that anyway. Envy could be a barking dog, or a pack of them. You spend half your life denying yourself because you're planning for some future. Then as the years go by, you tell yourself you're planning for a cosy retirement, but when retirement hits, you start planning for your death, and what you'll leave behind: no debt, a house maybe. So, if everything gets disrupted midstream, why not buy a sports car and drive through Paris with the wind in your hair?

Too much thinking. He stripped off and dropped onto the bed. The air-con was humming when sleep took him like a pressgang.

***

He had done what had to be done. Reparation had been made. Part-made, he corrected himself, there was still an invoice outstanding. The girl, who called herself a journalist – he seriously doubted that she actually held a professional job – well, that was regrettable, but action had been demanded. He had washed the knife down, seemingly for ages. Blood was more viscous than you realised. Perhaps he could have left the knife with the body, but that would certainly convict him.

After checking her phone and calculating that all the photos she'd taken at the pub that night were still there, and that none showed enough of him for any identification, his hope grew that he might actually slip through any net.

He dangled the knife from his fingers. Soon he would have need of it again, so he was glad that it looked clean and sharp. In a land where life often equates to water, the irony of wasting so much on cleaning what was an instrument of death was not lost on him. Although to be fair, he reasoned, the ultimate instrument of death is ourselves. Or, in their case, his victims. He was no more than the bullet, the arrow. The hand that pulled the trigger, held the bow, was theirs.

He slipped the knife back in its scabbard. Bella thought she could hide. She was mistaken. And if others tried to intervene, then they would have held the gun that fired the bullet that killed them. It was simple really.

23

Five a.m. found Clement and Earle in Clement's room, both dressed, sipping tea extracted from typically weak complimentary teabags. He'd used up his coffee allocation playing host to Keeble. First light had officially landed about ten minutes earlier, but it was only now streaking the hotel windows. Clement found himself trying to calculate how much a hotel would save in a year by having these reduced-strength bags. Twenty-five percent, he guessed, of whatever the budget was. Another two hours' sleep would have been most welcome, but he wanted to be ready from the moment the planes took off. That would likely be another five to ten minutes.

Two light aircraft would leave from Kununurra and another from Halls Creek. Helicopters would search from local cattle stations too.

'Lester's only got an old Commodore.' Earle sipped his tea and couldn't help taking a look at it as if his senses might be deceiving him. 'His chances of going off-road in that are minimal.'

This of course was a massive advantage. You had a region as big as whole countries, but most of it was sand and scrub. There were only a few roads and a few tracks. An off-road vehicle like Bella Tait's could just about make its own rules, but Lester's Commodore would be effectively handcuffed.

'He could have a second vehicle,' suggested Clement.

'You think he's that organised?' Earle finally gave up on the tea.

'Those diving boots. That was carefully planned.'

'The tape across the licence plate wasn't exactly *Mission Impossible* level.'

That was true. Lester could be falling apart. That could lead to him being quickly caught. It could also lead to much more bloodshed.

He told Earle what he'd learned from Keeble the previous evening: so far, they had no real confirmation to pin the Miller killing on Lester.

The dining room wasn't open yet, so all they could do was wait. There was no point driving off hoping to spy Lester's vehicle by chance. The Kimberley was the ultimate crucible, he thought, and we, we are no more than soft lead in its belly.

**

With the sun risen, Bella Tait felt calmer, stronger even. The rays were pitchfork prongs and there was a steaminess in the air like they were turning compost.

Breakfast was fried eggs with bacon. A tin of baked beans already heated waited in the can. She didn't mind cooking for her clients, male or female, although she noted that the women would often feel the need to help with the cooking. Occasionally a man would ask to cook, and she never objected. There was rarely much cleaning up to do but very few clients sat back while she did that.

Johan watched her objectively as she flipped the eggs and bacon.

'Good coffee.' He saluted with his mug. Another small bonus when clients booked with her was the plunger coffee from the best ground coffee she could get.

Johan's English was excellent. Yesterday he had hiked enthusiastically, taking a zillion pictures, the highlight of which was a long Ord snake. He had chatted enthusiastically like a child as he snapped away, Bella cautioning him to keep his distance.

She had never taken her clients' common sense for granted. Even with Ebba. But Ebba hadn't taken any risk seriously.

'So what do you do back home?' she asked as she dished the eggs and bacon. Bella had not asked this most obvious question until now for good reason. She had learned to give her clients space on their vacation. Often the last thing they wanted to think about was the work they had left behind.

'The worst, most boring. IT.'

'There are beans here if you'd like.' People turned their nose up at baked beans. Not Bella. Cheap and nutritious. 'I don't know anything about IT. I'm only on Facebook for business. Is that IT?'

He smiled, inclined his head. Clearly not what he considered IT.

'It can be,' he said politely, 'but that's not so much what I do. I help companies check their stock, and my firm has a program that tells them the optimum discount to offer if they are overstocked. A hundred years ago, I would have been a clerk.'

He was likely late thirties, a youthful face behind glasses but slightly hunched as if he'd been beaten by a demanding mother when growing up. He wore a wedding band.

'It's something I know nothing about,' offered Bella. She had to admit, it did sound boring.

'Every day is interchangeable. Nothing like we saw out here yesterday.' There was a sense of wonder in the IT man's voice.

She had taken him south of Kununurra around Lake Argyle, which for thirty-odd years had been famous for its pink diamonds, before the supply had been exhausted. It was spectacular scenery, blue skies overhead, and you might have been looking down upon a lake in Switzerland except there were no people, no forests, just red dirt, rock and patches of brush surrounding it. Today she planned to push west towards the Chamberlain River. A lot of rough ground but she carried two spare tyres.

'I try and get away at least once a year,' he said, tucking into the food. 'My wife isn't a big fan of the wilderness.'

'So what does she do while you're away?'

A tiny smile played on his lips. 'Good question. Sometimes we go away together. We had a beautiful time in Venice. That was my favourite. We would sit for hours outside a coffee shop looking at the people listening to a string quartet. And in the evening, we would just lie in bed with the window open, hearing the life outside: voices, laughter, arguments, music. When you're close to somebody you don't need to talk much even. Your minds are in synch. You know what I mean?'

Bella didn't. She would have liked that. But she nodded.

'Last year I went to the north of Norway, to Fauske.' Johan was basking in the memory. 'I watched the Sami herding reindeer. I wished she had been with me.'

'I would find that really interesting.'

He nodded thoughtfully. 'Yes, you should do it.'

Bella doubted she would ever have the funds for that.

—

While they finished breakfast, Bella ran through her proposed route for the day. Her client offered no objection. Then they cleaned up. Despite all of Bella's activity and Johan's presence, she had been unable to rid herself of the sense of a threat. It must have been obvious.

'You keep looking,' said Johan pointing to the horizon.

That brought her back. 'It's the weather. We don't usually get much rain this early in November, but I feel it's coming.'

***

Like a film over his skin, Clement could feel the moisture in the air growing.

'It's going to dump,' he said to Earle. After grabbing bacon rolls from the just-opened-for-the-day deli, they had driven up Kelly's Knob, the big hill overlooking Kununurra. The sky was stretched like a two-tone football jumper, light blue and deep black. The planes searching for Lester had now been aloft nearly four hours.

'It might pass.' Earle had finished his roll already. It was true, you could never be certain up here. There were a lot of false dawns – or storms, as the case may be. 'What did the boss say?'

Clement had just got off the phone from Scott Risely.

'He'd just spoken to Rebekka Dyson's parents. They're beside themselves.'

'He say anything about who's running the case?'

'No change for now.'

Whether he ran the case or was subordinate didn't matter to

Clement. All that mattered was getting a result, and in that regard, he felt that his staying in charge of the investigation would be the best call. But if they went with the Perth blokes, he could live with that. Especially now that he had spoken to Lena.

Another day when she had answered his call like she was in love with him, or at least missing him. He wanted to hoard those for winters that must surely lie ahead. How comforting it had been to speak with somebody about nothing much: the hot water system might be on the blink, there's a new film coming to the Sun. He'd unloaded to her about his disappointment. What he had not achieved on this case, his dread at the possibility of another body. With Marilyn he had made the mistake of keeping all that in. He hadn't wanted to infect her with the product of his job. Wanted to insulate her. All that had happened was he internalised all his frustration and anger. That became an ulcer. This time he would try to mitigate. Lena would soon tell him if he was boring the pants off her or bringing her down. You had to trust. That was the key.

'Why this crime, why now?' he asked Earle.

During an investigation, it was so hard to find any space where you could actually think. You found yourself pulled this way and that. Breakfast was an opportunity to recap, maybe stretch the brain.

'That comes from motive.'

'And we're guessing there,' acknowledged Clement.

'It seems Miller and Lester were an item at one point. So, it could be love gone wrong. Then again, those two were also witnesses to Ebba Olsson believed taken by a crocodile. However, we have only their accounts, and Bella Tait's, as to what happened.'

That was true.

Clement said, 'Tait told us she saw drag marks on the bank, but she doesn't know whether Olsson was alive or dead at the time. So it's possible that Lester, or Lester and Miller together, killed Olsson and that one of them was going to talk.'

'Or Tait herself is involved somehow.'

Also true. It was time to head back to the airport to collect the three Perth detectives. Graeme Earle volunteered for pick-up duty. He drove first to the station to drop Clement. There was already a contingent of media types assembling when Earle skirted them by driving through the gate to the rear entrance.

'This is just the start,' said Earle bitterly.

Nelson was waiting when Clement entered.

'You see the press?' asked the station boss rhetorically.

Clement nodded and made for the office they were using as their case room. He imagined himself in a big pot, the flesh flaking off his bones. Where the hell was Lester? His phone buzzed. It was Mal Gross.

'Yes, Mal.'

'Manners passed along Lester's social media contacts. I've got a number on the pastor of his church if you're interested.'

'Shoot it across.'

His phone pinged: Pastor Michael Vanderberg and a number. Clement checked the number and dialled Vanderberg. It rang for some time before being answered.

'This is Father Vanderberg. To whom am I speaking, please?' A slight accent. South African?

Clement introduced himself. 'I'm heading an investigation of the homicide of a young woman in the Kimberley, and I believe you know one of our persons of interest—'

'Jarrad.'

'Yes. Did he ever mention his relationship with the deceased woman, Lorraine Miller?'

'Not directly, no. Inspector, we are a small church, a spiritual group. My flock here is made up largely of people who have fallen through society's cracks.'

Clement wasn't sure where this was going but let it flow.

'They suffer from addiction, affliction, they were drifting without purpose. We give them that purpose.'

'You're saying Jarrad Lester has issues?'

'*Had* issues. He has discovered a new purpose here. Our people are very physically active. We have a small property near Mapleton.'

Clement tried to place the town, pretty sure it was Sunshine Coast hinterland.

'We built our church, our living spaces. We grow our own food.'

This sounds suspiciously like a cult, thought Clement.

'I apologise if I am rambling on but it's important you understand how far Jarrad has come. He was a lost sheep. But I believe he is incapable of harming another person. Not now. Not since he's discovered God's love for him.'

'I appreciate that, Father, but the facts I am confronted with suggest that whatever equanimity Jarrad had achieved there with you, he may have lost. We've had a young woman abducted in Jarrad's vehicle.'

There was a long pause.

'I can't imagine Jarrad would be capable of that. Unless ...'

He had aroused Clement's curiosity with that pause.

'Unless?'

A sigh. 'Unless Jarrad perceived the young woman to be in some kind of danger.'

Jarrad Lester the saviour? That was a new spin.

'How long have you known Jarrad, Father?'

'He first came here a little over a year ago. He had cancer. Quite severe. During his time here, the cancer cleared up. He was undergoing treatment but still he ascribed his healing ultimately to God's love. That's what he told me. He has been very devout. Harming another, that would be the last thing he would consider. I don't know that he would even be capable of it.'

'When I asked you about Lorraine Miller, you said he had not mentioned her directly. Had he said anything indirectly?'

Another long pause. 'I don't know if he was talking about that particular woman but he confessed to me – not a formal confession like the Catholics, more a therapeutic conversation – he confessed to me that he suffered the burden of great guilt about something some years previous.'

The crocodile attack? Surely that was the most likely.

'Did he give specifics?'

'No, but he suggested that whatever it was had been at the highest end of the scale. I assumed a matter of life and death in which he felt a degree of responsibility. He did not go into any detail but told me he felt he needed to bring his new insight to others who must also be affected, that reparation needed to be made, that the hurt that he had been instrumental in causing should be alleviated.'

'Eight years ago, Jarrad was on the scene up here, where a young woman was believed to have been taken by a crocodile. Was that something you ever discussed?'

'No.'

'But that could well be the incident.'

'It sounds like it could be.'

'The young woman whose murder we are investigating was with Jarrad at the scene of that attack. Might he have blamed her?'

'I believe Jarrad has learned the power of forgiveness.'

'What if she had rejected his overtures to make reparation as you say. How would Jarrad react?'

'I really don't believe he would be violent.'

'But you're not certain.'

'Inspector, I am sixty-six years old. I have learned that you can never be certain of being certain. But if there has been foul play there, I really don't think Jarrad is involved. Like I say, he may have been trying to save people, spiritually and physically. I don't think I can be of more use.'

'Has he phoned you or been in contact with you in the last week?'

'No.'

'Please call me immediately if he does contact you.'

'Goodness be with you, Daniel.'

Well, what to make of that? The pastor didn't believe Jarrad capable of this violence. Rose-coloured glasses? The pertinent point was that Jarrad seemed to feel great guilt over something. Surely, that had to be Ebba Olsson. But ... Clement pulled himself up ... that didn't necessarily make him a killer. Ebba could have gone swimming, found herself confronted by a crocodile, screamed for help. Really, in that situation, there wasn't a lot you could do but you could still blame yourself.

—

The sounds of arrival were unmistakable. Clement detected muffled greetings in the hallway and then Earle showed the Perth contingent into the case room.

My God. How much younger than me they all look. Questions whirred, turning his head into a slot machine: How much longer do I have in this game? Am I already over the hill? Such thoughts had never occurred to him before. Was it because with Lena came a realisation there could be another road down which his life might travel? Clement stood to greet them.

Introductions were handled by Earle. The oldest of the detectives, Dick Beare, must have been just on or under forty. He was a largish bloke with thinning hair. Maria Haynes couldn't have been over thirty-three. Anil Patel was thirty at a pinch. Callum Nelson joined, and they ran a Zoom link to Steve Eaton at Halls Creek, Scott Risely in Broome and Travis Page who headed up Fitzroy Crossing.

Clement wasted no time. 'We have a person of extreme interest, Jarrad Lester. Have you all seen his photo?'

They had.

'Lester was known to the first victim, Lorraine Miller. We know Lester has been in town these last few days. We are hoping we can place the two of them in the Kununurra pub on the last night Miller was known to be alive, last Wednesday. On that night, a young journalist, Rebekka Dyson, was taking photos. We believe that yesterday around midday Dyson was abducted from her motel room here in Kununurra. The security camera at the motel shows a photo of a white Holden Commodore arriving and leaving in the time window in which we believe she was abducted. The numberplates were taped over, but the car appears to be the same as the one registered to Jarrad Lester and known to have been in this area. The driver was male, but features were hidden behind sunglasses and cap.'

Earle distributed still photos of the vehicle and picked up the commentary, giving Clement a break.

'All major roads are being closely watched. The NT police have been alerted to look out for the vehicle their side of the border. We don't believe he can get far; however, he may have switched vehicles or have an accomplice.'

Clement resumed. 'Our priority has to be to find Lester. Hopefully that leads to a good outcome on Rebekka Dyson.'

He explained he wanted everybody looking for the Commodore. Being the end of the tourist season a lot of places were closed, so that made their task easier.

'He could have an associate up here hiding him, but otherwise he has to stay somewhere, has to fuel his vehicle. We'll be working the phones.' He directed Steve Eaton to check all tourist areas in Halls Creek and Wyndham. Travis Page was designated Fitzroy Crossing and surrounding areas. He split the newly arrived detectives up. Beare and Haynes were to review the Miller murder and Dyson abduction.

'We need to have a better idea of Miller's movements after she was seen at the pub. Callum's people have done a great job canvassing but so far nothing. Also, if anybody saw a vehicle near where Miller was discovered. Some of our potential witnesses are well and truly off the grid – fishermen, prospectors, tourists who rarely come into town – so we just have to persist. We don't think the Commodore could have handled that location, so does Lester have access to another vehicle? Also check the Emma Gorge campground where Lester was staying. Did anybody see Lester in the company of anybody else, or driving another vehicle. The campground is only open a few more days. Potential witnesses are pulling out.'

Nelson's uniforms, Clement explained, had already done a lot of this but so far had come up with nothing. However, he wanted everything checked. They hadn't necessarily interviewed all potential witnesses. The same went for Dyson's motel. Perhaps somebody got a good look at this man in the sunglasses and cap.

Patel was assigned to call all the petrol stations along the Gibb River Road asking for sightings of the Commodore and/or Lester.

Wishing them luck, Scott Risely pulled out of the Zoom link. Clement could imagine the pressure he'd be under from HQ, especially now the media were in a feeding frenzy. Patel was found a desk and phone, and Haynes and Beare a vehicle. They had not long left when Callum Nelson rushed back in on his phone.

'I think we've found the car.'

24

It had been Constable Fernandez from Kununurra, having split up with his mate Davis so as to cover as much ground as possible, who had spotted the flank of a vehicle hidden in scrub a few metres off the road between El Questro Station and Zebedee Springs, another camping spot as of the last week devoid of tourists.

For the time being, Clement had requested Fernandez park his vehicle in cover and observe while they made their way to join him. Jarrad Lester's mental state was unknown, and he was possibly armed. Clement didn't want another injured cop on his hands. Of course, the vehicle might have been dumped, but if so Lester or an accomplice may return at any moment. Better Fernandez was ready in his own car to pursue.

—

Earle, Clement and Keeble drove to Kununurra Airport where a helicopter was waiting, Geoff, a middle-aged pilot with a shaggy moustache, at the helm. Two medics were placed on standby at El Questro. On the flight to the station, Clement couldn't erase the suspicion that whatever had begun with Lorraine Miller's death was approaching a climax. There was little conversation, even after the helicopter landed.

The medics – Henry, in his thirties, and Cassie, Clement estimated younger – listened attentively.

'We don't know the situation, but it could present danger. I wanted to make sure you know.'

They were both good with that.

'It could also be extremely unpleasant.'

Up to this point Clement hadn't bothered to voice his dread to Earle. He knew his partner already shared it and there was no benefit to be gained by dwelling on the likelihood that Bek Dyson's body and an abandoned vehicle could be all that awaited them. The medics were terse but serious. They were prepared, they assured Clement.

A slim man, tall, about forty, came over and introduced himself as Seb, the station foreman. Clement thanked him for providing the vehicle.

'Happy to help any way we can.'

'And be careful,' warned Clement. 'We don't know if it is one person or more, whether they are armed or not.'

Seb said all his team were warned and alert. 'You'll be there in ten minutes or so,' he estimated. The light was growing dimmer by the minute, rain a certainty.

—

Clement, Keeble, Earle and the two medics climbed into the waiting four-wheel drive. Earle drove. As they set off, Fernandez radioed through that he had now been joined by his partner Davis, in a second vehicle. So far there had been no movement in the Commodore.

Logic told Clement the car was likely empty – of the living at any rate – but that didn't prevent a cocktail of excitement and trepidation swirling in his gut as they approached the scene. Right on cue, as if in a movie, thunder rumbled. It was distant but deep.

The two ambos were told to stay with Keeble at Clement's vehicle. Clement walked over to where Davis and Fernandez had both parked just off the track on the opposite side of the path to the Commodore.

'Any sign?' asked Clement.

'Nothing,' said Fernandez. 'I don't think there's anyone in it.'

'Stay in your vehicles just in case anybody turns up or the car takes off.' Clement and Earle started across the track towards the car. Clement signalled Earle approach from behind while he came from the front. They were armed but had no weapons drawn.

In only a few paces Clement was confronted by the branches hiding the car's flank. He pulled them down. From what he could see the car was empty. Flies were drumming. There was an unmistakable odour around the vehicle. Already Clement's heart was in his boots.

He stepped around the branches and was now tight to the car's passenger side. Earle had approached from the boot. Clement peered down to the rear seats. Nobody was lying on the floor.

He shook his head to Earle who pointed at the boot. The flies were concentrated there.

'Looks like blood,' said Earle, indicating the hub of black flies where the boot fit behind the bumper.

Smells like death, thought Clement. Pulling on latex gloves, he tried the front passenger door. Unlocked. When he opened it, intense heat rushed him like a linebacker. With the worst of it out he leaned over, found the boot release and popped it.

The volume of buzzing doubled; so did the number of flies. From God knew where they zoomed to the boot as Earle, also gloved, swung it open.

Clement saw his partner turn away reflexively from the assault of sight and smell. He joined him and looked in.

Scrunched into the space, bloodied from what looked like stab wounds, was a very dead Jarrad Lester.

25

'Cause of death, multiple stab wounds. Time of death, Keeble wouldn't commit. First impression, thirty-six hours.'

He and Earle were in the car heading back from the scene to the station where the helicopter waited. Keeble had remained with the body and other techs were on their way to support.

The first thing Clement had done after finding Lester's body was to text Risely. Rather than be distracted by phone calls, he'd wanted to concentrate on Keeble's first impressions.

'But there's no sign of Dyson?' Risely sounded dejected.

'No. It's not looking good.

'So there's an accomplice and they had a falling out?'

Clement really had no idea. And that's what he told his boss.

'We found blood in the bush by the car. We think that's where he might have been killed.'

'Or Dyson.'

'Yes, that is a possibility. Keeble's onto it. We need to find Bella Tait. She could be a victim. Or she could be involved.'

'Jesus. Faarrrrk!!' It was extremely rare for Scott Risely to give in to such emotion. Clement didn't blame him. He was fortunate to have Risely as his superior. He'd had previous bosses who at the first sign of pressure did nothing but stomp, shout and wave their arms as if imitating the singer Peter Garrett. He heard Risely take a deep breath. Perhaps he did some kind of yoga or mental exercise to help him keep the lid on. 'Gotta go. Media will be all over this. Leave it with me, keep me informed.'

For a moment the only sound was rubber on road. They took the turn-off to El Questro.

'You really think Bella Tait?' Earle looked over.

'We have to consider it. She could have been lying to us.'

As they emerged from the long driveway that led to where the chopper was parked, the station foreman, Seb, appeared in front of them waving his arms frantically.

Christ, what now, wondered Clement. He slowed, stopped, wound down the window.

'One of our choppers looking for the Commodore spotted something at Pigeon Hole.'

—

Pigeon Hole Lookout was a large waterhole about ten k from the station, a prime destination for guests and other tourists in properly equipped off-road vehicles. Because the wet season could lead to sudden and dramatic flooding, most of the more remote tourist locations closed around the end of October. Nobody wanted to be trapped for the duration of their vacation.

Within ten minutes, pilot Geoff had them over their destination. He pointed down and banked. As they came around, Clement could see the small helicopter from the station where it had put down in an open patch about a hundred metres from the ridge that overlooked the stream and waterhole.

His heart was pounding now. As they dropped, he was able to make out two people. So, the radio message they'd received as they had taken off was likely verified. Geoff put down twenty metres away from the first chopper. The ground was relatively flat, crewcut shrub on rocky dirt.

Waiting for the rotors to slow, Clement found himself in a state of near disbelief. To be honest he really had not expected what he was looking at.

Geoff signalled they could exit, and Clement and Earle lowered their height and did the well-practised TV bent rush from the landed chopper. His heart was drumming as his gaze fell upon Bek Dyson.

He heard Earle introducing himself to the other pilot, caught the name Todd. Clement had a million questions, but he held off, concentrating on Dyson who seemed not injured, not even really bruised.

'I'm tired, hungry, a bit sore, otherwise okay.'

He had expected to find a body here. While a more detailed interview could be undertaken back in Kununurra, there were things Clement had to know now.

'You were abducted. Is that correct?'

Dyson explained what had happened. She could not confirm it was Lester.

'He was wearing a cap and sunglasses. He must have used a taser on me, then injected me.'

The next she knew was waking up here sometime in the night. There was no vehicle, but he had left her a torch, a large bottle of water and a towel. She had no idea where she was. She had moved about two hundred metres away from where she had been left, and tried to hide as best she could, in case he returned. At first light she had walked further away, and then she had heard the helicopter and run to open ground.

'We'll get you back shortly, but can you show us as close as possible the exact spot where you were left?'

'I think so.'

They thanked Todd and told him he was free to go. Then Earle, Clement and Dyson made their way back to where Dyson had been abandoned.

'Looks like it's pretty much on the most-used track.' Earle was pointing to where earth had been flattened over time by vehicles. But they would have to be off-road vehicles. This terrain was too tough for an ordinary car. So, the abductor had driven up here in a four-wheel drive and left the presumably drugged Dyson with water.

'Do you remember him saying anything?'

'Nothing. I opened the door of my motel room: *zap!*'

'You don't have your phone?' Clement knew it was a stupid question, but it would be more stupid not to ask.

'I doubt he wanted me calling for help.'

Clement suffered her sarcasm. So perhaps all of this was just to get her phone and computer. But why not take those and leave her? And if the idea of getting the phone and computer was to delete photos that might identify him ...

No, that should wait.

Earle was marking the area with crime tape they still had from Zebedee Springs. It was an improvised affair to mark out a perimeter, using whatever bushes they could. Clement snapped photos. He turned back to Bek Dyson.

'Time to get you fed.'

They walked back to where they had started. There, Earle and Clement methodically bagged the torch, water bottle and towel.

'You're okay?' Clement asked again.

Dyson nodded, more vigorously this time. 'Can you imagine the story this is going to be? This will make me.'

Well, that was one way of handling the trauma, thought Clement.

—

Geoff flew them directly back to Kununurra. For now, the storm was on a break. That meant the media was building again out front of the station, slickers and raincoats like the sideline of a kids' footy game. Bek Dyson was placed in the capable hands of Simone Livesy to be fed and clothed and medically examined before being interviewed. For once, Callum Nelson had good news. Keeble's search of Lester's car and surrounds had turned up a phone in the bush near a pool of dried blood.

'Lester's thumbprint opened it,' revealed Nelson, unable to suppress the smile.

'That is excellent news.' Clement and Earle allowed each other a rare grin.

Keeble was uploading the data to Manners. Clement immediately called Risely.

'You hear about the phone?'

'Manners told me. He's onto it now. Maybe the tide has turned.' Risely was suitably cautious.

Clement left him to it. Earle was demolishing a cream biscuit.

Breakfast was wearing off but Clement didn't dare break stride.

Earle said, 'You think it was too lucky with the phone? The killer's been careful and all of a sudden cocks up?'

The thought had occurred to Clement. 'Perhaps Lester was the organised one. This might have happened in a panic. I mean, it could be that an accomplice didn't want to harm Dyson, so they got rid of Lester. Or, it was night, moving the body ...'

Of course, he had doubts. But on occasion, the luck did break your way. Livesy poked in her head to say Bek Dyson was ready to be interviewed.

—

The interview lasted about forty minutes. Clement did not want to prolong it. Afterwards he wrestled with the information she had provided, which had been minimal. The photos she had taken at the pub had already been uploaded to the cloud, although without her computer and phone, she couldn't remember her password. Regrettably, Dyson was certain that there was no wider shot of whoever had been chatting with Lorraine Miller on the night she disappeared. When shown photos of Jarrad Lester, she had been unable to recall him from that night.

'Can't say I remember seeing him.'

They could confirm if he was there or not when they got into her account on the cloud. Livesy had been tasked with sorting that out with Dyson's assistance, and whatever help they needed from Perth.

Beare and Haynes were still out trying to follow Miller's, and now Lester's, movements up to their deaths. Clement put in a call to Risely, placing him on speaker. He asked Callum Nelson and Anil to step into the case room.

'The ground at Pigeon Hole where Bek Dyson was dumped is too rough for the Commodore. So either she was transferred to an accomplice's vehicle or Lester himself switched vehicles. It's unclear still why Dyson was abducted.'

'Did he interrogate Dyson?' asked Nelson.

'No. Which makes you wonder. Perhaps Lester planned to kill her, and the accomplice, unwitting or otherwise, cottoned on, removed

Lester and dumped Dyson far enough away to give themself a chance to escape. Let's continue to look and see if anybody might have seen the Commodore with or near a four-wheel-drive vehicle.'

Clement was thinking that Bella Tait had just the vehicle.

'The third person involved in Ebba Olsson's assumed death was the guide, Bella Tait. We interviewed her. She was about to leave with a client on a tour. Now, it's possible she could have been in this with Lester. She's an experienced bush person so she could have put Miller in the river. She looked strong enough to kill Lester. Personally, I didn't get that vibe.'

'Maybe the killer is going after her next,' said Patel.

The thought had haunted Clement over the last hour.

'Can't rule that out either.'

'Could it be a member of Ebba's family? Her fiancé?' asked Risely.

Clement had beaten himself up on that too. He could have called the family earlier but had been focused on finding Lester or his vehicle.

'Graeme's on that now. He's waiting for a call.'

'Keep me posted.'

His tone said 'This is a clusterfuck'. Didn't Clement know it. Risely rang off.

'I'll get eyes out for Tait's vehicle,' said Nelson.

'Anil, could you help on that?'

Those two left the room. Earle's phone rang and he got up to take the call.

Clement found Bella Tait's mobile phone number and dialled. No signal. Next, he tried the satellite phone. No answer. He told himself that didn't mean anything, but he was uneasy. If somebody did wish her harm, how could he track her down out there?

—

He walked into the adjoining kitchen, made himself a coffee. Earle appeared, phone call over.

'That was Ebba's brother, Tomas. The parents don't speak good English, and the father has early dementia anyway. Tomas says the family sold up the old home a year ago because of the father's condition. The home was in a little town, Hammarstrand. Tomas lives closer to Stockholm, in Uppsala. He has another brother in Stockholm. He claims he spoke to him this morning, their time. He hasn't heard from August Sorensen in about three years. They had stayed in touch for a while, then so far as he knew, Sorensen moved overseas but he wasn't sure where. His mother might know. He'll try her for me. And he's sending me the most recent photo he has of Sorensen.'

That reminded Clement, Hanna Lund the assistant at the production company had been going to send him photos if she could find them.

'They'd never heard from Lester?'

'Not according to Tomas.'

—

Through the kitchen window Clement saw forked lightning in the distance to the north. Assume Tomas wasn't lying. Nobody from the Olsson family had travelled here to exact revenge. He had texted Hanna Lund again, asking for any photos of August.

Earle said, 'Even if August believed these people had been responsible for Ebba's death, how would he know they were going to be here?'

There was truth in that. Why look for an international perpetrator when there were local possibilities? One big one. Bella Tait had said she had a client, but they'd not seen one. She worked for herself so there was no head office to confirm. And in fact, they only had her account that Jarrad Lester had appeared during the day, and then possibly stalked her in the evening.

She could have been caught up in some affair with Lester and Miller. Then the diving boots would make sense as a diversion. And the false claim that somebody was watching her would feed into the idea of a malicious third party.

Clement pulled car keys, left his coffee. 'Let's go.'

—

It was hard to gauge the age of David Holcroft, the neighbour of Bella Tait. He could have been a prematurely aged mid-fifties or a fit seventies. He wore his long silver hair in a ponytail, his torso was thin, his arms muscular. As the rain spattered over his bare shoulders – his attire comprised black footy shorts and nothing else – he was completely unconcerned.

They were standing out the front of his shack, which was twice the size of Bella Tait's but equally handmade.

'She dropped the dog off yesterday. Scrounger's used to me now.' He pointed to where Scrounger looked on from under the cover of a crude porch. 'Bella's okay, isn't she?'

He appeared genuinely concerned. Clement wasn't inclined to tell him the truth: I'm checking up on her in case she was lying about having a client and might in fact be a psychotic killer.

'We wanted to ask her about a few things. You heard about the young woman and the crocodile?'

'Oh, yeah, bad business.'

'Were you around eight years ago when the Swedish girl was taken?'

Thunder sounded so close it could have been a bowling ball dropped in the gutter beside them.

'No. I was in Cairns then. Got too commercialised for me there. Needed to get back to basics.'

Earle asked if Bella had been on her own when she'd dropped off the dog.

'Yes. She was going to meet her client at his hotel.'

Clement asked if he knew the name of the hotel, but he didn't. Really, Clement already had what he needed: Bella had dropped off the dog. If she'd made up the client, would she still have done that? Maybe. Or maybe she was going to run, wanted the dog looked after.

'You have any idea of what route she would take?'

'Nah. From what she says, I think she does a different one each time. Gets an idea of what the tourist might want to see and then tries to deliver.'

They thanked Holcroft. This time the thunder boomed right overhead, and the ground lit white. Scrounger bolted indoors. They leapt into the car as rain dropped like a bucket of marbles.

'Well I think she's probably genuine,' said Clement. 'But I can't be sure. You?'

'We have to assume both, don't we? She's in danger, or she's a danger and she's on the run?'

Great. Clement had continued to try her numbers on the drive over but there was still nothing. He tried again now. Nothing. Maybe she didn't want to be found?

Earle said, 'I don't think you'll get anything in this storm anyway.'

And once more, Clement found dread curling in a tight ball in his gut. What are you, Bella Tait? Killer or potential victim?

***

Bella Tait had cut across the Victoria Highway en route to the Chamberlain Gorge, the dark section of sky spreading. She had stopped east of the gorge, a little track she knew that gave access into the rock gullet and, more important, shade and shelter.

'Feel like coffee?'

'Great.' Johan climbed from the car, stretched. It had been around a hundred minutes of solid rough driving. 'I need to pee,' he said, and grabbed his camera and headed towards the taller bushes on the fringe of the rocks at the periphery of the gorge.

Good, I need to pee too, thought Bella. 'Careful of snakes,' she called out. She fixed the small pot of water and headed into the low scrub. The feeling of being stalked had not completely abandoned her, even in the heat of day, yet she knew now that it had to be in her head. They had seen two vehicles so far today, both of those in the stretch she'd driven on the Victoria Highway.

She pulled down her pants and squatted. Poor Lorraine. She shuddered. The only thing they had in common was a trip they would surely all prefer to forget. Could Jarrad really have done that?

He must have. He'd seemed nuts when he'd pestered her in Kununurra. He must have snapped. She pulled up her pants and stood.

When they caught him, what would he say? Would she again fall under suspicion? Lose all that she had worked so hard for? Whatever his claims, she would deny. She didn't want to think about it.

The water had boiled. She made the coffee, the smell alone giving her strength. Lorraine was gone. Whatever Jarrad said, it would be her word against his.

'Johan,' she called. She plunged the coffee and called again. Nothing. She started towards the bushes where he had disappeared. Maybe it was more than a wee he'd needed? She gave him another couple of minutes and called again. No reply. Okay, she wasn't having another tragedy on her watch. She followed the narrow track, her apprehension building. Even if you were keeping an eye out for them, snakes could strike.

'Johan?'

She stopped. It was the point where the boulders suddenly got bigger at the rocky perimeter leading into the gorge. His camera was perched on top of one of the taller rocks. If he wasn't answering, and he wasn't taking photos …

Too late she heard the rush of leaves from behind and felt a powerful jolt. Her muscles instant soup, she collapsed. Something swooped and pricked her, and in that moment she gave in to the dark terror she had been trying to keep at bay.

Whatever it was had found her.

***

The twenty-minute drive back to town was roof-pounding. The car threw deep fans of water in its wake. By the time they made the police station it had eased but was still solid. Bella Tait remained incommunicado. The thunderstorm had thinned the waiting media to only two vans.

News awaited them. Manners had managed to pull data from Jarrad Lester's phone and curated what he considered the most important photos. One showed Lester in Halls Creek outside a church. The time stamp showed the previous Wednesday at 6.10 p.m. The next one selected by Manners showed the car pulled over by the side of the road and a long snake slithering across. It was time stamped for the Thursday at 9.12 a.m. In the distance could be seen a sign indicating a turn-off to the Bungle Bungle ranges. With that as a guide, Clement could calculate Lester would still have been a few hours' drive from Kununurra.

If Keeble's estimated time of death on Miller was a few hours out, it was not impossible that Lester had driven through to Kununurra, met up with Lorraine Miller, and organised her gruesome death. Not impossible but as good as. Following was a screenshot of his booking at the Emma Gorge caravan park, confirming his booking from the Thursday. Again, that didn't mean he wasn't in Kununurra before then. But what was telling was that there were no photos of Lester and Lorraine Miller. No photos of her caravan park. Sure, if he'd been planning to kill Miller, had the diving boots ready, then maybe he was smart enough not to give himself away like that, but Clement's gut said Lester hadn't arrived in Kununurra by the time she was killed. And that made Lester another victim.

His phone buzzed. He saw it was Dick Beare. Last he'd heard Beare was at Emma Gorge to recheck potential witnesses.

'Yes, Dick.'

'I'm here at the campground at Emma Gorge. Fellow just came back after a couple of days away. He is one caravan over from Lester's van. He says he heard Lester outside his van on a phone call Saturday night speaking with somebody. Said Lester was a bit annoying, loud. Anyway, he remembered the end of the conversation. Sounded like Lester was arranging to meet the person. Lester finished off with, "Okay, Augoost, see you soon." This bloke thought it was a funny name, like a goose, that's why he remembered.'

It had to be August Sorensen. And if Lester had been planning to meet him soon, he had to have been nearby.

26

The investigation had a new momentum. August Sorensen had to be in a four-wheel-drive vehicle to have gotten to Pigeon Hole. But what vehicle?

The news from Perth HQ was frustrating. So far, the Danish police had tracked Sorensen to the UK but that was all. Clement requested Perth check with Immigration, see if August Sorensen had entered Australia and what contact he might have left.

'And – sorry, what was your name again?'

'Danielle Lee.'

'Danielle, could you see if the Danish authorities have a passport photo or ID photo on record we can have?'

'Onto it.'

One big question: if August Sorensen was responsible, how had he managed to coordinate being here with Lester and Miller?

He saw Graeme Earle approach and offer his phone to him.

'This just came through from Tomas, Ebba's brother.' He leaned over, showing Clement a photo of a man about forty, thinning hair, a high forehead; beside him, a very attractive young woman. 'August Sorensen and Ebba Olsson.'

Clement called in Callum Nelson, passed the photo on to him and suggested he get his people asking all over town if they had seen the man in it.

'It's about eight years old,' he added.

Better than nothing, but people could change a lot in eight years, and Sorensen might well be disguised. Clement would have called

206

Bek Dyson to see if she recognised him as being around the pub when Miller had been there, but Dyson was without a phone. Instead, he called Livesy who was with her.

'Graeme's sending the photo over now. Explain he would be nearly ten years older.'

He hung on the line while it arrived, giving Dyson the opportunity to study it.

'She can't recall if she's seen him anywhere,' said Livesy.

'Anything else she's been able to remember?'

'We did a bit of a reconstruction in the room here, and she thinks he was about a metre eighty-eight.'

That would put him a good four centimetres taller than Jarrad Lester. They could try and get an idea of August Sorensen's height.

As soon as he ended the call his phone buzzed with an incoming message. This time it was Hanna Lund, apologising for taking this long to get back with a photo, and explaining it had been hard to find one with August. The photo must have been taken about the same time as the one sent by Tomas Olsson. It was clearly the same person.

'How tall would you say August is?' he asked.

'I'm not certain. One metre eighty-seven?'

He thanked her for her time.

Thunder sounded close again. The windowpanes reverberated. Once more he tried Bella Tait. Still nothing. Dick Beare poked his head in.

'We just got back. We got Lester's last credit card purchases here in town. Haynes has already started checking them out, see if they can confirm who might have been with him.'

'This is August Sorensen,' he flashed the photo. 'We have no confirmation he's in Australia, let alone the Kimberley, but if this whole thing has to do with Ebba Olsson, he has to be a person of interest.'

'Copied you,' said Earle. A ping from Beare's phone confirmed transmission. Graeme Earle said, 'If these guys need a hand, I can help. We could split up the places where Lester used his credit card.'

Again, it was a good idea. Maybe they would get lucky, and somebody would remember a vehicle. They didn't need two of them here coordinating.

'Works for me,' said Beare.

—

When they had left, Clement began flicking through the rest of the photos Manners had found stored on Lester's camera roll. As he did so, he methodically reassembled the facts in his head as he knew them. Miller had been killed in what was potentially a long-planned murder. And a very personal one. It was extremely unlikely, Clement now believed, that Jarrad Lester was responsible. Lester himself had been murdered. Everything pointed now to August Sorensen.

Two down, one to—

Clement froze. He was looking at a photo of an envelope. An envelope addressed to August Sorensen, c/- Mrs Monica Olsson of Hammarstrand. Presume Monica Olsson is Ebba's mother. The photo was time-dated August seventeenth this year. Lester must have taken a photo of the envelope so he had a record of sending it. Okay, allow two or three weeks to get to Sweden from Australia. Say Mrs Olsson has an address for Sorensen. She forwards the letter. Add another week to two weeks. So, mid-September Sorensen gets a letter from Jarrad. We can only speculate on the contents, thought Clement, but half of all detective work is speculation.

He felt himself go to red alert. A thought was worming through Clement's brain. The pastor said that Lester at one stage had cancer. Bella Tait mentioned it too. If Lester thought he was going to die, and there had been something off about Ebba's death, maybe he contacted August and confessed. Or, equally, he'd been cured of his cancer, a cure he ascribed to a spiritual entity. To God. Lester felt his belief had saved him. Would it now be incumbent upon him to come clean?

As a boy, Clement had asked God to make Susan Woods love him as much as the schoolboy Clement loved her. 'I'll do anything you want, Lord,' he'd promised. His entreaty had fallen on deaf ears, and his life had played out.

Yet what if it hadn't? What if his prayer had been answered? Might he not therefore, in keeping with the covenant, have altered his life, done his very best to excise all his bad behaviours, confess past wrongdoings?

Of course, having received no succour, he'd promptly drifted back to his impious life. He wondered where Susan Woods might be now.

He ran with the hypothesis: Lester felt obligated. Lester needed to confess. Ergo, Lester was the driving force in bringing everyone together, prevailing on Miller and possibly Tait to follow his example.

Clement could see it, Lester getting in touch with Miller, saying he wanted to meet here to pay respects to Ebba.

The first step might have been to notify Sorensen. Perhaps he couldn't locate him by email, or, given the deeply personal nature of its contents, felt that an old-fashioned letter was more appropriate. Lester may well have exchanged addresses with Ebba. Perhaps she had given him her family's address because she was often away, shooting her series. Young people always invited one another to come visit their country.

So, cured of cancer, Lester writes a letter to Sorensen, the contents of which apologise for some action, either deliberate or some sin of omission that contributed to Ebba's death. Why not write to the family as well? If he had, Tomas, the brother, seemed not to know about it. Regardless, Sorensen gets in touch with Lester. Perhaps a phone call. They would have to check Lester's phone log from late August.

An arrangement is made for Sorensen to come to Australia, the Kimberley. It could just be to celebrate Ebba's life, but it might also be an opportunity for Lester and Miller to seek forgiveness.

Speculation indeed. Yet it fitted with what he had so far learned of Jarrad Lester. His phone buzzed. He recognised the number of Perth Headquarters. It was Danielle Lee, the woman he'd spoken with earlier.

'Immigration says an August Sorensen entered Australia in Melbourne, September sixth. They are trying to locate him.'

'Do you have details? A photo?'

'They have a contact phone number and address and are working on it. But I have a passport photo from Danish authorities of August Sorensen as of three years ago. I'm sending it through now.'

Yes! He watched as his phone lit up. 'Got it.' He opened the photo. The five years had taken their toll. His hairline was well and truly receding, more lines on his face. It being a passport photo, he wasn't smiling as he had been with Ebba.

'Thanks, Danielle. Could you get this updated photo out to all our agencies please. And go back to Immigration and ask them to get a copy of any video of the August Sorensen who entered Melbourne at the arrivals gate, and request they find and fingerprint his entry card. Also, we're currently chasing the call charge records of Jarrad Lester. Please call the AFP and ask them to get that process underway.' It was unlikely the Feds would get any quick results but every little bit helped. She said she would do all of that.

He ended the call, his mind aflame with possibilities now. He rang Earle and asked him to get back there. Okay, suppose Sorensen is the killer. He is wherever he is, living a miserable life, when he gets this letter from Lester. It implies some wrongdoing. August becomes bent on revenge. All well and good. It could easily explain how he found and killed both Miller and Lester.

If Bella Tait was an intended third victim – a big if, but one that must be considered – how could Sorensen possibly stalk Bella Tait, an experienced bush person? Well, if you were going to do it, you'd need some kind of electronic tracker ...

Wait up.

Clement's mind was a slot car speeding around a track. Bella Tait thought she was being stalked by Jarrad Lester. She claimed she'd heard someone on her property. What if that was Sorensen planting a tracker on her car?

Shit. He could stay half a dozen k behind her, and she'd never know.

And now she wasn't answering her phone.

There had to be a way to find her. Planes and choppers in this weather? Hopeless.

Think!

Sorensen has planned this meticulously. He wants to savour his triumph. He wants the punishment to come full circle.

An idea slammed Clement's brain at the exact instant that Graeme Earle stepped through the door.

'I think he's after Bella Tait. And I reckon the location he'll choose will be where Ebba disappeared.'

—

The moment he stepped back out into the open air, Clement realised they would need more than the exact location of where on the Pentecost River Ebba Olsson had met her end. They were going to require a very dedicated and fearless helicopter pilot. The clouds were thick and dark, masking any early afternoon sun. The rain was steady, and the threat of lightning had not completely receded. Two pilots volunteered. Geoff insisted he do it.

'Because I'm divorced, no kids, and no one will miss me. I'll get down there now and get the bird ready.'

Clement was more than aware that all of this was being enacted upon nothing more than a hunch. He didn't want lives lost, including his own, in some tragic helicopter crash that might prove to have been completely unnecessary. He did decide, however, that he wouldn't risk more police on this.

'Graeme and I can handle it,' he told Dick Beare, who had offered to come. 'Take the updated photo, revisit hire-car companies, accommodation sites. Somebody must recognise him.'

—

Callum Nelson had pulled out the original reports to try to get the exact location on the Pentecost River where Ebba had apparently been taken. Clement had then called Mike O'Donnell, the former cop, to make sure the reports were accurate.

Just as well. 'That sounds like where we set up the investigation post,' said the former cop when Clement gave him the estimated location. 'The actual site was about two hundred metres east of there. What's the weather like?'

'Thunderstorm.'

'You're crazy. Bit of water and those crocs will be sliding around there like ...' he struggled to find the right simile, 'crocs in mud.'

The plan was to land at Home Valley Station again, the station that had helped them out when they found Nicholas Cooper. They would borrow a vehicle from there. They could drive down the station track, link up with the Gibb River Road and head south about ten k to the crossing. Hopefully they'd make it across to the eastern side of the water. They then needed to cut up north-east cross-country another four k to the site of the camp.

—

Geoff already had the rotors spinning when Livesy dropped them on the tarmac. As if to spite them, a terrific clap of thunder smote the heavens and the sky flickered like carpark neon. Their shoes slapped through sudden puddles.

This could be my last ever journey, thought Clement, then chided himself for being so dramatic. He found it curious that for the first time the image that pushed to the forefront of his mind was not his daughter Phoebe but Lena. He immediately felt guilty.

As they hauled themselves in, Geoff reassured them, 'I've flown in worse.'

I haven't, thought Clement.

27

Of some comfort, the wind was not gusty. The rain grew heavier as they lifted off. Clement found himself gripping the underside of his seat. He looked over at Earle, who shook his head and smiled: Are we fucking nuts?

It was surprising just how dark and blurry the sky was, a kind of viscous vapour where rain and cloud mixed. At one point the helicopter jolted, then shuddered, and Clement threw automatically to Geoff's face, a picture of deep concentration, jaw clenched, neck muscles rigid.

Over the next few minutes, they seemed to level out, no more sudden jolts. And then the sky ahead suddenly illuminated, the sun shining a massive spotlight on the sodden ground below.

Clement's stomach began to churn. He had often suffered travel sickness as a kid, but these days only rarely. He found himself being more concerned about throwing up than actually crashing, taking that as a good sign.

And then they could see the station below. Just a few more minutes, he told himself. Geoff banked and brought the chopper in to a large, flat landing zone where two helicopters sat already, huge droplets glowing on their sealskins.

'Got any spare underwear?' Earle cracked as the engine shut down.

'It was a little hairy,' said Geoff. 'But you've got a story to tell the grandkids.'

The raindrops were like tennis balls.

Waiting for them was Mark, whom they had met earlier when he'd shown them the track that led to Nicholas Cooper. He explained he'd taken a chopper up before the storm got bad.

'It might be better if I drive you,' he said. 'I know these tracks. The rain's gonna make it treacherous. It'll be worse tomorrow, but we should be able to get over the crossing.'

Clement didn't like the sound of 'should'. He said he appreciated it and was obliged to warn yet again, 'It might be nothing, or it might become dangerous.'

'Any shooting, you can handle.' In classic Outback style, Mark said it without even the hint of a smile. 'I'll stick with driving. We have radio too. And GPS.'

Within a few hundred metres of setting off Clement was pleased to have an expert at the wheel. The four-wheel-drive track was muddy and churned and the car slid, slipped and bumped. The rain had intensified and was slamming against the windscreen. Clement found himself gripping the strap above the passenger seat. Graeme Earle was in the back seat. It was like they were back in the vibrating chopper.

After about ten minutes they came out onto the Gibb River–Wyndham Road. It was a notch up from the track but that was all. The road was unsealed. Frequent and random potholes turned the surface into a bagatelle table. Every so often red soup would splatter over a window. If Mark was fazed by any of this, he didn't show it. His headlights probed the misty rain.

'The crossing is about three k from here,' said Mark. Clement had punched in the coordinates he'd got from Mike O'Donnell. Their route was in a V shape. South-east to the crossing, then on the other side of the water, back north-east.

Already Clement had begun to doubt himself. Maybe he should have sat tight. For the umpteenth time he tried Bella Tait's phone numbers. The result was the same.

The rain eased. They saw headlights coming at them. As it drew closer, the vehicle flashed them. Now Clement could get a visual on it, he saw it looked like Bella Tait's.

'Stop,' said Clement, and Mark eased his foot off the accelerator, letting the engine continue to run. The other vehicle had stopped already.

'Is that Tait's car?' asked Clement.

Earle leaned forward for a better look. 'I think so.'

—

The driver door opened. A tall man in a t-shirt and dungarees almost tumbled out onto the road and ran at them as if flagging them down. As the man ran to the vehicle, Clement's hand went to his gun. The man's features were blurred by rain, his wet hair plastered over his forehead. Mark stopped completely and Clement heard Graeme Earle behind him climbing out.

Clement opened his door. The running man had closed to within ten metres.

'Stop!' commanded Clement, beginning to draw his pistol.

The man pulled up abruptly. 'Please, I need help! I was attacked.'

'That's Bella Tait's car.' Earle was behind him, but Clement knew he would have his hand on his gun even though this man seemed unarmed and terrified, his eyes on stalks.

'She's my guide. Somebody zapped me. Taser, I think.'

Clement calculating. He had an accent, possibly Scandinavian, but his hair was curly, different to the photo of August Sorensen and, even allowing for the out-of-date photos, he was a little older. It wasn't Sorensen.

'Where's Tait?'

'I don't know.' The man's voice was quivering. 'Somebody zapped me from behind. The next thing I knew I was lying on the ground in the rain. I don't know whether they drugged me or what, but I couldn't stand. I called out for Bella. She was gone but the car was there. I thought I should get out of there while I could.'

'The keys were in the car?' Graeme Earle.

'Yes. Please!'

'We're police officers.' Clement stepped towards him. 'What's your name, sir?'

'Johan Andersen. I'm Norwegian.'

The rain momentarily eased.

'When were you attacked?'

'More than an hour ago.' His eyes darted, guilty. 'I thought to stay and look for Bella, I did. But then I think, what if they come back?'

'How many people attacked you?' asked Earle.

'I have no idea. I heard nothing. Next thing I felt this … like my brain jolt. Then I wake up in the mud. My neck is sore. Maybe they injected me.'

Clement checked where Andersen was pointing. Hard to see in the rain, but there might have been an injection site there.

'Where were you when you were attacked?'

'I went to pee. There was a track through to the gorge. That's where they got me. When I get back to the car, Bella is gone, so is my phone.'

A quick internal debate by Clement. He could send Andersen on to Home Valley, but perhaps he'd sustained an injury that had not yet manifested. The road was tricky. On the other hand, he didn't want him around if things got hot. But what choice did he really have?

'Park the car and climb in with us.'

He radioed Kununurra and told Nelson of the developments. Nelson said he would get eyes in the sky as soon the weather eased.

'Meantime I'll notify everybody in the surrounding area and Livesy and I will get a chopper to Home Valley.'

'Bring a medic,' said Clement.

Andersen joined Earle in the back of the car.

'Let's go,' said Clement. Mark needed no encouragement.

We have to move fast, Clement was thinking. He grabbed the radio handset, raised Home Valley and asked for Geoff, the pilot. Clement realised he didn't even know Geoff's last name. He explained the situation. The river crossing loomed dead ahead.

'What do you need?'

'As soon as you consider it safe, I'd like you in the air just northeast of the Pentecost River Crossing.'

'It's safer now than it was when we landed. Less lightning. I'll have her up in a few minutes.'

'You're looking for a vehicle, or a person or two.'

'Gotcha. Over.'

The river was churning when they reached the crossing.

'It's pretty deep,' warned Andersen.

It had been a few years since Clement had driven over the crossing and even back then it was hairy. The dumping rain made the waters rush and swirl around the tyres. They needed every centimetre of the vehicle's extra height. You got stuck here, you had big saltwater crocs on every side.

Mark shifted gears with practised skill and then the car was hauling itself out of the water and up the muddy bank on the other side. There was a brief respite as they followed the Gibb River–Wyndham Road for a couple of k. But then they had to turn off-road and follow the track down which Andersen had driven. It was alternately boggy and slippery, but the rain had eased to a fine mist.

About ten minutes in, Andersen pointed.

'This was where we stopped, just in there.'

Yet again Clement found himself debating whether to stop and search here. His gut told him otherwise.

'I think he's taken her back to the original location. Keep going.'

Mark could see the GPS location on his screen, there was no need for Clement to talk him through it, so Clement turned his attention back to Andersen.

'Your attacker never said anything?'

'Not a word. It was just … *wham*.'

'When you got back to the car did you see any other vehicle tracks?'

'It was raining. Heavy. I was calling out. Then I just wanted to get out. I'm sorry.'

The ground flattened and was a little rockier for a short stretch, and this helped them pick up speed. The rain eased off further. Now it was a constant misty drizzle. The lightning had vanished; thunder was distant.

'We're pretty much here,' said Mark.

They had reached a clearing. This must have been the site Bella Tait had chosen to camp eight years ago. Directly ahead the foliage grew thicker.

'That's the river, I suppose?' Clement pointed in that direction.

Mark nodded. 'Yeah, straight down there.'

'Let's get a bit closer.'

Mark edged the vehicle forward.

'Look at that.' It was Earle from the back seat. He tapped Clement on the shoulder and pointed at churned muddy earth.

Vehicle marks for sure, but no definition, just a sloppy trough. There was no proper track here and the foliage swatted the car as it nosed towards the river. And then the greenery was gone and before them was a muddy flat, branches strewn over it like whitened bones.

Clement checked his weapon. 'You guys wait here.'

'Be careful, fellas,' said Mark. 'It's thick with crocs.'

Clement and Earle climbed out. The misty rain did not abate.

This has to be the spot, thought Clement. 'You go that way.' He pointed left and Earle set off in that direction. Then he turned right. What did the killer have in mind for Tait? Maybe simply to drug her and leave her on the bank, for sooner or later a croc would come to investigate.

With all the adrenaline flooding through him, Clement doubted that his heart could beat any faster. However, as he moved along the narrow strip of muddy flat between the water and the wet grasses, he was sure his heart rate kicked up a notch. He reached a jutting chin of rock that forced him to clamber around it, looking for a handhold on decaying branches.

There was no way of seeing what lay on the other side. He could pretty much step on a big croc. He edged around, breathed a sigh, clear. But as his left foot landed, it skidded on the mud and sent him tumbling. He picked himself up, glanced up, and his heart stopped. Ten metres ahead was another mini-promontory, a paperbark trunk near its tip and one of its branches hanging out over the river. Dangling from the branch, her hands looped by rope, her arms stretching up and head lolled forward, was Bella Tait. From the navel down, her body was below water. Clement did his best to run. Was she alive? He couldn't tell. He yelled her name but there was no reaction.

Close now, Clement saw the rope was secured around the tree trunk. Even if he could cut it, that would only drop her into the water.

And now as he looked directly out towards the middle of the river, about thirty metres offshore he saw a tiny mud island and, lying on it, a large crocodile.

Shit. He had a gun but no knife. But Graeme did. He fumbled for his radio, no time for protocol.

'Come in, Graeme.'

'Yes, mate?'

'She's here. I need a knife. Fast.' He told him to head along the bank to the promontory. All the time his gaze never left the island. The croc hadn't moved. He tried to estimate the time, wondered about hypothermia. The temperature wasn't too bad, and a wedge of sun was just now breaking through.

But maybe that was a bad thing. Had the croc just moved, or had he imagined that?

'Mate!' Earle had made good time and was calling from the first promontory.

'Toss it,' called Clement, trying to run towards him over the treacherous mud. Earle looped the small pocketknife through the air. Clement snaffled it.

'Get ready to shoot that bloody thing,' Clement yelled, but as he turned back, the crocodile was no longer visible.

He raced, almost slid, back to the tree. There was no getting up to the bough. The only way he was going to free Bella Tait was from the river. He charged out into the water.

'See anything?' he yelled, and his feet plunged down a hole.

'Nothing!' From the sound of it, Earle was close by now.

Clement had his back facing the direction from which the crocodile would attack. Water was just above his hips. He was at full stretch to get the small pocketknife above Tait's hands to the rope. One thing about Graeme Earle, he maintained his equipment well: boats, car, knife. The blade was small but sharp and bit easily into the rope.

A rapid volley of shots erupted just as the blade sliced the last strand. Clement dropped the knife, caught Tait's body, the plunging weight dragging him down for an instant.

'Fuck it!' Earle shouted and the next thing Clement felt his partner's hands reaching to help. They pulled backwards, calf-deep water now, then ankle-deep … Clement was aware of the sound of a helicopter, still a way off …

A heave, and they were out onto the muddy flat. No stopping.

'I've got her!' Clement cried and hauled Tait's body onto his shoulder, allowing Earle to draw his weapon again in case the croc decided to chase them.

'How close did it get?' asked Clement as his chest heaved.

'You don't want to know,' said Earle.

The noise of the chopper was growing quickly louder.

'She's breathing,' said Clement. And he almost burst into tears.

28

Nearly two hours had passed since they had loaded an unconscious Bella Tait into Geoff's helicopter. He had landed on the Gibb River–Wyndham Road to make the transfer as quick as possible. In spite of Johan Andersen's protests, they had loaded him in too. Clement had travelled with them while Earle stayed to drive Bella Tait's vehicle back to Home Valley Station. The chopper had been met at Kununurra Airport by an ambulance, and the patients transferred to the hospital.

Callum Nelson and Steve Eaton had light planes and helicopters in the sky within about thirty minutes after that, for the storm had cleared. So far, they had not been able to isolate the perpetrator. Keeble was at Home Valley Station going over Bella Tait's vehicle, and Earle had hitched a return flight to Kununurra from Geoff, who had gone back to Home Valley after delivering his first load of passengers to Kununurra.

After a quick shower and change of clothes, Clement had called everyone together at the Kununurra station house. As before, those bods who were not in Kununurra were on Zoom. Outside the weather had calmed but Livesy, who had spent the most time up there, reckoned they would likely cop another dose tonight.

To start, Clement thanked everybody for their efforts. He was indeed proud of what they had all achieved, not just his fellow police officers but those civilians like Geoff and Mark who had found themselves in a pile of trouble but had brought courage and skill to bear. These days, when the world we grew up in seemed to be ever slipping backwards, taking its values with it, it was reassuring to see a demonstration of the opposite. Not that Clement said that publicly, but that's what he was thinking.

'The most important result has been delivered. No loss of life. I just got off the phone to the hospital, and Bella Tait is conscious, and in good health. She was tasered and injected. The same with Johan Andersen, but it would appear he was given a lesser dose. Alas, no luck yet on finding the perp or their vehicle. They would have had at least an hour start. August Sorensen entered Australia in September, but so far he has not yet been located. That might be further confirmation he's our man. After this meeting, Sergeant Earle and I will interview Bella Tait. Maybe that will clear up a few unknowns.'

Scott Risely spoke. 'So your assumption is that this has to do with the Ebba Olsson case?'

'I think we have to assume that.' Clement said. 'Anil, I would like you to keep looking for any video that might link a vehicle to these crimes. Maria, check with every hire-car company and every accommodation place in the Kimberley and see if you can find any trace of August Sorensen. Unless he has false papers, he will be on record somewhere. Dick, I'd like you to continue to look for witnesses who might have seen somebody in the company of Lorraine Miller or Jarrad Lester immediately before their abductions.' He looked back at Scott Risely. 'Look, I have no idea how many August Sorensens are. Any chance you could give our Danish brothers a call and see if they can locate Sorensen, confirm if he's in Australia or otherwise?'

Risely said he would get onto it.

—

Before they left for the hospital, Simone Livesy slipped Clement and Earle fresh ham and tomato sandwiches. Clement was grateful. He was starving. But he was also embarrassed that the most senior woman in his team was the provider.

'I'm sorry this fell to you, Sergeant.'

She laughed. 'I'm the only mother in that room. Somebody had to feed you.'

Some wheels turn more slowly than others, thought Clement.

Women might fly helicopters, run police departments and interrogate suspects, but it also seemed to be only women who genuinely considered the needs of those around them. I'm the worst of the bunch, he scolded himself. So far, he had done nothing for his assembled team. He needed to get his act together.

—

Bella Tait was sitting up in bed, staring at the ceiling, earphones in. She had not been allowed visitors up until now. Though that was the doctors' edict, it suited Clement. When she saw Clement and Earle enter, she pulled out the earphones.

'How are you feeling, Bella?' The policemen pulled up chairs. The last thing Clement wanted was to appear threatening. She had a little colour in her cheeks.

'Pretty good, thank you. I heard you rescued me.'

Clement wondered who'd told her.

'Everybody helped. Everybody did a great job to see you were safe.'

'And Johan?'

'He's okay. He had the same things happen as you, but not so severe. Detective Sergeant Earle and I have some questions for you. Are you up to answering?'

She nodded.

'Firstly, do you have any idea who did this? Did you see or hear—'

Already she was shaking her head. 'I went looking for Johan. He hadn't come back. I really don't remember what happened after that. Not until I woke up here.'

Perhaps, thought Clement, that was a good thing.

'Earlier today we found Jarrad Lester stabbed to death. His body was left in his car.'

He saw the fear in her eyes, heard her intake of breath.

'You don't think he killed Lorraine?'

'No, we don't.'

'Perhaps he had help?' She seemed to be clutching at straws.

'It's possible but we don't know who, and we can't figure out why, exactly. I spoke to Jarrad's pastor. He genuinely believes Jarrad couldn't have done that.'

Graeme Earle picked his moment. 'We have a few ideas we would like to run by you.'

Now she looked nervous.

'Do you need a water or juice or anything?' Livesy's kindness was still fresh in Clement's mind.

'I'm fine.'

Clement told Bella Tait that they believed the deaths related to Ebba Olsson's disappearance.

'We might be wrong, but that seems to be where this is inevitably heading. August Sorensen, Ebba's fiancé, may be in Australia. Naturally we have to consider him as a possible suspect in what is happening. This is him three years ago. Have you seen him anywhere around here?'

She studied the photo closely, then shook her head.

He could see the pressure on her now. Her gaze dropped to her hands. He swapped a look with Earle, who took up the baton.

'We think that somebody might believe that the three of you were in some way responsible for Ebba's death.'

At that, Bella Tait looked up sharply, her lips parted, and she seemed about to speak but didn't.

Clement said, 'We had to consider the possibility that you hadn't been completely truthful about what happened, but we wondered how, even if that were true, anybody else would know.'

Risely said, 'And then we learned that Jarrad Lester, perhaps worried he was going to die with cancer, or grateful that he wasn't, wrote to August Sorensen. Perhaps others.'

'It seemed he wanted to get things off his chest. Make things right.'

Clement studied her closely. She sighed, looked off into the distance. Clement and Earle waited. Clement knew there was something. The question was whether she would spill it.

She swung and met their eyes. 'I lied about what happened. We all did.'

And then she told them the truth about that night eight years ago.

—

That night had never left her. No matter where she was, what her mood – happy, anxious, desperate – it would just come drifting back to her on a magic carpet.

'Most people evaluate their lives over time, I think. You know, "I should have done more with my life, or studied harder, or never broken up with that person". Or "I wouldn't change a thing". Like their lives roll gradually this way or that. But some of us, usually the unlucky ones, we are defined by a few moments, or hours. The boy who dives headfirst into the surf and becomes a quadriplegic. The drunk who loses his temper and king hits somebody who cracks their head on the footpath. The one who is hit by the angry drunk. That you can't undo an action, no matter how much you wish you could, that is terrifying.'

As she was telling the detectives, every detail appeared before Bella in three-dimensional real time. She could even smell the heat in the night air.

'Come on, Bella. You're twenty-one and you've never tried an E?' Jarrad holding the pill out on his palm. It was always him pushing the hardest. Why wouldn't he; he was the supplier.

'It's just us. You'll be fine. It's the most amazing experience.' Ebba with those beautiful teeth. 'We'll look after you.'

She'd realised that one of the reasons Jarrad may have been invited along by Ebba was exactly that. He was the one who supplied the drugs. Although to be fair, none of them, not even Jarrad himself, was excessive. Not up until that night.

Every night she'd watched them, her curiosity, or was it envy, building. They would drink, smoke dope. Jarrad was annoying, and Lorraine seemed sweet but was his lackey. It was Ebba who made the idea attractive. She was everything a young Bella aspired to be: confident, beautiful, and soon to be married. At university Bella hadn't indulged in drugs. It wasn't her scene. Sure, she'd puffed on a joint, three times all up, just to fit in a bit. No raves, no dance parties though. No friends like Jarrad. Yet Ebba was saying it was okay. Ebba who had told her that she might propose a TV program about Bella.

'A young, sexy female tour guide surrounded by crocodiles, why not?'

If she had been a tourist herself, a client, well okay. You turned a blind eye to a little bit of moderate drinking or a joint around the campfire. But she was the guide, the one in charge. She should never have been tempted.

—

For a few hours she had felt so free. So this was what the fuss was all about? They drank wine, sang. She should have known then that no good fortune comes to those who cross from their designated role in the world, trying to be other than what they are. Ebba had been insatiable when it came to pushing boundaries. Too close to edge of a crumbling ledge, or getting up close and personal with a snake. Or holding up a bag of pills.

'What are these like?' she'd asked Jarrad.

'Don't know, haven't sampled, but they come highly recommended.'

The wine was going down easy. She and Lorraine and Ebba had been dancing. Like she'd always wanted to at those university events, yet never dared, standing at the back with a plastic cup half full of chardonnay. Watching everybody else.

The tiredness had hit her suddenly. Maybe it was the wine, the joint. She'd taken one tablet an hour back. She'd staggered to her tent and fallen in.

—

Despite everything, next morning she had still been the first one awake. A terrible hangover. A vague memory of throwing up sometime in the night. She'd staggered to the car and popped a couple of Panadol. Drunk a large bottle of water to hydrate, shuffled towards the little gas cooker to get water on for tea and coffee. Lorraine and Jarrad were flaked in the tent. No surprise. Of Ebba there was no sign. Her first thought was she must have got up early and gone to do her yoga. Before the excess of the evening had begun, Bella had impressed upon them all how dangerous it was closer to the river. Now, she began to worry that Ebba might have ventured down there regardless. The girl just had no idea about a safety buffer.

Bella's head was thumping as she forced herself down towards the riverbed, which was still a good eighty metres off. She caught a glimpse of white clothing through narrow knotted trunks and yellow grasses, probably twenty-five metres away.

'Ebba,' she called. Then, as the little path she was following twisted around, giving her a better view, she saw Ebba sprawled facedown. She wondered how long she could have been there. All night?

'Ebba,' she said more quietly, almost on top of her. There was a smell of vomit around the prone figure, magnified by the risen sun. She'd probably passed out and thrown up. Thank God she hadn't wandered down to the riverbed from here. She was probably disoriented, so even more fortunate this was where she had wound up.

'Ebba.' She knelt over her now. Ebba was so still. Even then, Bella wasn't thinking straight. Her mind was running to how she was going to clean Ebba up, and whether she might need treatment.

When she touched Ebba's back, it felt stiff. With difficulty she tried to roll her over, gently tapping her cheek and exhorting, 'Ebba, wake up.'

But now she could see the glassy eyes staring up at her. Even so, even though she felt not a tremor of life in the body, Bella resiled from the obvious fact confronting her. She poked and pushed and cajoled. 'Ebba!'

And then she could no longer find a blind in which to hide, had to acknowledge the awful truth.

She stood up quickly as if to scream. But the effort was too much, her head spun, and the water she had downed just moments before came gushing back up, sluicing over the vomit of the dead woman.

—

It must have been a full thirty seconds since she'd finished talking, but it was as if Bella Tait only now realised it.

'Sorry ... where ...'

'You'd found Ebba dead,' Clement prompted gently.

She nodded, wiped a tear. 'Yes. She was dead. Whatever that drug was, whether it was cut with poison, or she was allergic, none of us knew. I told the others, and then I went to call it in. But Jarrad and

Lorraine freaked. "What are you doing? You'll fuck your own life up too, not just ours." I'd always done the right thing. But the more they talked about it, especially Jarrad, the more I got swayed. "She's dead. We can't bring her back. And if we tell people how she died, that comes back on her and her family too." That was the thrust of it. Would her parents want to know she'd died sampling drugs? Would August? My life as a guide would be over.' She gave a bitter grunt. 'Well, as it turned out, even with the lies we told, I looked incompetent.'

She had said to the other two: 'But what can we do? We can't just leave her there.' And Lester had replied, 'Why not? Won't a crocodile come get her eventually? And then the story can be tragic.' He had constructed a whole story already: Ebba must have come down to the bank – where Bella had warned her not come – she had been doing her yoga, communing with nature, and nature had taken her. Her love of freedom, her desire to be one with nature had cost her her life.

Jarrad had had that talent. He could paint a graphic picture.

And that's what they had done. They had dragged the body to the bank and left her there to be taken by a crocodile. The drugs would be out of their systems by the time they called in the tragedy. Nobody was around. They could take days if they needed.

Nearly forty-eight hours Ebba's body had lain there.

Bella Tait was sobbing now. 'Maybe I should have died like them. Now I'm the only one who has that horrible memory. Going back, hour after hour, to see … to see if …' Unable to finish, she simply shook her head.

—

It was gruesome, yes. Deplorable. Yet Clement could not find it in his heart to condemn Bella Tait. Ebba Olsson had made her own choices. Even Jarrad Lester, who maybe was a poser and an idiot, hadn't forced the drugs on her. They had all made poor, ultimately tragic choices, but it was the living who bore the terrible guilt. By her death, Ebba had been absolved of responsibility.

It had been an awful demise, but now two more people were dead, and another's life in ruins because they had wanted to – what? Flourish in a career?

Which of them would not willingly have reversed that choice now if given the opportunity?

And the killer of Miller and Lester, if it was indeed August Sorensen, how would Ebba have felt about that? Yet another life destroyed because of her actions. The man she loved locked up for most of his life.

We are so stupid.

Clement's thoughts floated above Bella Tait's guttural sobbing.

So very stupid.

29

Clement and Earle shared a pizza at the station. Not normally a pizza person, Clement had abstained completely since Lena had appeared on the scene as his dietician. They had to eat something though, and this was easy.

The frustration inside him was mounting. Eight p.m. already and nothing much to show except a never-ending mountain of paperwork that he and Earle were trying to level in this downtime, waiting for word on August Sorensen. Immigration hadn't found him, Lester's phone records weren't complete, no accommodation booking in the Kimberley with that name. Thunder and lightning had climbed back into their cave, and the rain had stopped.

Now it was steamy. No wonder so many who lived up here eventually made for the opposite end of the state, closer to the Antarctic.

Anil Patel was working in Livesy's office, trying to find evidence of the perpetrator on video. No luck so far. He was checking every camera in town and on the roads. Clement had told Beare and Haynes they could go back to their hotel. He would call if he needed them. Haynes had so far found no bookings for anything in Sorensen's name in the Kimberley. Maybe Sorensen had bought a vehicle over East and driven it across the country. He'd been in Australia long enough. He could be living out of it. Dick Beare had thoroughly canvassed the town. One shopkeeper thought he had recognised the photo of Sorensen but when Beare hunted down the lead, it crumbled. The service station attendant was pretty sure the shopkeeper was confused, mistakenly identifying a fellow he knew who looked very similar. The credit card sale the shopkeeper was able to call up pointed to the same fellow the servo bloke had suspected.

'Bek Dyson has published her story.' Earle had taken a break to check his phone.

'Good for her. I hope she's flown back to Perth though.' Clement didn't mind the young journalist getting a career boost but if that had been Phoebe, he'd be wanting her well away from here. He was consolidating his notes. *It is thought that the perpetrator planted a tracking device to follow Bella Tait.*

'Did Keeble say she was coming back or is she still at Home Valley?'

'Not sure.'

Keeble had called earlier with a familiar story: she had found no useable prints on the Jarrad Lester vehicle. Bella Tait's vehicle had had prints from three people. One was Graeme Earle from when he'd driven the vehicle. She assumed the others to be Tait and Andersen. Clement dialled her.

Keeble answered swiftly, explained she had decided to spend the night at the cattle station. 'By the time the rain cleared I thought I may as well stay here.'

'And the accommodation is better,' he poked.

'You know me so well.'

'Did you find a tracker on Tait's vehicle? I was thinking … fingerprints.'

'No tracker. I looked inside and climbed under the vehicle myself looking for anything. A tracker I would have spotted.'

Earle, who was listening in, offered, 'Probably took it with him.'

Yes, thought Clement. This bloke leaves no loose ends.

'Any luck on those diving boots?' Her turn to ask him.

Clement explained what he had heard from Perth. 'They found the distributor, but orders are worldwide.' However, it jolted him. Perhaps the distributor had recorded a sale to August Sorensen? That would be solid evidence. If they could find a way to tap into Sorensen's financial records, they could also come at it from the other angle: see if a purchase that he had made matched with the diving boots.

'On Lester's body there was an injection site, and there were traces of fentanyl and benzodiazepine. The same with Andersen and Tait. Probably mixed the concoction up himself. Knock them out quickly then keep them groggy.'

'Presumably the same person then.'

'Certainly the same batch. With the rain there was no chance of finding tyre tracks, but it had to be a four-wheel drive with high clearance. The rope is the same as was used on Lorraine Miller.'

'So if we find who did this, we might be able to prove they did it, but none of what we have actually gives us an ID?'

'That's about the size of it.'

'Okay, thanks for everything. Rest well.'

His eyes met Earle's. 'I'm losing it. I should have been onto those leads hours ago.'

'We've had a bit on.' Dry as a cracker.

Clement leaned back and stretched. His phone rang. It was Scott Risely. Clement put him on speaker.

'The August Sorensen who entered Australia in September is not our guy.'

Clement wasn't sure he'd heard correctly. 'What?'

'He's not the same one. This August Sorensen lived in Malmo. He's been working in Melbourne for an engineering firm and is currently holidaying in Hobart. He took himself into the police station there when he got a text to contact police. I'm sending you his photo.'

The phone pinged. Feeling like he was decaying from the inside, Clement clicked on the photo. Okay, the photos he'd seen of Ebba's August were old, but this guy seriously looked another five years on top of that. His hair was thinning, true, but the remnants were dark. The nose and eyes were all wrong.

'It's not him,' Clement was forced to confirm. He slid the phone across to Earle.

'We've spoken to the Danish police. They're trying to find our August Sorensen. All we have is that six months ago he was living in London. I'll call with any news. Gotta go, the big cheese is calling every five minutes.'

'Sorry we've left you hanging.'

'Just bring him in, all will be forgiven.'

Clement felt pancake flat. He had been sure about Sorensen even though he hadn't admitted it. Earle slid the phone back.

'It's not the same August Sorensen. The name was a coincidence.'

'But it's got to be him, right?' Earle was as disbelieving as him. 'The conversation at the caravan park. Lester was going to link up with August. It has to be him.'

'Immigration only has a record of the one August Sorensen. And we can't find a record of accommodation, or car, booked in his name, anywhere near here.'

'False passport, got to be.'

Perhaps, conceded Clement. Normally out of the reach of ordinary citizens, but if the guy had organised those diving boots …

'You spoke to one of Ebba's brothers.'

'Yes. He mentioned another brother but said he had spoken to him that morning in Sweden.'

'Obviously he didn't sound like he was lying.'

'No. I'll ring Tomas Olsson now. See about this brother.'

Earle started looking through his contacts.

Trying to get his brain to shift was like trying to move a bogged car. He just kept pushing down, and the tyres continued spinning on the same point: logic says this has to do with August Sorensen. Like Graeme Earle just pointed out, Lester was overheard on the phone to him.

Clement heard Earle making contact with Tomas and switched in. He gestured for Earle to give him the phone. He introduced himself.

'Yes, Detective. Is there any news?'

'We're still looking, I'm afraid. You mentioned your other brother?'

'I don't think Martin knows any more than me.'

'He's in Sweden at the moment?'

'Yes, I told the other detective. I spoke with him this morning.'

'Could I have his phone number please? I should check with him as well.'

There was a sigh, possibly annoyance, maybe frustration, then he gave the number. Clement wrote it down.

'Did your family receive any communication from Australia, by phone or letter? Or from August saying he had received information from Australia about what happened to Ebba?'

'No. I wish that had happened.'

Think, Clement commanded himself. There had to be something. He was almost on automatic pilot now, the muscle memory of a thousand investigations moving his jaw and tongue.

'Tomas, when Ebba died, was there anybody in the family, or the village, who took it particularly badly? An old school friend ...'

'We all took it badly.'

'Of course.'

'Everybody loved Ebba. I know people say that but I mean it. Some too much.'

Clement was about to pass on that but pulled himself up. 'What do you mean, "too much"?'

'The worst of all was her ex. He was very controlling, and she left him. They'd been broken up for months when she met August, but he wouldn't accept it. August had to threaten him to stay away. When Ebba died, he rang my parents and blamed them. Said if she had been with him still, this wouldn't have happened. He was upset. He was always aggressive. That's why Ebba left him.'

'What is his name?'

'He's Norwegian. Johan.'

***

I nearly managed it all. Johan Andersen studied himself on his phone screen. There was no mirror here in his hospital room and he wanted to see how he presented on what would be the last minutes of his quest. He pressed Record.

'Everything has been for you, Ebba. The others didn't know the pain of truly loving you. The *wonderful* August, he moved on with his life, very quickly. Like you were a pet that had died. So easy to replace. Even your family. But my life remains dedicated to you. I love you, always.'

He pressed Stop. He would never forget their time in Venice, which had been just as he had described to Bella Tait, although of course, he had no wife … In fact what he had was much more: Ebba, the love that would be forever with him, no matter what.

All in all, he was satisfied. He had done his best. From the moment that letter, meant for August, had been directed instead to his address at the flat he'd once shared with Ebba, he had set out on a single, unwavering path. First make contact with Jarrad Lester: inspire him, make him feel his path to redemption could be completed by all of them meeting here to lay to rest the wrongs of the past.

Fate had put the letter into his hand. It might as well have been a sword.

—

Everything he'd planned had worked so well. Lorraine Miller had been easy prey. He'd followed his points to a T: make contact briefly in the hotel and then, as she left, away from cameras and witnesses. All done in the blink of an eye. If anybody had seen, it was just another drunk girl leaving the pub. And Jarrad Lester. That had worked even better than he had hoped. Pretending to Lester that he was August, arranging they meet before Miller's body had been discovered. Getting him to drive out to Zebedee Springs to meet him there.

Lester had at least repented, so his death was kinder: stabbed to death rather than taken by a crocodile. Then he had the bonus of having Lester's car to drive around in. Take the journalist girl, because he needed to make sure there was time to deal with Bella Tait. Make it look like it was Lester. Swap cars again, leave Lester's body, dump her not too far away but far enough she wouldn't be found quickly.

And then join Bella Tait on her tour.

He'd thought the thunder and lightning were a guarantee of success. Thought the conditions would delay the police enough.

But the easy way for him, the one of least sacrifice, was not to be. Sure, even when they brought him back here to Kununurra he could have slipped away. However, that would be leaving things unfinished. And they had to be finished, whatever personal price he must pay.

He placed the phone down and stood. He was ready. He would not abandon what needed to be done, simply to save his own skin. It was more important that Bella die than he be free. After all, what sort of freedom could there be if he knew he had failed Ebba?

—

For eight years Bella had lived with the shame of her actions. The policemen had been kind, really. According to them, if what she had told them was a true account, which it was, then she had officially done nothing to contribute to Ebba's death. At worst, she had been professionally negligent. It might have insurance implications for her former company, but it was not a crime she could be charged over. The disposal of the body, hindering a police investigation, yes, there could be charges laid. But not right now.

'We have a more urgent problem,' Detective Clement had said. 'Somebody murdered Jarrad and Lorraine and tried to kill you.'

All these years to climb back onto her feet, only to be swept over again. She did not think she could come back from this. She would never again be able to make a living as a guide. And she would forever be haunted by the memories of eight years before. What was worse: walking to the bank to find Ebba's body still there, or arriving to find it had been taken? They were equally horrific.

I'm not even human, she thought. Who had tried to kill her? Ebba's fiancé? Well, she could hardly blame him.

She felt a presence in the doorway. The hallway light caught somebody's outline. She only had a very low light on the headboard.

Johan stepped into the room.

'Thank goodness you're alright.' She could not hold back her genuine relief. Losing another client would have been the end.

Johan moved closer to her.

'I'm so sorry,' he said.

She had not blamed him for running. Why should he stay there and lose his own life to protect hers? She was not worth saving anyway.

'There's no need to be. It wasn't your fault.'

'No, it wasn't.' He walked right over to the bed. Then he pulled up one of the chairs and sat down. He almost whispered into her ear. 'We must own our actions, don't you think?'

For an instant she wondered if this was a phantom Johan, one her conscience had conjured. But no, he was the real deal. She could feel his breath. He had a bead of sweat on his left brow.

'Ebba and I would have been together by now. Probably with children.' He sniffed, wiped around his eye. Tears?

Bella was trying to piece this.

'You're … August?'

'That dog!' Spittle flew from his mouth, which set into a rigid square as if it were a cartoon drawing. 'He wouldn't have lasted. Ebba would have realised her mistake and come back to me. But Ebba never had the chance. Thanks to you.'

Now she understood. Johan was the ex that Ebba had been so glad to be rid of. Two days back, Bella would have been terrified. Now, what did she have to lose except a worthless life?

'That was you in the shadows outside my place.'

'I wanted to see you. How you lived. I'm glad your life has gone nowhere. That's what you deserve.'

'I did an awful thing. That's true. But you're wrong. Ebba would never, ever have gone back to you.'

In one movement his hands were around her throat, cutting air to her lungs. She flailed, tried to scratch him. He was too strong. She was going to die right here. Despite everything, she desperately wanted to live, but it was too late. Everything was fading, grey …

At the outpost of her consciousness, she heard a growl. The monsters of hell coming to collect her. Then a sudden weight landing on her … She was coughing, there was colour again, her lungs sighing. A familiar smell assaulted her.

—

They had just run into the corridor when Clement heard the unmistakable sounds of a dog snarling mid-attack. A stunned David

Holcroft stood at the room's doorway, screaming for Scrounger to stop. Clement shoved past him into the room. A nurse and an orderly were at the bed, covering Bella Tait, while on the floor Johan Andersen was attempting to fight off the dog. Clement tried to drag Andersen away, but Scrounger had a go at him too. Then Earle came to the rescue and helped pull Andersen back to the doorway.

'It's okay, Scrounger. It's alright!' yelled Clement, Holcroft joining in, reassuring the dog. Realising the threat had been removed, the dog quietened and leapt onto the bed, ready to attack the nurse ministering to Bella Tait.

Now Clement could see her, pale and white, but her lips were moving as she whispered something, and the dog nuzzled into her.

30

What had started only a week or so back seemed to have lasted months. Clement couldn't believe how relaxed he felt just walking the jetty at Derby with Lena. The sun was already low by the horizon, the heat moderated by a light ocean breeze. He'd only been back an hour from Broome. He'd been commuting, tying up the paperwork and criminal case from there and returning every other night to Derby. This evening the sex had been immediate, hot and sweaty.

Perhaps I'm living two lives simultaneously, he mused. This was so different to what he was used to, there had to be a glitch, like you saw on all those sci-fi series: an abnormal weather event slides you through the portal. Before Lena, the typical day's end would have found him alone, lying under a fan in his steamy room above the chandler's, trying to piece where his life had gone wrong, and terrified it would never be back on track, certain that he was destined to play out his days in a retirement village, then a high-care home with progressively softer food.

Yet here he was, as alive as a flowering marri.

He'd been talking Lena through the case.

'How did Andersen learn what had happened?'

Lena had that ability he so admired, to lope gracefully. A group of boys were fishing. One was hauling something wriggling and silver from the water. Triumph. He remembered that feeling as a boy. These days it was a rare feeling for him but wonderful when it occurred. Yet while he felt satisfaction in the case of these recent killings, any triumph remained elusive.

'Jarrad Lester, who was the one who had provided the fatal

drug, had developed oesophageal cancer. He finally began to take responsibility for his actions, and wrote to Ebba's fiancé August Sorensen, apologising and setting out exactly what had happened. I think, I can't be sure, this was after his recovery had started, though it doesn't really matter. The point was, he was genuinely remorseful. The problem was that he had no address for August, so he sent the letter care of Ebba's family home. By that time though, they had moved. A neighbour was forwarding mail. It seems they rang Ebba's new family home to get the address. The father, who has onset of dementia, gave the address as the one he remembered, the former boyfriend's, Johan Andersen.'

'So a letter for August arrived and, being the asshole he is, Andersen opened it?'

That, according to Andersen in Clement's interview with him, was exactly what had happened. Andersen had suggested to Lester a healing service back in Kununurra: all four of them there. Lester had adopted this idea with fervour.

'We confirmed an order for the diving boots used on Lorraine Miller in Andersen's PayPal records. Lester located Miller and talked her into returning to Kununurra. He learned Bella Tait was still working there and tried to convince her in person to seek some kind of redemption. Meanwhile Andersen turned up and began to eliminate them, one by one.'

'I suppose he at least spared the journalist.'

'Yes. He only wanted to punish those he considered responsible.'

'And you didn't pick him?'

No, I did not, thought Clement. In fact, he explained he had estimated Andersen to be more ingenious than he really was by assuming he had planted a tracker.

'He never actually did that.'

Lena laughed, 'If you hadn't thought of that, you would have known he was the killer when you found him in Bella's car.'

'Certainly would have been more suspicious. But he was careful. He did taser himself, and inject himself, at very low levels – but then that also fitted with the profile he'd established when he abducted Bek Dyson, the journalist. And of course, by then we were sure it was August Sorensen we were after.'

They were heading back to shore. Clement evaluated his performance: he'd been clever yet unlucky for a lot of the case, and stupid but lucky for the remainder.

'What will happen to Andersen?'

'No death penalty in Australia. He'll get a long prison stint.'

'And the guide?'

'Bella, I'm not sure. She is never likely to reoffend. In the end she made a stupid mistake. She nearly lost her life. Just lucky her neighbour turned up and thought nothing of bringing a dog into the hospital. We'd rung the hospital to warn them to guard Bella, but without the dog intervening I don't know if they would have been in time. I think Bella will get a suspended sentence.'

But she'd be hounded for a year or three. And her vocation, to be an Outback guide ... Clement couldn't see that continuing.

'Could Andersen have got away with it?' asked Lena.

'At least for a time. He had an air ticket booked to Thailand. It might have been a long time before we turned up that Johan Andersen was Ebba's ex.'

'So revenge has wrecked his life too.'

Or love. Or obsession. Yet Clement did not say that.

—

Lena cruised her motorcycle into a spot near the supermarket. Clement had no embarrassment about riding pillion. Tonight, he would be cooking. He was thinking chilli con carne, and what he didn't have was chilli or jalapenos. He removed his helmet and started towards the supermarket.

'You may as well wait here,' he said, leaving Lena on her bike on low idle.

At the same time as he began his journey, across the road two guys were walking towards a parked car. It looked like they'd just purchased sixpacks.

Clement had taken two more paces before he stopped.

He knew that bloke.

He swivelled and starting walking fast now. The two guys were still ambling.

'Anthony Edmonds!' Clement's voice was clear and strong. Even as he called out, he was calculating that he was unarmed and that there were two of them. But he could not let Heather Lawson's attacker go free.

Edmonds turned and took an aggressive step towards him, his mate at his hip.

'Detective Inspector Daniel Clement, Broome. We've been looking for you, Anthony.'

The mate hung back but Edmonds kept coming.

'What do you need me for?'

'Heather Lawson was assaulted. She's your girlfriend, right?'

'That slut.'

'Let's go over the station and we'll talk about it.'

There was hesitation and a moment of calculation in Edmonds' eyes.

And then a sixpack of cans was hurtling at Clement.

No time to evade, Clement thew up his hands, the steel cans thumped into his arms. Edmonds was already running.

Clement gave chase down the crumbling road. He was gaining now. Then ahead, Edmonds stopped, pivoted and swung around. A short branch had appeared in his hand. Clement saw it too late. The branch caught him in a blow to the temple and he went down. He was dazed, his backside half on grass and half on bitumen.

'I'm not going to prison for that whore.'

Edmonds took a step towards Clement and raised the branch high. Clement tried to push himself away, but his legs were jelly.

Then he heard the powerful motorcycle roaring their way. Edmonds turned and his mouth opened in an O. He turned to wield his branch, but the cycle was heading right for him. He threw the branch and tried to run.

The bike did not alter its course. Lena had her extendable baton in her hand. As she passed, she swung. The baton caught Edmonds in the kidneys, and he went down in a heap.

Clement had picked himself up. He could feel blood trickling down his cheek, and he was fuzzy-headed. The cycle had stopped up ahead and now swung around in an arc. Edmonds was on the ground moaning.

Clement reached him and looked down. 'Anthony Edmonds, you are under arrest for assaulting a police officer.'

It gave him immense satisfaction to utter those words. Lena watched on, still astride her motorcycle.

Her, Clement would have to deal with later.

Three days of solid rain. The Martuwarra Fitzroy River was swelling. Clement was one of those who, though a non-believer, found himself praying they didn't cop another flooding down there. Di Rivi was at a desk filing reports, Graeme Earle was flicking through a fishing magazine while eating a pastry. Clement himself was double-checking the personal letter he had written to Ebba Olsson's family. Two weeks to get around to that, but there was so much official paperwork in the job that everything else piled up. And criminals didn't stop just because you caught a bad guy a couple of weeks back.

'Rehab is coming on good. I'll be right for the season.' Josh Shepherd back at work, practising leg-spin with an orange. Clement wasn't sure who he was talking to. Most likely anybody who would listen. Nobody was paying any attention. James Matar had been charged with assaulting Shepherd. So much had happened so quickly, but now everything was back to normal.

Di Rivi had been disappointed that she hadn't been the one to arrest Edmonds. He and his mate had been camping up on the May River. Apparently, Heather Lawson had burst into tears of relief when di Rivi broke the news that he'd been caught.

As for Johan Andersen's case, that was a way off yet. But all the evidence had stacked up. The clincher was the tiny bit of DNA under the nails of that surviving hand of Lorraine Miller's.

Clement sensed a presence, looked up and saw Scott Risely at the threshold of the room. He beckoned with his eyebrows.

—

Risely's office was always sparsely furnished and neat, but now even more so. He was starting his new job next week. Risely had been proven right. With everything ticked off neatly, the superiors had gone quiet.

'So, you've had a chance to think about it?'

Clement confirmed that he had. 'When I was out there, there were moments I really resented it, you know? Catching crooks was the only motivation I ever needed, but there I was thinking, shit, I'm going to be fifty in a heartbeat, and I'm not as good as I used to be.'

'It was a tricky case.'

That was true, but ... 'Five years ago, I wouldn't have accepted the assumptions that I did this time. I just wanted to be right, to put the case to bed. I didn't dispute myself enough.' Risely did not interrupt, letting him get his thoughts together. 'I thought, maybe this is it. Maybe this is the sign I should go more to administration than in the field. When sportspeople retire, they always say they know, they don't have the passion ...' He was aware he had trailed off.

Risely said, 'Your salary will be much higher. You can impart your investigative skill to your staff.'

It's very final though, Clement thought. You don't go back into the field. He continued. 'And I thought of Lena, too, and our relationship.' It was unlike Clement to be open about such things, but Scott Risely was the person within the job in whom he tended to confide. Graeme Earle sometimes. 'On the one hand, more regular hours would be good.'

'Not getting punched up, shot or stabbed also has its advantages,' said Risely.

That provoked a smile. 'True. I won't say that hasn't crossed my mind. Especially when Lena winds up in the middle of it, like with Edmonds. But I still don't know where we're at, Lena and me. She's still talking of going to Darwin.'

And if she did, and he didn't, would she ever return? Would she hook up with some other guy? Yet if he went with her, and they busted up, how could he ever get back on his feet without his job? He needed the job for him to know who he was. Otherwise, who was

Daniel Clement? He didn't fish, or waterski, or play bowls.

The rain suddenly dumped on the roof with increased weight.

'So, what have you decided?' asked Risely, leaning forward to be heard above the drumming rain.

—

She was lying on her stomach in her underwear on the thin bed in the small apartment above the chandler. She was on her Kindle, and looked sideways at him when he stepped in, soaked.

'You better get those wet clothes off,' she joked.

The rain was thumping on the roof, dribbling through the small space she'd left in the sliding window. He didn't say anything, just wanting to freeze that moment, frame it, hang it in his memory.

'So?' she prompted, rolling now on her back. How did anybody get that flat a stomach?

'I spoke with Scott.'

'You turned him down, didn't you?'

'You think?'

She sat up, hugged her knees. 'You don't want to give up the chase. Not you. Even though you think you're losing it, and you're not as good. Of course, I don't know if that's true, I don't know you long enough.'

'That's the perfect reason, the perfect time for a change. And better for us.'

She made a kind of snort. 'This is not about us. It's about you. I told you before. You have to trust.'

'But can I trust you?'

'You can trust me. That's not the same as me promising to be with you forever.' She swung off the bed and stood up. Her tone was mildly accusatory but really more matter of fact. 'You think if you stop doing what you do, and put all your eggs in this basket' – pointing at herself – 'the eggs might break.'

'You're getting good at this language.'

'Because I am prepared to make mistakes so I can learn.'

They stood facing one another. He ached to have her in his arms.

'You're right. I didn't take the job.'

She wasn't angry, she opened her hands. 'It's your choice.'

'But I'm not sure if I should be in the field. People's lives are at stake: colleagues, the public ... I'm taking leave. I've got three months to decide what I'd like to do next.'

She draped her arms over his shoulders. Her breasts almost touched his chest.

'The coward's way out, huh?'

'Yeah, I'm nothing if not that.'

Their lips met and they kissed deeply. The rain was still thundering, and so was his heart. He was once again standing in thigh-high water in the Pentecost River trying to cut down Bella Tait, unable to monitor the threat behind, his life out of his control.

I have no idea where I'm headed, he thought.

The idea was both exhilarating and terrifying. But if he had learned one thing from this case, it was that you can't bury your fears.

The rain would end ... sometime.

ACKNOWLEDGEMENTS

These books sneak up on you. *When It Rains* is my thirteenth crime novel, and my seventh with Georgia Richter editing. Georgia is a brilliant editor and really a collaborator in my criminal escapades. To have somebody you trust looking over your shoulder means a writer can take risks. I can think, well if I've miscued here, Georgia will set me right. Thanks so much, Georgia, for everything.

This novel required a fair bit of genuine research on policing methods, and I was fortunate to have made the acquaintance of Rob Kirby at one of my previous author library sessions. Rob has worked in numerous policing roles in his career, a detective across multiple divisions, Motor Squad, CIB and in his last role as Duty Inspector at the Police Operations Centre. With a stint or two in the Kimberley, Rob brought firsthand knowledge to bear. I can't thank him enough for his insights.

The marketing and sales team at Fremantle Press and Penguin Australia have been superb in their assistance. Claire Miller has been championing my books for years now, and Chloe Walton has been spectacular on the event front, so big thanks to you all.

Special thanks to the Kununurra Writers Festival, who had me as a guest in 2022. Not only did I make great friends among guests, organisers and authors but I was inspired to get that part of the East Kimberley into a book.

None of this would be possible, however, if it weren't for my fabulous wife Nicole. She is still my inspiration and always my biggest supporter.

I'd like to acknowledge the traditional people of the Kimberley and East Kimberley regions in which this novel is set.

ABOUT THE AUTHOR

Dave Warner is an author, musician and screenwriter. *When It Rains* is his thirteenth adult novel, with previous novels winning the Western Australian Premier's Book Award for Fiction and the Ned Kelly Award for best Australian crime fiction. Previous Dan Clement novels are *Before It Breaks, Clear to the Horizon* and *After the Flood*.

Dave first came to national prominence in 1978 with his gold album *Mug's Game* and his band Dave Warner's from the Suburbs. Dave continues to write and record music, has been named a Western Australian State Living Treasure and has been inducted into the WAMi Rock'n'Roll of Renown.

Connect with Dave here:
davewarner.com.au
Instagram @davew.author
X @SuburbanWarner
facebook.com/Dave-Warner-370719336278939
Youtube @mrmugsgame
TikTok @davesuburbanboy

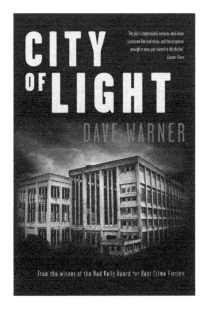

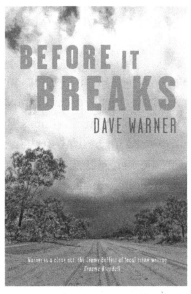

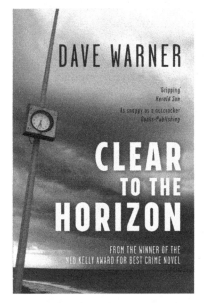

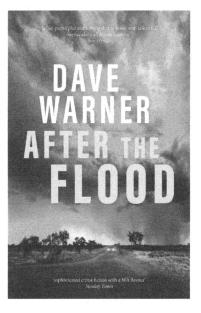

ALSO FROM DAVE WARNER

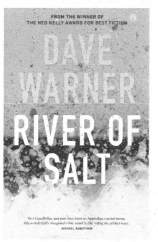

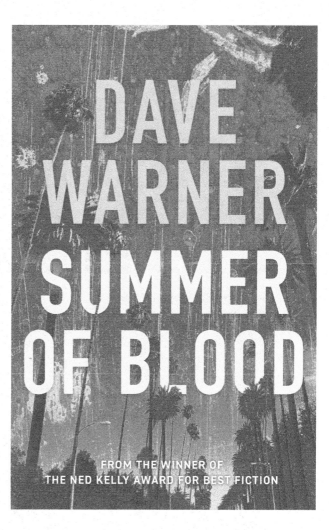

AND IN ALL GOOD BOOKSTORES

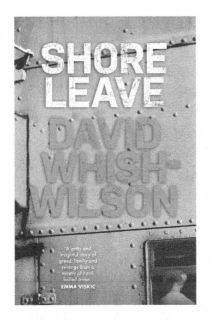

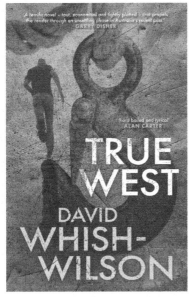
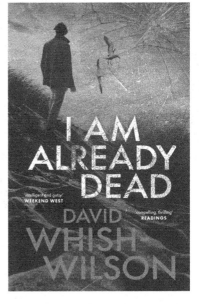

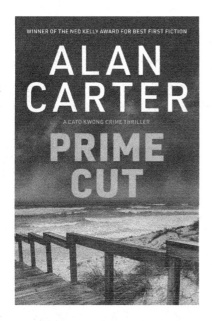
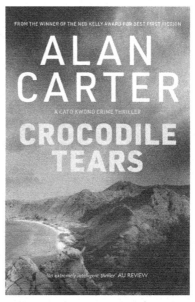

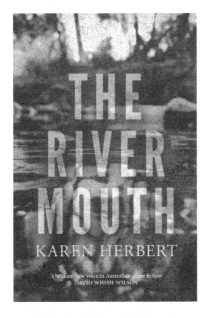

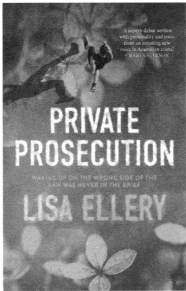

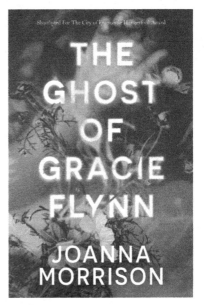

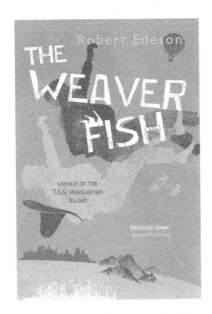